BOOK 5 OF COURAGE ON THE OREGON TRAIL SERIES

WILD PROMISE

A.T. BUTLER

WILD PROMISE

An Oregon Trail Western Adventure

A.T. BUTLER

CHAPTER ONE

"After you, Mrs. Tenney," her husband said, near bursting with pride at even holding those words in his mouth. He gestured broadly through the open door.

There was a slight chill in the late afternoon air, and Rebecca Tenney (née Stephens) stood with her husband on their front porch, about to enter their new home for the very first time. She and Andrew had just stepped under the wild overhang of marigold growing along the eaves of the old Bailey house. All through her childhood Rebecca had walked by this house almost daily, admiring the pair of dormer windows that gave the house such an air. She had never dreamed that she might one day get to live there.

"Are you sure?" she teased looking around. "It's this one? This whole house is for us? No one is going to come throw us out?"

"All for us. For as long as you want. And when you want something new, we'll see about that too."

This man knew her so well. He loved her so well. It

wasn't as though she necessarily wanted anything other than what was right in front of her—Rebecca just wanted the option in case she changed her mind. And Andrew had long ago learned that about her, and supported her through all of it.

It was early spring in 1849 and it sounded as though all the birds in the neighborhood were singing just for her. For the two of them on their wedding day. She could almost cry with joy; all that she had ever wanted was now here right in front of her. She had loved Andrew Tenney since she was ten years old. There, of course, had been ups and downs during that decade—as one might expect of fifteen-year-olds—but Andrew had always been her anchor and stalwart at the end of the day.

Andrew had been the first boy to ever dance with her, back when she was twelve at the Marwood family's holiday party. Andrew had been the one to help her home when she sprained her ankle trying to jump over the creek on a dare. And then later, when she turned eighteen and had been so distraught at the prospect of being stuck in one place forever, Andrew had been the one to promise she would see another state. He couldn't say where specifically, or when, or how, for that matter, but his faith in the two of them to find new avenues and opportunities was unceasing.

Now after all the milestones they had passed together, Andrew and Rebecca were finally well and truly married. Now they finally got to start their life together, wake up next to each other every morning, and lay down at each other's side every evening. Sharing laundry and farm chores and cakes and headaches.

Now Andrew Tenney would be Rebecca's forever.

Not ten minutes ago they had left their friends and family at Rebecca's parents' home to continue the wedding supper, as the newly minted Tenneys went to their own home for the very first time.

Andrew swung open the front door, and though the interior seemed well lit and welcoming, Rebecca still hesitated in crossing the threshold.

"Is it ...?" he began, in an uncertain whisper when she had been standing there too long. "Is there anything wrong?"

She shook her head fiercely, but still couldn't bring herself to speak. She was too happy, so happy it scared her. Surely such joy was sinful. Mere mortals shouldn't be so happy and her bliss seemed overwhelming. There was a surge of tingling all through her arms to the tips of her fingers. She wanted this moment of anticipation to last, but at the same time she wanted to prowl all over her new house with her new husband.

She wanted it all, all of the time.

As soon as they had set a wedding date, Andrew had rented the old Bailey farm, promising Rebecca the world if she just stuck by his side. They were staying in the same neighborhood, with the same church, same community as they had both known their entire lives. But now they were doing it together. Now they would wake up every morning, side by side, working toward their future.

Maybe they would have a chance to buy this farm. Maybe some other adventure would be presented. The future was wide open to them, and Rebecca just had to take this first step.

From the neighboring farm, Rebecca could smell the

woodsy scent of a bonfire. The young Valenti boys had been begging for one all week, she knew from Andrew's stories, and their parents had evidently relented in celebration of the Tenneys' marriage. Just earlier that day more people had stuffed themselves into the Stephens parlor than had ever been there before. It seemed as though everyone in Indianapolis had been eagerly waiting for this day, not just the Tenney and Stephens families.

The couple was loved and supported from the very start.

"We can go back to the supper with everyone else," he teased. "You know your mother would love to see you."

Rebecca laughed, relaxing somewhat. "Absolutely not. You know my mother; she'll have me donning an apron and washing dishes. 'Well, if you have nothing else to do, why don't you make yourself useful?' She would think nothing of assigning me chores on our wedding day."

He laughed.

She smiled at the sound. Her goal every day had been to make this man laugh. She wanted nothing more than to be a source of his joy.

Finally, she felt ready to look at her new husband, ready to weather the wave of love and exhilaration that washed over her.

"I love you," she whispered.

"I love you," he whispered back.

Andrew offered his hand, and she slipped her small fingers through his own. Together, they stepped through the doorway into the sitting room of the farmhouse. It was sparsely furnished—Andrew had been able to get a few pieces from family members, but they would have to save money for more purchases to fully outfit their home. In spite of this, the room was cozy and welcoming. Mrs. Valenti had cut across the field that afternoon to light a fire for the newlyweds before they arrived; warmth permeated the space.

Everything was perfect.

Even the things that were imperfect—Rebecca would want to move the small kitchen table to the space under the window—were still perfect, because they were hers. Hers and Andrew's.

There was the big, gilded mirror that she had so admired at Andrew's parents' home. On the other side of the room was the trunk of linens and quilts that Rebecca had spent the last several years sewing for their future home. The braided rug in front of the stove that Rebecca's aunt had sent as a wedding gift. There was even a vase of freshly cut flowers, collected from her new garden. There was still plenty to be done, plenty of ways for Rebecca to add her own touches.

Rebecca's brother, their family, their friends, their neighbors, everyone who had loved Andrew and Rebecca for the last ten years had worked so hard to make this day special for them. Every tiny thing that could be done for the new couple had been done. While she had been enjoying the plummy wedding cake the pastor's wife had made, someone had brought her hope chest over and left it at the foot of the staircase. While she had been worried about her veil staying put, someone else had cut a bowlful of blooms to rest on the kitchen table. Rebecca had not had to lift a finger.

Their house was transformed into a home before she even walked through the door. She saw at once that this would be a haven for them; no matter what other adventures came their way the Tenneys would have each other here.

"I thought we could get a piano to put here," Andrew was saying, gesturing at the empty space next to the staircase. "If you want."

"Can we afford it?" she asked, eyes lighting up. "Really? A piano?"

"Of course. With enough time." He still held her hand, and pulled it to his mouth where he kissed her fingers gently. "Anything you want, my love."

"Oh, goodness, if I had known we would get a piano, I would have married you years ago," she teased.

"I don't doubt it."

She leaned up to kiss his cheek.

"Come look at the kitchen," he said, pulling her toward that corner of the house.

The space was smaller than the kitchen in her childhood home, but the pantry was a glory of pantries everywhere.

"Root cellar down here," Andrew was saying, pointing. "And I've arranged with Bobby Valenti to help me with plowing in a couple weeks. It'll be a late start, but I think there's still time to get the crop in. Give this place a couple months, Becks, and you'll have everything you need or want."

"And I think I'll pull up the flowers outside the kitchen door," she added. "That seems like the proper place for a vegetable garden, don't you think? Although,

I suppose I should wait and see how the sun hits that side of the house."

"Whatever you think best. We have plenty of time."

"We do, don't we?"

He squeezed her hand. "The rest of our lives."

"Let's go upstairs," she exclaimed, as giddy as a schoolchild.

He laughed as she ran on ahead of him, stopping at the foot of the stairs to smile at him over her shoulder.

"You going to wait for me?"

She shook her head saucily and nimbly climbed the stairs, the skirt of her cream-colored wedding gown in her hands. At the top of the staircase, Rebecca paused again, but this time to take in the space. Just a handful of rooms, but all hers. Hers and Andrew's. Theirs and whatever family came along. Closing her eyes, Rebecca imagined the laughing children or sleeping babies that would one day fill these rooms.

Andrew caught up with her, and placed a hand at the small of her back.

"The largest room," he said quietly, as though unwilling to disturb her reverie, "*our* room, is in the western corner, there at the end of the hall."

Again she felt unworthy of such joy, but she dropped her hem, slipped her hand into his and started the few steps down the hall.

As she stepped across the threshold to her married woman bedroom, Rebecca squeezed Andrew's hand so tightly she heard him gasp. The room itself only had a narrow bed, so small Rebecca imagined her husband's feet hanging off the bottom, and a washstand, but the potential was there. She could imagine all the comforts and personal touches that they would bring to this room.

To their new home.

Their home together.

Rebecca sighed deeply.

"Do you love it? Are you happy?"

Rebecca heard the uncertainty in his voice. This man who knew so well how to love her and what she needed was now somehow worried that he wasn't doing enough.

She laughed, a joyful sound that immediately relaxed him.

Bless this man for wanting so badly to make her happy.

Rebecca was tall, but Andrew was taller, and she felt him draw his arm around her shoulders and tuck her into his side, close, tight, inseparable.

"Is this all right?" he asked.

She turned to him, beaming up into his face. "My love, this is exactly what I wanted."

CHAPTER TWO

That first day of their married life together was arguably perfect, but Rebecca soon learned that the reality of living with a man wasn't always. He somehow never noticed that the water in their washstand needed to be refreshed, and he tended to lose track of time when she had supper all ready and waiting. In spite of all their best intentions, and all the purported support of the families in their neighborhood, acclimating to married life was not quite the easy transition Rebecca had hoped it would be. The adjustment was manageable, of course. Anything was possible if two people loved each other. But the disillusionment stung.

Rebecca didn't want to be ungrateful, but it did seem as though getting married should have been a bigger adventure. Creating a home of her own, she thought, should not involve so much tedium. Waking up next to Andrew was wonderful, yes, but it didn't make any of the mountain of chores she had to do any more interesting. But, she pushed such thoughts from her mind, focusing only on the best parts of her new life, the opportunities and discoveries, the joys and celebration. Andrew loved her, and he was doing his best and that's all that really mattered.

She reminded herself of all this when having to peel yet another potato brought her spirits down.

Weeks went by like this, Rebecca trying to infuse some excitement into the daily chores while Andrew seemed apologetic but unable to do anything. Cows needed to be milked. Fences needed to be repaired. Wishing things were different would not make them so, and then the long day would be over and they would fall exhausted into bed.

Late in the summer, Rebecca and Andrew were weeding the plot of land she had set aside for their vegetables. As they had moved into the home later in the spring, the Tenney garden had gotten a bit of a late start. Alongside the tomatoes and squash, the weeds seemed to be flourishing, and the two found it much more agreeable to do the chore together rather than burden one or the other with all of it.

They'd had a little spat that morning over breakfast; Rebecca was growing increasingly frustrated that they had been living in this home without any furniture in their spare room for several months. How were they supposed to have guests with nowhere to welcome them? But Andrew had smoothed it over, reassuring her that once the harvest came in they would have more available in the budget to use for treats and other frills. She still felt the residue of that disagreement, but being outside and getting her hands in the dirt had a calming effect on her. Not for very long, mind. She would soon be ready to go, to move, to get up and find something else to hold her attention.

But she knew that this chore needed to be finished. She hurried through, snatching up the small plants as quickly as she could.

As they worked side by side, Andrew kept looking at her, acting as though he was about to speak, but then not. Rebecca didn't have the patience to try to draw him out. It had been a long day of hard work and she was tired out.

Finally, he cleared his throat, and sat up a little straighter, as though resolved to do the thing without shirking.

"I've had a thought."

She sat back on her haunches, tilting her head up to look at him. "Oh?"

"I'm not sure you're going to like it."

That got her attention. She turned to face him fully, setting the handful of greens down.

"I think you need more than all this." He gestured broadly and indistinctly. To the house, to the farm, to perhaps the town as a whole.

"I don't— What do you mean?"

She was too stunned to even protest. What else was there for her but this life that she had been expecting since childhood? As long as she had known Andrew she had known that he was the man for her. That this life with him would be what she wanted. True, her youthful daydreaming never extended to weeding all afternoon under a summer sun, but that was to be expected.

"What more could there be?"

"I think we should—" He cleared his throat. "Lots of

folks are migrating to the Oregon Territory, and I think we should go with them."

Rebecca gasped so deeply she started coughing. In her speechlessness, Andrew pushed forward.

"We don't have to leave now. We don't have to decide until maybe January or so. Then we can get to one of the jumping off towns before the summer migration and the wagon companies form. I've learned all about it, everything we'll need and everything we can expect. It will be hard, there's no doubt about that. And you'll have just as much work to do on the trail. There's no getting around work anywhere we go, but at least as long as we're moving you can't be expected to weed." He grinned.

"I... I don't understand why you think that this is a good idea."

"Rebecca." He took her hand in his, both heedless to the dirt. "Would you really be happy here doing the same thing every day until you die?"

She pulled back, startled at such a bald assessment of what their life could be like.

"There's a safety there, and a security," he went on, "but I wonder if you've already had plenty of that."

"What are you saying? You think there's something wrong with me? That I won't be satisfied here?"

He took a deep breath. "There is nothing wrong with you, my love. But I do think there's a chance that you won't be satisfied here. On this farm. In this life. I could be wrong, of course. And there will obviously be hard parts about anything we choose. But when I think of you trekking across the continent. Seeing places like the Bear Valley or Courthouse Rock. Soaking up all the wonder that this amazing country has to offer, even maybe one day the Pacific Ocean, I know that I have to at least offer you the chance."

"The chance to see Courthouse Rock? What even is that?"

"It's in the territories, a bit farther west than here."

She frowned. She felt herself thawing, interested in following this line of thinking, but was too dumbfounded. She had been blindsided. Never before had they talked about any kind of life other than here where they had both spent their entire lives. He knew, of course, that she had big dreams, but that had never before seemed truly attainable.

"How long have you been thinking about this?"

"A few weeks. Months, maybe. Since not long after the wedding. You just seemed so—"

"Don't you blame me for uprooting our entire life, Andrew Tenney!"

"No! No, my love, I'm sorry, you misunderstand. I just started thinking of your favorite things and ways I could make you happy. Remember when we went into the city to hear the senator speak?"

She nodded, a faint smile playing on her face. "Back when I was trying to convince Jasper to one day run for office."

"Right. You lived on the wonder and novelty of that for months, it seemed like. There are not many other times I saw you so happy."

"There are not many other times we have had that kind of opportunity."

"But that's what this could be. Don't you see? The journey and the destination and all the people we would meet along the way. Every step could be an adventure."

"I don't understand. You want me to leave my family? Our friends? Everything we know?"

"No, that's not it. We'll miss everyone we leave behind, of course. But we can write letters, and we'll meet new people. And, Becks, I really think that the joy you'll find in the change will outweigh your heartbreak."

"I don't know…"

"In fact," he said, looking down in embarrassment, "I've already spoken to your father about it. If you are willing, I believe your family will be joining us in emigrating to the west."

Rebecca started to laugh but stopped when she recognized the earnestness in her husband's face.

"You must be joking." Her mouth hung open in wonder.

"I'm not. Of course, he didn't agree right away. It took a few conversations to bring him around to my way of thinking, but now I think he's just as enthusiastic as I am."

Rebecca blinked in surprise, a million questions soaring through her mind. "But— What did my mother say?"

He shrugged. "Not much. You know your mother. She saw plain that her husband had made up his mind and just turned all her efforts toward that. No doubt she'll have plenty of thoughts and opinions along the way about the best way to take every step."

Rebecca laughed in recognition of the truth.

"But she seemed agreeable to the plan as a whole," he finished.

"That's frankly… well, it's shocking," Rebecca said.

"I know." Andrew laughed self-consciously. "It all was actually much easier than I expected."

"And you did all this before you even spoke to me?" she asked warily.

He took a deep breath. "I just wanted to be prepared. To give you all the choices. I know how you get excited about possibilities and I just... I wanted to make sure this was actually a sound chance before I said anything. The last thing I want is to disappoint you."

She didn't know what to say. It was all so much to be taking in at once.

"I should also add, this is why we haven't yet gotten the piano I promised you."

She frowned.

"I started thinking about going to Oregon not long after our wedding, and thought if we did make that trip it would be impossible to take a piano with us. I didn't want you to get too attached, but... Well, if you decide you want to stay in Indiana, Rebecca, I promise that buying you a piano will be my first priority."

"I need to think," she said, getting to her feet.

Wiping her dirty hands on her apron, Rebecca walked away from her husband, away from the mess of a garden, the overturned earth and all the other minute little tasks that needed to be done. Only an hour ago she had assumed that this would be her life, that this small farm just outside Indianapolis would be the whole of her world until she died. She had been weeding the garden in anticipation of putting down deep roots there. But now her husband had offered her something else, another chance.

Did she want this chance, though? That was a question only Rebecca could answer. She turned and looked back at Andrew, who was busying himself with the garden, head down and focused, giving her the space she needed.

There was no doubt that this married life had not turned out to be the idyllic happily ever after that she had envisioned. Would Oregon be any different?

Maybe not, but at least between here and there Rebecca would see more of the world, would get to meet people that this town would never give her. It might not be better, but it certainly could not be worse. Rebecca knew herself—Andrew knew her—and if she stayed in Indianapolis she would always wonder what she had missed by not taking this chance.

She turned back to her husband, closing the few feet between them and squatted where he still sat in the dirt.

"What do you think?" he asked.

"Well..." There was a last flash of indecision, of uncertainty, but then Rebecca looked at her husband's face. In that expression she saw the hope and the pleading of the man she knew so well. This was what he wanted, and what he believed to be best for them both. "This is really what you want? Even after all we've done to build this home? Don't misunderstand, dearest. I just want to be sure that Oregon is what *you* want, not just what you think I want."

"It is." He took both of her hands in his own. "It really is. I think that the freedom and the newness will be exactly what we both need. Think of it, Rebecca. The rolling green hills and the ocean only a few days' journey beyond. We'll have our pick of land to build our own home, instead of just renting the little available to us here. We can build our life to be exactly what we want. Something new. Something just for us."

"I thought that's what we were doing here," she murmured. "But, yes, my love, if this is what you want, I am..." She teared up a little, proud to be married to such a man. "I am honored to be by your side. Let's go to Oregon."

"Let's go to Oregon," he whispered just before drawing her into his arms.

CHAPTER THREE

"You're sure?" Andrew asked quietly. "You haven't had much time to think about it. You're ready to tell your parents?"

"I'm sure. I've had plenty of time. It's all I've thought about for the last day. I'm not going to change my mind."

The Tenneys were on Rebecca's parents' porch the following evening, having a whispered consultation before knocking on the door. They were to be having supper with the Stephenses; it had been planned for more than a week, though no one had known what big news the Tenneys would be bringing. Rebecca didn't think she could even wait as long as sitting down for the meal to talk about their upcoming journey to Oregon. She seemed to thrum with excitement.

"I'm sure," she said again, as she rapped smartly on the wooden farmhouse door.

Before Andrew could respond, the door was flung open and Mrs. Stephens stood before them, a broad smile on her face. Her mother was tall, like Rebecca, but far wider and sturdier, and she pulled her daughter into a tight hug. Rebecca closed her eyes and breathed in her mother's scent; she had always seemed as solid and comforting as their very house.

"Come in," Ada Stephens insisted, ushering them inside. "Supper will be ready soon. Jasper is just out doing the milking, and then we can eat."

"We have news," Rebecca began, excitedly as her father took her hat.

"Goodness," her mother said looking from one to the other. "Already? Why, you've only been married a couple months!"

"Already what—" Rebecca began, before realizing what her mother had assumed. She blushed and laughed, glancing at her father who was awkwardly pretending not to be listening to such female talk. "No, Ma. No baby. Not yet. Goodness! Don't rush us. We have other news."

Her father looked at Andrew meaningfully. "So, you finally talked to her then, did you?"

"Goodness, Pa!" Rebecca whined through her laugh. "Just— I want to say it. Stop stepping on my story."

"Oh, yes, of course. Your news. Go ahead now. You tell me." He held his hands behind his back, waiting expectantly.

It was difficult for Rebecca to even pretend to be mad when she saw that twinkle in her father's eye.

"Wait, no, not yet," her mother said. "Jasper's not here."

Rebecca and Andrew exchanged an amused look. Everyone in the room knew exactly what Rebecca was dying to say, but they were all pretending otherwise for the sake of the experience, of letting Rebecca have her moment. It was very likely that Jasper knew they were going to Oregon before Rebecca herself, but if waiting another few minutes was what her mother wanted, she could manage it.

"How's your corn?" Michael Stephens asked Andrew.

The two proceeded to discuss all the vagaries of farming that Rebecca had all but forgotten in her excitement of their future travels. The men would need to coordinate their harvest schedules, as all the families in the community helped each other with the enormous project each year, rotating the whole team of labor to each farm one by one. That was one of the things Andrew had assured her would continue on their trip to Oregon, that they'd be surrounded by other families and help and support. Though the journey would doubtless be difficult, they wouldn't be doing it alone.

Jasper came in from the barn only minutes later, called his greetings before going upstairs to change his shirt and wash his hands.

"Hurry!" Rebecca called up to her brother.

But, in no time, the five sat down at the supper table and Michael said grace over the food. As each member of the family lifted their head, there was a brief lull of charged silence, as though everyone knew what was about to happen, but no one knew how to start.

Finally, Rebecca's mother poked Rebecca's arm where it lay on the tabletop.

"Go on, then, dear, tell us your news."

Rebecca laughed. "You know, I guess."

"Maybe," her mother allowed, "but say it anyway."

"Well..." Rebecca exchanged an excited look with her husband. "We have decided to emigrate to the Oregon Territory."

"What a coincidence," her father said dryly. "So did we."

Amid the general laughter all around the table, Rebecca felt a peace that she hadn't expected. Just taking this chance on a new life with her beloved Andrew would be thrilling enough, but to know her family would be there every step of the way helped Rebecca feel even more confident in this choice.

Things would likely go wrong—she wasn't so naive as to think otherwise—but at least they would be together.

The rest of the evening was taken up with planning and excitement. Both families would have to sell belongings and livestock, and they would need to leave Indiana after the first of the year in order to get to Oregon before the winter snows the following season.

It was all quite a lot to be thinking about. Rebecca sat back, listened, and left everything to her husband.

With this new goal to look forward to, Rebecca found herself less resentful of the little day-to-day maintenance that had consumed her time. Now, she no longer had to worry about what would deplete the soil of their garden long term. She didn't have to try to budget for a new spare room bed. Not only did they need to save that money for their journey, but there was no certainty they would even have a spare room when they made their home in Oregon. Any time that she would have otherwise spent knitting or quilting, for example, she could instead spend checking in on friends and soaking up every moment with the people she would leave behind.

These were people that had been dear to her most of her life, and who she only had a few more months with. As Rebecca kept telling Andrew, it wasn't as though they would be able to fit a dozen quilts in the wagon along with everything else; she might as well save her energy.

In late August, as the first hint of autumn coolness began to make itself known in the early evenings, one of Andrew's friends, Paul Murphy, invited dozens of the neighboring couples to a dance.

"This will be a far cry from any raucous gatherings under the prairie stars next summer," Andrew said as they walked up to their friend's door.

"I plan to memorize every detail," she responded.

When they walked into the large parlor, Rebecca's breath caught in her throat.

The room was a hum of bodies, conversation, and the tinkling of glasses of champagne being passed. Paul Murphy had certainly come into some kind of money since last they had been here. Beyond the immediate crowd of friends, the dance floor extended through the rest of the room. Though it wasn't quite a ballroom, it certainly was plenty large for several couples to take turns about the floor, as well as having room for the musicians that Paul had brought in.

Rebecca could not take her eyes off of them.

"Tenneys!" they heard from somewhere in the middle of the crowd. People parted to allow Paul to squeeze through and greet his new guests. "Andrew. Rebecca."

She felt him kiss her cheek in greeting, while she kept trying to see what the musicians were doing. The song they played... She couldn't quite place it but it was exquisite.

"It's good, isn't it?" Paul continued, after he had seen where she was looking. "That four-string quartet is set to be in the area for a month and I managed to find one of the few free nights they had in their schedule. Not that I needed an excuse for a party, of course."

"It's incredible," she agreed.

"Then you best get to dancing. Let me take your coats."

In no time at all, the Tenneys had taken their own spot on the dance floor, and Rebecca was in a haze of music, love and happiness.

As they turned about the floor, Rebecca fairly felt as though she were flying. Andrew had always been a wonderful dancer, and somehow the joy and freedom of being actually married now lent a thrill to their coupling that had not been there before. By the end of the night her face hurt from smiling so, and the heels of her feet were beginning to smart from the beginnings of blisters.

But it was all worth any pain. She couldn't remember a night that she had enjoyed as much since she had become a wife.

"We should do that more often," she said, as they walked home hand in hand later that night.

"Yeah? We could invite our friends over anytime you like. I'm sure they would love to see our home. Especially if we're moving."

"Oh, I meant the music. Yes, of course we can have your friends over, but... Andrew." She sighed happily and clung to his arm a bit tighter. "The music. The dancing. It was just heaven. Do you think there will be music like that in Oregon?"

"Like that?" He laughed. "Probably not. Paul told me

the quartet is from New York City. I can't imagine anyone near as talented makes it as far west as Independence, let alone the Willamette Valley. But, I do think there will be music. Of some kind. Oregon Territory will not be the stark frontier forever. Maybe someone will even bring their instrument west in our wagon company."

"I hope so." She nuzzled in closer to Andrew, and he wrapped his arm around her as they finished their walk home in silence.

The magic of the stringed instruments was enough of a delight for Rebecca to live off of for weeks, but combined with the wonder of dancing with her beloved helped Rebecca soar to new heights of happiness.

Summer passed into fall and with every day Rebecca grew more and more excited about everything they had ahead of them. She couldn't sit still long enough to read the guidebook, but Andrew had read it and was happy to answer any question she had. How easy was it to cross the rivers? How steep were the hills? What animals would they be able to hunt along the trail? How many pairs of shoes would she wear through? So many different possibilities just in the surviving of the journey.

Every time she drew water from her well, she had to remind herself that this was a convenience she would not long have. Every time she lit a fire in the stove, she gave a little thanks for the stack of already cut firewood just outside the door. So many things about her life she knew she took for granted and would soon be out of her reach when she was on the trail.

But alone, Rebecca allowed herself to daydream about the people they might meet along the way.

Andrew had explained to her all about the importance of joining a wagon company, and how those other families would be what helped them most over the six months that they traveled west. Rebecca loved the friends that she had here in Indianapolis, but her closest childhood girlfriend had moved to the next town over when she got married. Andrew didn't have any family. There were neighbors here that she would miss, of course, but she looked ahead to who else was out there that she might meet. People from all over the country would be coming to Missouri to prepare for their own trip west.

And Rebecca would be part of it.

All they had to do was get through another few months here in Indianapolis, and then the Tenneys and the Stephenses would be on their way to a new life in the Oregon Territory.

Rebecca could hardly wait.

CHAPTER FOUR

There was a chill in the air as Rebecca looked up at the late October afternoon sky and wrapped her scarf around her neck. A basket hung on the crook of her arm, and she held it close to her as she walked through the field, following behind the Tenneys' wagon at a leisurely pace. Andrew and the oldest Valenti boy were out in the field that morning. They'd hired Bobby to help clean up the stray stalks and leaves after the harvest and Rebecca had tagged along to share lunch with her husband.

Ever since they had decided to move to Oregon, she had been less and less interested in their home here in Indianapolis. She should be spending the afternoon preparing the harvest for canning. Andrew had purchased several bushels of fruit from the Jorgensens across the way, to help stock their cellar for the winter, but really why did that all need to be done today? How much would that really matter once they had packed all their belongings in a wagon come January? It would all get done somehow.

In her daydreaming, Rebecca lost track of the wagon. The farmland dipped down into a shallow hollow, and the wagon had crested the hill. She heard vague sounds, the hum of urgent conversation as she followed behind. As Rebecca reached the top of the low hill, the thrum grew louder. Andrew's voice shouting commands carried over the field.

At first, she wasn't quite sure what she was looking at. She had thought Andrew had everything under control. They were nearing the end of the row, and should be ready to take a break to eat together in just a few minutes. All of these assumptions crowded her mind as Rebecca stood on the top of the low hill watching the wagon, Bobby and her husband not far below her.

But the longer she looked, the more she saw to concern her. Bobby stood at the front, leaning over the side of the vehicle, indicating something behind Andrew. His weight was shifting the balance of the wagon, little by little, but inexorably. Andrew, meanwhile, had turned to look where Bobby pointed, and didn't notice the wagon leaning.

"Andrew!" she cried, frantic.

He glanced up toward her, smiled to acknowledge he heard her.

Her mother had been in full planning mode ever since that day in late June when Rebecca had confirmed that they would all be going to Oregon together. Somewhere in the house was a list Ada had made for her daughter about all the preparatory tasks she should be doing, everything they had gleaned from the guidebook; Rebecca wasn't sure where she had put that list, though. Between all the paring down of certain belongings, and then buying more of other supplies, it was all a bit much for Rebecca to bother with. She was too excited about the chance of seeing a real Indian or of meeting folks from as far away as Georgia to think about something as mundane as buying enough nails for the journey.

Today's detour to accompany her husband had been a last-minute impulse. As she'd watched Andrew pull on his boots after breakfast, suddenly Rebecca could not bear to be stuck in the house one more moment. Especially as there may only be days left of weather pleasant enough for such an outing. She might regret not finishing washing all the jars she needed for canning as she had been planning on, but right now, as she smelled the bonfires and dying leaves all around her, she couldn't wish to be anywhere else.

"Look out!" She pointed, as she ran down the low hill toward them.

Andrew turned again at her pointing, noticing that the mules had become agitated.

In a flash, everything changed.

Andrew took a step closer to the animals, at the same time that Bobby leaned forward with the reins to try to calm them. That small gesture finally upset the balance of the wagon and, as though time had stopped, Rebecca watched the whole structure, Valenti boy and enormous animals hitched to it, come crashing down on her husband.

Rebecca noticed the ache in her torn throat from her screaming before she realized that she had screamed at all. Time seemed to stop and then stretch and all she had room for in her mind was that her husband was stuck under the overturned wagon.

Bobby had tumbled off, rolling into the field over Andrew's prone form. He stumbled to his feet and took in the sight.

"I'm sorry, I—" he said frantically, looking at the scene.

"Andrew!" Rebecca wailed.

"I'll run for the doctor," Bobby said breathlessly before he darted off.

"But—"

Rebecca looked around helplessly. There was just her. Alone in the field. She had no idea how to treat him or what to do. She couldn't lift the wagon. She couldn't staunch the blood. There was so much blood. Too much. His once-green shirt was now a muddy brown where his chest had been caved in.

"Andrew," she exclaimed as she fell to her knees at his side. "I don't— I can't— Tell me what you need."

He opened his mouth, but instead of answering her, he coughed up a mouthful of blood, spraying it into the dirt and across her apron.

Rebecca gasped.

"No no no no no..."

As though rejecting the sight in front of her would make it not real. As though saying 'no' would turn back time.

"Please," she whispered. "Andrew, hold on. You'll be okay. Everything will be okay. Bobby will bring the doctor. You'll be fine."

She fumbled for his hand, wincing when she saw the pain cross his face. His arm had broken in at least one spot. His shoulder had come out of his socket. There was a wide, but shallow, scrape that ran from his left temple to his jaw. But those were the least of his injuries. She held his hand tightly, resisting the temptation to squeeze it as hard as she could to keep him here with her.

"Rebecca," he managed, before coughing up more blood.

"I'm here. I'm here. What can I—" She stopped herself, starkly aware that there was nothing she could do. "I'm here. I love you. I won't leave you."

His gaze seemed clear in that moment, piercing and lucid, even through whatever pain he must be in. Leaning over her husband, Rebecca felt a wave of anguish as she looked into those light-brown eyes that she loved so much. Those eyes that would not be long for this world, no matter how she pleaded.

"There is something," he said, with more strength than she would have guessed he had. "I do need you to do something for me."

"Of course," she agreed immediately, almost to rising to her feet to attend to whatever it was. Anything to save this man.

"This is... When the doctor gets here it will be too late for me, I'm afraid."

"No..."

"Rebecca, I need you to know... I want..."

"Anything," she whispered, tears stinging her eyes.

He coughed up a mouthful of blood, turning slightly to spit it in the dirt. Looking at her with a piercing, intense gaze, he said, "I want you to go on. After I'm gone. Live your life. You have so much ahead of you still, I don't want you behaving as though your heart is in the grave."

His tone was almost jocular, as though he was making light of the situation, but they both knew how his death would crush her, as hers would him. Rebecca hung her head and let the tears drip down her nose, mixing with the blood now pooling on his crushed chest.

"I can't."

"You must. I know you, Rebecca Tenney." He seemed to be using all of his strength remaining to inject conviction into his words. "You were born for adventure, and I don't want to be what holds you back from that, even if I'm not around. I want you to go on, and I want you to follow the plan we had set. Please."

"What plan? How can I do anything without you?"

"I want you to go on to Oregon. Please. Promise me."

Rebecca laughed an ugly, disparaging chuckle.

"You must be joking."

"Promise me," he said in a hoarse whisper.

Rebecca shook her head stubbornly. "I won't. I won't say a word about it. You will be going with me Andrew Tenney and—"

"Please. Becks... please."

"Andrew..."

Her tears choked off her words. All Rebecca had wanted her entire life was to be this man's wife, and now that was all ending almost before it began. It wasn't fair. How could God do this to her? She had a vague memory of her mother invoking the story of Job, when she had been a child complaining about staying home with a cold, but Rebecca refused to think of herself in that context.

"You are everything to me," he said in a whisper. "Every single thing I've done in life has been for you, to give you the life that you wanted. Rebecca Tenney, my heart. My love. I need ... *You* need to do this for yourself. This is the last thing you can do for me—to give yourself this chance. Promise me you will go to Oregon and find a way to be happy."

"I will never be happy without you."

"Promise me."

She felt his hand holding hers loosen. The little strength that remained to him was quickly fading. Whatever she had to say to him, whatever last moment she wanted to share with this man would have to happen now. Did she really want their last memory to be a fight?

Swallowing hard, Rebecca whispered, "I promise."

The smile that broke across his face was like the

sunrise, lighting up her life for what she knew was the last time.

"I promise."

CHAPTER FIVE

Making that oath to Andrew was the last moment Rebecca felt like herself. She clung to that moment, to that dream he had for her. With that one wild promise, he had given her a purpose in life and that small, sacred thing was all that kept her from collapsing completely.

She was wholly unprepared to deal with the death of her husband. That was not the way life was supposed to go. She was supposed to have more time; they should have had decades together, time for her to slowly acclimate to the idea of losing him. Time for them to discuss what his final wishes were, time for Rebecca to envision that next phase of her life.

But instead, she found herself twenty-one years old, and already a widow, making decisions about burial plots, ironing Andrew's Sunday suit, starching his collar and accepting all the heartfelt condolences that their neighbors had to offer. All she really wanted to do was crawl back into bed and sleep through all of the decisions, steps and events. But even that reminded her of

Andrew, reminded her of that very first day after they had been married, walking through their new home.

Ada Stephens was a godsend to her daughter in this darkest moment of her life. Where Rebecca was lost to her emotions, Ada was the type of woman to push up her sleeves and wade into the worst situation with determination. While Rebecca was finding it difficult to even get dressed for the day, her mother was making sure all who loved Andrew Tenney knew to say their good-byes.

Two days after his death, when Andrew's body rested in the parlor downstairs, Rebecca remained curled up in bed. Her eyes were closed, so she only heard her mother entering her bedroom late that morning. She heard the purposeful steps crossing the wooden floor. She heard the heavy curtains being pushed open.

"It's time, Rebecca. You have just enough time to get dressed before you need to go down and greet your guests."

Rebecca groaned and turned over in the bed, burying her face in the feather pillow. The bright light of midday was bad enough, but to be expected to be pleasant and welcoming to other people was simply beyond the pale.

"I know," her mother assured her.

Rebecca heard her cross the room to the side of the bed, then felt the bed tick sink down where Ada sat. Gentle, probing fingers sought out the top edge of the quilt, and pulled it back slowly.

"Ma," Rebecca protested, still facedown and breathing in the sweaty pillow where she had lain for days.

"I know," she said again, softer this time. "We all have things to do that feel like they might crush us. I'm sure it seems to you like sleeping away the day will make you feel better."

"It will," Rebecca said, as she finally rolled over to face her mother.

"It won't. The same pain and circumstances will be waiting for you when you wake up." She pushed a heavy lock of brown hair off Rebecca's face. "This is never going to go away until you face it, dear."

"It might," she mumbled half-heartedly. Rebecca pulled the edge of the quilt back up to her chin.

Ada took a deep breath, and ran her fingers through another of her daughter's curls.

"Have I ever told you about my first love?"

"What?" Rebecca was distracted out of her pain enough to sit up in bed. "You got married at eighteen, Ma. Isn't Pa your first love?"

Her mother shook her head. "There was another boy —Levi Griffin. He lived across the road from my family and we used to walk to school together. I tried to hide my crush; at times I could be rather mean to him, truth be told, in my efforts to disguise how desperately I adored him. I'm still not sure he ever knew."

"What happened? Why have I never heard of him?"

"When we were about fifteen years old, he died. It wasn't wholly a surprise. He'd contracted consumption the year before. But it seemed to come on so quickly. Neither of my parents ever told me the true severity of his illness until he was already gone. And then... this sweet boy who I thought I would grow up to marry was gone. I was... Well, I was fifteen, of course, but even so, I was quite lost."

"That's so sad, Ma. I'm sorry. But, you know," she

added bitterly, "a youthful crush is not quite the same thing as losing the love of my life, just as we're starting our marriage." Her voice cracked under the strain of emotion. Grief. Anger. Did no one understand what a tragedy this was for her? "He loved me. I had that. That was real. And now it's *gone*. All of our plans are gone. Everything I thought I would have, everything I was promised is now over."

The wave of tears overcame her then, and Rebecca couldn't say any more. Her mother silently rubbed her back, letting her daughter sob out all her anger and frustration and grief and pain. No one would ever understand what she had lost, Rebecca thought. And she could not face such emptiness stretching out before her.

"Did you or did you not make a promise to that man?"

Rebecca started. The iron in her mother's voice did not bode well, but more than that her question brought Rebecca up short.

"I don't deny that you have every right to grieve, dear," Ada continued. "You're right that you were promised a life that now you'll never see. But don't you forget that you made promises too. There are reasons that Andrew's dying wish was for you to go on without him."

"But ... I know I should. He wanted it so badly, I think. But, I can't. How can I?"

"You can. You will. It will be difficult, but don't forget that your father and Jasper and I will all be doing it with you. You will make a new life for yourself in Oregon, and Andrew will be so proud of you. And you will have kept your word to him."

"Don't make me think about this right now, Ma," Rebecca pleaded, trying to sink back under the bedclothes.

"No, you're right. Right now, you need to put on that dress," she pointed to the black widow's weeds craped over the back of the chair by the door, "and go downstairs."

Rebecca imagined Andrew's face, sympathetic, kind, assuring her she didn't need to do anything she didn't want to do. But even in the midst of so much pain, Rebecca also knew that he would have been so grateful and so honored to know that she was downstairs representing him for their friends. She had made that promise to him, after all. And she intended to keep it.

No one was more surprised than Rebecca Tenney to find her calmly, pleasantly getting through her husband's funeral service. And then she made it through the next day, though she did turn in for bed immediately after supper, leaving the dishes for her mother. And then a week had gone by since Andrew's death. And then a month, and Rebecca found she had gone a full day without crying.

Christmas—what would have been their first holiday together as a married couple—was a somber affair, but Rebecca found by then she had built a wall around that broken part of her heart. She could still be interested in the festive treats at the holiday parties, or her cousin's delightful new baby, around what social limitations were put on a new widow. The part of her that had so loved Andrew was blocked off from her, though. That vulnerability was protected and subsumed, otherwise she would be lost. She'd found that was the only way she would be able to get out of bed every morning. Despite all the other things, she had no real choice in that matter. She had made that promise to Andrew and she had to continue on each day.

Finally it was the middle of January, three months after Andrew's death, and the Stephens family was finalizing their plans to pull up stakes and begin their journey to Independence, Missouri. The house had been sold, all the extra furniture had been given away or sold, though Ada seemed a bit ambitious about what all would fit in their wagon. In the months since the decision had been made, Michael Stephens had commissioned a new wagon to be built, though it had been intended only for himself, his wife and son. After Andrew's death, it was the unspoken assumption that Rebecca would be joining them, rather than try to drive her own wagon by herself.

That had required some adjustments, mostly to cutting back what treats and luxuries they had room for, given the need to carry food and supplies for an additional person. But the family had always made-do, and Ada didn't complain when her husband suggested that they leave her maple vanity with the marble top behind, so there would be room for a narrow cot for their daughter.

Rebecca had let go of her own home at the end of December, and would be living with her parents until they finally set west for Missouri. Now that the date of departure was closer, Rebecca was eager to get going, to put Indiana and all its memories of Andrew behind her.

"Hang these from the wagon bows," Ma said, handing Rebecca two carpetbags. "Low down if you can, so we're not always bumping our head."

They were scheduled to leave in three days, and had a mountain of tasks to finish before then.

As she climbed into the wagon to pack their clothes, her father and brother were packing the outside of the wagon. Jasper was underneath, fastening a couple hooks and hanging empty buckets that would stay upright as the wagon rolled. Pa had lifted his wife's rocking chair up, leaning against the wagon and perched on one knee as he tried to lash it to the outside of the wagon.

Rebecca took one look at it and laughed.

"Rebecca," her mother scolded as she came out of the house. "Your husband is barely in the grave."

"I know, but—"

"But nothing. Of course, we know how you are; your family," she said gesturing to the men. "But what if anyone else were to hear you? How would you explain that?"

Rebecca sighed deeply. It wasn't as though she had forgotten her husband or his death. "Andrew had made me promise to go on to Oregon anyway because he wanted more for me than to pine away in grief."

"I know, dear. But there are expectations to adhere to. Think of the gossip if Charity Dutton were to hear you laughing a mere three months after burying your husband."

"Heaven forbid we upset Mrs. Dutton," Rebecca said sullenly.

Her mother shot her a warning look, but said nothing more.

"It looks so silly," Rebecca whispered to herself.

Instead of responding, Ada directed her to the stack of crates sitting on the front porch, and over several trips, Rebecca transferred them all to the ground surrounding their wagon, where Jasper was trying to pack.

"Where are we going to sleep?" Rebecca wondered, as she watched her brother lift their mother's rocking chair up into the wagon.

"There's room," Ada assured her.

Rebecca doubted that, but she also knew that she didn't have a choice. If she didn't leave Indianapolis with her parents, she would be stuck trying to make her own way as a young widow with limited resources.

Or she would have to remarry.

Just the suggestion that she could find a man worthy of taking Andrew's place—even in order to stay fed and sheltered—was ridiculous to her.

So, relying on her parents to help her was Rebecca's only option.

And wherever her mother wanted her to sleep, even if it was sharing space with a bag of potatoes, would have to be good enough for her.

CHAPTER SIX

"Jasper, come *on*," Rebecca called to her brother.

He only grinned at her and continued his flirtation with Laura Dutton. What he had to gain from such an interaction, Rebecca had no idea. He should be saying his final farewell to her—to all their neighbors—but instead he was twisting the end of her blond curl around his finger and offering her a teasing grin.

Just barely nineteen, Jasper had been the favorite of the neighbor girls for years already. None could resist his slow grin paired with his quick wit. Rebecca and Andrew had quite enjoyed watching her younger brother get himself into scrapes and unlooked-for attachments, but that was before she was waiting on him to begin the next big adventure of her life.

They had finally reached the morning she had been looking forward to for months. This was the day they were to leave Indianapolis and travel west to their jumping off point. Independence, Missouri, was often called the gateway of the west, by those who used that final bastion of civilization to purchase supplies, join up with a wagon company, and send final missives back east. The Stephens family, with Rebecca, had only a few weeks to get there during the ideal window of time, before all the best wagon companies were full and all the stores had sold out of the thousands of pounds of flour, beans and meat they would need to make it to Oregon.

Even since the very beginning, when she thought she would be traveling west with Andrew, they had dreamed and imagined the day that they set out on the Oregon Trail officially. And now it was here. Granted, the day looked very different than she had expected—she was crammed in a wagon with her parents to start with—but still the excitement and wild possibilities that her husband had promised coursed through her.

"Jasper," Rebecca called again, this time with more bite in her tone.

Her brother leaned down to kiss Laura's cheek—far too familiar for someone he would never see again, Rebecca thought—and ran over to his sister.

"Well, then," he said, "I'm ready."

Their parents were both inside the wagon, doing their final check that everything was in place that they would need before they reached Missouri, that every last loop was tied down and secured. Rebecca herself stood at the head of their team of oxen, rein in hand, waiting for the rest of her family to finally be ready.

The animals were each at least two thousand pounds of pure muscle, and were possibly the most essential part of the Stephenses' equipment. Even so, Rebecca was glad that her father and Jasper would be in charge of driving the wagon, not her.

A small crowd had gathered to see the Stephenses off. It was just after dawn, and though many of their friends had said their goodbyes over the previous several days, just as many had put off their morning chores in order to wave goodbye when the wagon finally set off. Mrs. Dutton—Laura's mother—had spent the last several months making dire predictions as to the family's survival, but even she couldn't stand to miss such an event.

The Stephenses would be setting off from Indianapolis to travel the five hundred miles to Independence, Missouri, from where they would then leave for the Oregon Territory. As Rebecca stood near their wagon, waiting for the rest of her family, her impatience threatened to get the best of her. The only person in Indiana that Rebecca would miss was Andrew Tenney. She had the idea that getting away from the places where they had lived and loved together would help her get away from the pain.

But she wouldn't know until they left. Every other member of her family was hugging, promising to write, or waving enthusiastically. Rebecca waited with a scowl, and tried to stay invisible as was expected of a widow.

But soon they had said all their good-byes, some more than once. Soon, Michael called to the team, which then set the wagon in motion. Finally, after nine months of preparation, they were on their way.

With her parents and brother, Rebecca settled in to travel the five hundred miles across frozen landscape. Together, the family weathered the rough crossing of the Mississippi River in winter, the couple of blessedly warm nights staying in a St. Louis hotel, and a delay when

Michael injured his back while hitching the team. They traveled across the plains through the biting cold of February, finally arriving at the edge of Independence, a bustling frontier town.

Their wagon rolled into the campsite in the afternoon of a bright day early in March. Rebecca had been walking with the animals, alongside her father. She was bursting with questions and thoughts and excitement, but it was clear from Michael's silent reticence that any such display from her would be unwelcome. Instead, Rebecca clutched her coat more tightly around her and allowed the sting of cold to invigorate her. With the shorter hours of winter sunlight, there had been many days when they were only able to travel for four or five hours, but all the planning had paid off and now they had arrived just as the first signs of thaw were making themselves known.

Michael led their wagon to a campsite maybe ten yards from the next closest wagon. Rebecca noticed a tall man, leaning over to stoke the fire. It was a bit too early for supper, but as she watched, two small children climbed out of the wagon and ran to him, throwing their arms around his knees and warming themselves in the glow.

"We'll stop here," Michael said with a sigh. "Looks like we're not the first, either, so we should ask where they've established the privy and where the water source might be."

Rebecca stood off to the side, out of the way, looking at their surroundings. Beyond the closest family was another wagon with two small children shoving each other playfully. Another twenty yards beyond that was a pair of wagons, with three young men Rebecca's own age working together to repair a wheel. Maybe half a dozen other wagons filled the space, all families getting ready to launch off into the west. While Rebecca watched interestedly, Jasper unhitched the animals and brushed them down.

"Why don't you go ask that gentleman, Rebecca?" her mother instructed, pointing at the man who was now getting the children settled on a quilt.

Briefly, Rebecca flushed, embarrassed at having to make such an intimate inquiry of a stranger. But she didn't protest. If she had been an unwed girl, of course, her mother would never have asked such a thing of her. The black she had worn since October shielded Rebecca in such social situations.

Over their weeks since Indiana, making camp each evening had already become a habit for the family, each person knowing their role. Rebecca, specifically, knew better than to try to help her mother with supper or cleaning before she was specifically told what to do. Goodness knew how Ada kept all the details in her head, but it was fine for Rebecca. She could give her attention to more exciting things, and just get to work whenever given specific instructions.

And now, she could use her widowhood the same way other women used their husbands to shield them from gossip. No one would give a second thought to a woman whose heart was in the grave asking about a privy.

While the rest of her family made camp, Rebecca marched resolutely to the stranger. He didn't seem to notice her, or at least didn't look up, as she approached.

The children, a boy and girl both aged around six or seven, stared boldly, though.

She paused shortly just outside the circle of warmth, but still the man didn't notice her.

Rebecca cleared her throat.

"Can I help you?"

Rebecca spun around to see a woman carrying an armful of sticks joining them at the campfire. Out of the corner of her eye, she noticed the man had finally looked up.

"Good afternoon, I'm sorry," Rebecca began. "My family and I just arrived. My parents. My brother." She indicated over her shoulder. "And we'll be making camp here for a few weeks."

"You all going to Oregon too?" the woman asked, as she squatted to feed more wood to the fire.

"We are, yes. And you?"

"Oh, I can't wait," she answered, beaming. "We've been planning it for more than a year now."

Rebecca thought with a pang of her first conversation with Andrew about emigrating. She nodded.

"We're the Buchanans," the woman said. "Maybe we'll see more of each other, if we end up in the same company. Have your father come speak to my husband once you're settled. He can introduce you to William Sullivan who is putting together a group."

"Thank you very much." Rebecca only had the vaguest idea what Mrs. Buchanan was offering, but it sounded important.

"But first, you need water. I know." Mrs. Buchanan grinned. "Jeb, will you show her?" she asked her husband.

He grunted his assent and gestured for Rebecca to

follow him, though still without truly looking her in the face.

Was this what she could expect from now on? To only be treated like a person by the women?

Ten minutes later, Rebecca returned to her own family, where her mother already had a roaring campfire going and was busy mixing up the corn meal for the johnnycakes they'd have for supper. She filled in her parents on what she had learned from the Buchanans, but kept her personal concerns to herself.

"How long will we be here, Pa?" she wondered.

"A few weeks yet. Depends on the wagon company we're able to join, but we might plan to leave toward the end of April."

"That's weeks from now! And what are we supposed to do in the meantime?"

"I will have plenty for you," her mother cut in.

"Well," her father said, "town is about a mile west of us. If you need anything before we leave for the Oregon Trail, you can let me know or you can walk it. We can go to church in town, of course. There's bound to be a post office, if you want to mail any letters back home."

Home. Who would Rebecca have to correspond with back in Indiana? No, she would look ahead, at their future home, whatever that might look like.

While her mother started a batch of biscuits, Rebecca hung back. There was so much to see and do already, and they hadn't even left the jumping-off town. She looked up into the blue sky, shading her eyes against the brightness. It wasn't too hot yet; maybe if she made the walk in the mornings she wouldn't sweat clean through all her clothes. Not that she could even imagine what she would need from town.

But there would be people there. That was something.

With Andrew gone, Rebecca felt as though she didn't have a place. She was no longer an unmarried daughter looked after by her parents, but neither was she a wife with her own household to look after.

She felt pulled between the freedom of few responsibilities and the chains of social expectations. There was plenty of new people and sights to catch her eye just in this small campsite on the edge of Independence. What other wonders could be waiting out in the west for her?

CHAPTER SEVEN

It took all of about forty minutes for Jasper to find the prettiest girl in the camp and introduce himself to her. Rebecca watched from her perch on the seat of their wagon, while Jasper laughed and teased a cheerful, smiling girl in the wagon closest to the main road. It was not that Rebecca wanted such attention herself, but the freedom with which her brother went through the world was certainly something to be envious of. He charmed everyone he met, while she was expected to stay quiet and somber in her black attire.

So, rather than mortify her family or draw unwanted attention to herself, Rebecca stayed close to home. She didn't laugh too loudly. She didn't seek out entertainment. Her heart was truly in the grave. But other than thinking about how much she missed her husband, she didn't know how else to spend her time. If Andrew had been with her still, he never would have wanted her to so shrink herself on his account.

"What's her name?" Rebecca asked, practically

ambushing her brother when he returned to their camp the second night. The girl's laugh had carried across the plains.

Jasper turned to see who was speaking to him, and smoothly continued in a full rotation before continuing on to their bucket of drinking water as had been his original destination.

"Why, whatever do you mean?"

"Yes, very funny. We'll pretend you've not been doing anything, banter back and forth, until you finally can't stand but brag about her. Let's just skip all that, can we? What's her name?"

He grinned at her over the top of the tin cup as he drank down a draught of cold water.

"Jasper," she insisted.

"Rebecca," he whined back.

"Her name is Rebecca? Isn't that weird for you?" she teased, before sticking out her tongue at him.

He was only a couple years younger than her, and she supposed an adult in his own right, but there was something about their sibling interaction that always seemed to revert to childhood. Rebecca was sure that if she had her hair down, Jasper would find a way to pull her pigtails.

Even so, they were alike enough that Rebecca knew the one way to get Jasper to do what she wanted: ignore him. The man couldn't stand to not be the center of attention.

"Fine," she said, sitting down again with her journal. She pulled it close on her knees, so he couldn't see that she still hadn't written a word.

She counted silently to herself, and only got to twenty before Jasper gave in.

"Her name is Nora Cole. She's eighteen. Oldest child."

"Eighteen like you. And she's going to Oregon too. What a fortunate coincidence."

"I am nineteen now, big sister, lest you have forgotten." He refilled his cup.

"Well, I hope if her family ends up as part of our wagon company that you don't break her heart. Two thousand miles is a long ways to have someone angry at you."

"I would never. You wound me," he claimed dramatically, before tossing his sister a wink.

But even that little protestation gave Rebecca a glimpse. No matter what else happened, she didn't think he intended to break the girl's heart. Only time would tell what actually happened between the two of them.

After a couple of days waiting around their campsite, playing with the young Buchanan children and failing again to journal, Rebecca had gotten bored enough to venture out into town. She'd put it off as long as she could —the memory of Mr. Buchanan simply ignoring her still stung and Rebecca had had virtually no practice talking to strangers since her husband's death. But there was only so much time she could spend collecting firewood, only so many times the family's clothes need to be washed.

But Rebecca needed other people. Even if she didn't speak to any of them. Even if she was treated like a piece of the furniture, insignificant and uninteresting in her widow's black. She could not be entertained by books and chores the way other women could. She needed interaction and conversation.

The boredom would make her crazy if she didn't get out of this campsite.

And so, the next morning, when Ada was talking through her plans for the day with Michael, Rebecca spoke up.

"Can I come?"

Ada looked at her in surprise. "Goodness, Rebecca, are you sure you're ready? Independence is not the quiet neighborhood we left behind, you know."

"Yes. No. I don't know. I'm not ready to talk to other people, but also I need something. I don't know. But, I guess we'll never know if I don't try. Besides, I can help you carry things back. Since Jasper is probably going to make up some reason why he has to stay here to talk to Miss Cole."

"That's true," her mother said thoughtfully.

"I just want... I need to get out of this one spot, Ma. I'll help you, and can see the town and maybe get an idea of what we're all doing."

"You know what you'll have to do, though, Rebecca. I won't make you wear a veil, but you'll need to keep your head down all the same, not look folks in the eye if you can help it, stay quiet and subdued. It seems like that'd be a lot easier for you here."

"I know. I know all that. It's just ... I have the whole day ahead of me and no idea how to fill it. Give me something to do. You shouldn't have to do all the shopping by yourself just because I'm in mourning."

She couldn't interpret her mother's expression, but after a moment, Ada smiled and nodded.

"Stay close to me, dear. And if you want to come back, you just say the word."

The walk into town from the campsite was only a mile, but it seemed to take forever. Rebecca had been so secluded for so long that every person, every signpost was new to her. She wanted to stop at every thing they passed, to compare it to what she knew from Independence, to ask her mother how it might be different in Oregon.

But when the two women finally turned onto the main street of Independence, Rebecca's exhilarating fascination with every detail was like a wave breaking over her.

Rebecca felt as though her eyes were going to fall out of her head, as she struggled to take in the sight of every man, woman and child that crossed their paths. The closer they got to the center of town, the more crowded the streets were. And the more crowded the more Rebecca wanted to stop and take it all in. Indians riding bareback with stacks of beaver pelts tied in front of them. Dirty children of all ages playing tag in the mud while their parents were who-knew-where. Braying shopkeepers calling to every soul that merely looked their way. It was noisy and bustling and Rebecca could not get enough.

"Where are we going, Ma?" Rebecca asked, looking around. Why had she been hiding away at the campsite? There was so much in this bustling frontier town to see that she might run out of time before they had to leave again.

"We need to stop by the post office to see if your aunt sent anything. Check in with the tanner who is making us new reins. They were supposed to be done two days ago. And I want to get some eggs from Mrs. Case for our breakfast the next few days. The more fresh food we eat while we can, the better.

"In fact," she continued, "she's just down this side street here. Follow me."

Over the next hour, Rebecca followed her mother from store to store, saying hello to new friends, checking on the Stephenses' orders, adding more tasks to their to do list. Ada Stephens was vibrant and social; Rebecca got her fill of company just standing next to her.

"How many of these new friends are actually in our wagon company?" Rebecca asked in a low voice as they left the tanner.

"Maybe half. It'll be a shame to miss the Armstrong family, though. You would love their daughter. But maybe when we all get to Oregon..."

When they all got to Oregon, there was no saying what might happen. Though there must be plenty of fear and trepidation among the emigrants, to Rebecca, that unknown and that possibility was a source of excitement.

"I'm sure they'll all come looking for you no matter where in the territory they end up," Rebecca said, teasing. "That Mrs. Stephens who was so kind to sew our wagon's canopy with her own two hands, or some such nonsense."

As they left the tanner, stepping out onto the boardwalk, Ada spotted yet another friend coming out of the store across the street. Lifting their skirts out of the mud and the muck, the two women picked their way across.

"This is Mrs. Hudson," Rebecca's mother said, gesturing to the other woman. "Her family will be part of our wagon company, I believe."

"That's right, and please call me Margaret. There are going to be too many Hudsons around; I don't want it to get confusing."

"Oh!" Ada gasped, turning abruptly away from Margaret. "I forgot something. Stay here," she said to her daughter, putting the basket in Rebecca's arms. "Just hold this. Wait for me. I'll be right back." She darted off down the street after whatever she had suddenly remembered.

Rebecca and Margaret shared a smile as her mother walked away.

"She doesn't mean to be rude..." Rebecca began, before Margaret laughed.

"Please. No explanation needed. It's nice that you all are able to come west together. That's what my family is doing too. I couldn't imagine being left behind, making my son grow up without his aunts."

"Aunts?" Rebecca asked. "How many of you are there?"

"Four sisters including me, plus my teenage son. My youngest sister has accepted a marriage proposal in the territory, and, well, if you meet Louisa, you'll understand whose idea it was for us to all go with her."

Rebecca could not help but laugh. "Funny, my mother is the same way. With just a hint of a suggestion, she'll barrel on through and make everything happen."

"It's easiest to just let her have her way," Margaret said with a twinkle in her eye. "I only married into the family, and even I know that."

Rebecca looked around guiltily but her mother was not within earshot.

"I don't know what I would have done without her, when my husband died," she said, finally.

"You'd like Annie. The youngest. You might have a lot in common," she suggested gently. "Her fiancé died before they were married, so though she can't rightly be called a widow, I know she's done a fair bit of grieving in her life."

"Annie? She's not the one who is getting married again is she?" Rebecca tried to keep the judgment out of her tone, but couldn't do much about the expression she was sure had flashed across her face.

"She is, yes. It was an ad placed in our local paper, a correspondence situation. I've not heard all of the story, myself, but I try not to pry. It'll come out in time. I'm sure there's a reason she's decided it's time to move on from her past."

Rebecca looked down, cleared her throat, and changed the subject. "And what about your son? Is he excited about Oregon?"

"He was one of the loudest voices in our decision to leave Virginia. That boy..." She shook her head in marvel. "He's fourteen and already the man of the family."

"You sound very proud," Rebecca said.

"I am. His father died when he was too young to really know him. The way he's grown up to be so kind and so responsible is a wonder to me."

"He sounds like quite the gift to be accompanying you on the trail."

"No more than any of the rest of us, I think. You'll

see, Mrs. Tenney. I believe traveling the Oregon Trail will bring out the best of every single man, woman and child that makes it to Oregon."

Rebecca felt a chill at the unsaid part of her declaration—that there would be some who did not make it to Oregon.

But she put that detail from her mind. She didn't have to worry about it today; there would be time enough to think about it in the future.

CHAPTER EIGHT

Now that she had had a chance to meet some of the other women that would be on the same journey west, Rebecca was even more excited to get moving. The longer they stayed in Independence, the more she felt her grief dragging her down. Andrew had been exactly right—this change of scenery was doing wonders for her. She was so grateful she had made that promise to him and had it to guide her.

Day in and day out, the Stephens family hustled to get everything settled for the inevitable day that they left the last vestiges of civilization behind. Once they left Independence there may be opportunities to acquire more supplies at the forts along the way but they couldn't be certain of it. That meant that Ada checked and double-checked and triple-checked that everything was set that they would need before they left. It kept Rebecca busy, too, but not so busy that she wasn't anxious to get going.

Finally that day arrived. The wagon company

captains had committed to their schedule, committed to the trail and it was time to get started. The Stephens family, Rebecca, and at least a quarter of the families who had been camped outside of town with them, pulled up stakes to join the Sullivan-Mills wagon caravan in leaving Independence, heading west and beginning their adventure. Rebecca schooled her face to remain as somber and withdrawn as her mother expected of her as a widow, but inside she was fit to bursting.

This was the very day she had been looking forward to for nearly a year. She made every effort she could to not think about the circumstances the choice had been made under, and kept her eyes looking ahead toward the horizon, toward the future.

Many of the other families in the wagon company had been staying in Independence itself. They had been scattered among its dozens of small hotels and boarding houses that were now full to the gills in the spring with all the wagon trains moving west. In order to be included in their caravan leaving the town, the Stephenses had their own wagon at the town's edge first thing in the morning. In no time, wagons and families rolled past them out of town.

"That's Captain Mills," Michael said, as the head of the caravan passed them. He pointed out the lead wagon, driven by an older man, while a younger man rode a horse alongside. "He's one of the men leading us to Oregon."

The train of wagons followed close behind, and the Stephenses waited for an opening where they could join, in between the sprawling families, the livestock and the dogs trotting along the road. Nearly all of the wagons that were coming from Independence seemed brand new, with stark white canvas tops that had not yet been exposed to the rain and the elements. As they crossed the plains, the white should reflect the sunlight to keep the interior cool, but also provide a beacon to guide the immigrants should they become separated.

"What does that say?" Rebecca asked.

One of the wagons approaching seemed to have big black writing on the side of the wagon canopy.

Michael peered at where she pointed. "I can't tell from here, but it's probably their town name. Or maybe a phrase like 'Oregon or bust.' I saw some examples of that in town last week. There's some folks that want to shout from the rooftops who they are."

Rebecca smothered a smile; she would have wanted to do that very thing. If Andrew were here. If the Tenneys had had their own wagon. If she had any modicum of independence. Instead, she was a young widow, tagging along with her parents as though she were still a child. Well, no matter. She would enjoy the adventure either way. She would fulfill her promise to Andrew.

As they watched, several of the other families that had camped outside town had a chance to slip into the long train of emigrants. The Buchanan and Waters families found a spot near the front of the train, while the Coles waited almost as long as the Stephens did before tucking into the line. Rebecca caught the look of disappointment on Jasper's face when he saw that the Cole family might not be too close to them in the travel.

Finally, about three-quarters of the way through the long line of wagons, one of the drivers had slowed to fix a twisted bridle. Michael called to his team, getting the wheels of his wagon rolling and guiding them artfully into the caravan. As he straightened out the vehicle, bringing it in line with the wagon in front of them, Rebecca followed joyfully.

"Well! We're on our way," Ada said cheerfully. "It's really here."

The two women walked together alongside the wagon, and Ada wrapped her arm around her daughter's shoulders.

"Are you still glad you kept your promise?" she whispered to her daughter.

Rebecca nodded, but couldn't say more as she fought tears. She was imagining her husband leading their wagon, helping her around their camp, building the Tenneys a new home on the other side of the continent. She could so easily picture Andrew at her side through every bit of this. But it was a dream that would never come true. Everything that they had talked about doing together, Rebecca was now doing on her own—or as an ancillary to her parents, which was hardly the same thing at all.

Her mother squeezed her again and let her go, before making her way to Jasper's side for a similar encouragement. Rebecca was left alone with her thoughts on the several-mile walk to their first campsite. Though she kept to herself—and no one tried to speak to the widow—Rebecca managed to have a full afternoon of watching the new people around her, soaking in every detail.

Finally, at the end of the day, the long row of wagons pulled into a campsite. As her father and brother took care of the animals, Rebecca's mother handed her two empty buckets with instructions to collect them water.

"We'll be here all day tomorrow, too, your pa says. To give any stragglers time to catch up. You'll have plenty of time to go exploring then, dear. Don't dilly-dally around tonight."

Dilly-dallying didn't seem very likely. She'd be lucky if anyone even noticed her, let alone took the time to speak to her, since she was wearing her mourning attire. As Rebecca walked through the camp, she kept her eyes open for any of the other women she had met when they were in Independence. There were nearly fifty families in the Sullivan-Mills wagon company, and she hoped to make friends with all of them.

Being virtually invisible had its perks, however. As a widow, Rebecca slowly strolled between the wagons and barely any head even turned toward her. She saw interactions and heard snippets of conversation that most people would be embarrassed to have a stranger overhear. The small Buchanan boy was getting a spanking when she walked past. The Cole family seemed to be pulling everything out of their wagon in order to repack it. Margaret Hudson was gesturing excitedly, with what Rebecca guessed was her sisters gathered around her.

There was even a Black couple, with their camp far on the edge of the circle of wagons. Rebecca tried to walk casually past their camp, on her way to the water, but this woman did not ignore Rebecca in her black mourning dress; she locked eyes with Rebecca. The expression on the woman's face was inscrutable, though Rebecca sensed no hostility.

Rebecca put her head down and kept walking toward the stream, away from the woman, away from the camp.

The stream and privy for the camp was somewhat busy, with all of the immigrants in a hurry to settle in for the night. Rebecca waited her turn to get to the water's edge, and even then had to squeeze between an older woman grumbling about the crowd and a child who seemed oblivious to the fact that she was in the way. In her waiting, Rebecca ached to have someone to speak to.

As she got to the water, she noticed a young woman approaching, maybe a few years older than her, with her blond hair pulled tightly back and tucked under her bonnet. Peering closer, Rebecca realized it was one of the women she had seen with Margaret Hudson. The youngest.

The bride. The one Margaret thought she might be friends with.

At that thought, Rebecca almost fell over her own feet in her haste to get her water and get to this woman before she left again. When Rebecca pulled her full bucket up carelessly, a little splash spilled over the side onto her feet. The Hudson woman approached the spring near her, and meticulously held her bucket under the surface of the water.

"Are you one of the Hudsons?" she called as the woman hauled her bucket out of the spring.

The other woman set the bucket at her feet and turned toward Rebecca.

"I am," she said with a returning smile. "Have we met? I'm sorry I can't place you at all."

"Oh, I guessed as much," Rebecca said with a dismissive wave and grin. "But your sister Margaret talked all about you, so I feel like I already know you."

She laughed. "Yes, that sounds like Margaret. My name is Annie."

"Annie. So you're ... the youngest? The bride-to-be?"

Annie blushed, but laughed. "She really does talk about me, doesn't she?"

"Only kind things, I assure you. My name is Rebecca. Or, I suppose, Mrs. Tenney."

"Tenney," Annie repeated. "I'm sorry, but that name doesn't sound familiar at all to me."

"That's probably because I'm the only one," she said. "Just me. My husband died before we even left Indiana, and I'm traveling with my parents and brother. The Stephenses." Rebecca felt her throat tighten at these words, but tried to keep her tone light. She would have to get used to telling people about Andrew without letting the sorrow overtake her. She pushed it from her mind.

"Mrs. Stephens, yes. I'm sure Margaret has mentioned her."

"My mother."

"I'm very sorry for your loss," Annie said. "It must be very trying to be going through all of this without your husband, Mrs. Tenney."

"Please, call me Rebecca." She smiled brightly, in an effort to hide her pain. "Everyone calls me Mrs. Tenney and it just makes me sad all over again each time."

"Forgive me," Annie said hastily. "Rebecca."

"I don't want to talk about me, or the past," she said with brave cheerfulness. "I just wanted to introduce myself. From what Margaret has told me I thought we might be friends. I used to play piano, too, you see."

"Did you? I miss it ever so much. But of course it's completely impractical to haul one all the way across the continent."

Rebecca laughed. "I've only ever played our church's piano, so it's not as though I had any idea of bringing one to Oregon. Sometimes at night, though, I find my fingers playing a hymn against my knee when my mind is elsewhere."

"I was the piano teacher in our town." Annie shook her head. "Without one, I'm not sure how I will spend my time there. It's all so new!"

"There will always be something, I'm sure."

"You're right. Just like there's always some chore to do here." Annie gestured to the buckets she had set in the dirt at her feet. "My sister will be wanting these."

"Of course! Yes, well, it was lovely to meet you, and I do hope we can be friends."

"I hope so too. Until then."

Rebecca watched her walk away, and immediately thought about how she would have described Annie Hudson to her husband. This was a woman she could be friends with—and all it had taken was leaving Indianapolis to find her.

CHAPTER NINE

Her stroll back to the family's campsite was even more distracting than when Rebecca had gone to the water. There were people everywhere she looked. More and more families were crowding into the space, far more than belonged in a single wagon company. All around her people were making camp, turning their children and their animals loose, and starting to cook all manner of delicious-smelling meals. Some women had started to repack their wagons. Some men had settled in to clean their guns. Rebecca found herself trying to look in twenty different places at once.

"Hurry up with those," her mother called, as Rebecca returned to her camp with the buckets of water. "We won't have coffee with supper if we don't get it started soon."

"Heaven forbid," Rebecca responded with a grin.

The look her mother gave her warned her what kind of scolding would have been in store for her if Ada had just one extra minute—but she didn't.

Rebecca kissed her mother's cheek in repentance as she set the buckets near the fire. Wiping sweat from her brow, she looked around at the chaos. Several of the small bags and barrels had been pulled out of the wagon, but to what end Rebecca couldn't say.

"What else would you like me to do?"

"Peel three of those potatoes," she said, pointing with the wide wooden spoon in her hand to the burlap bag that rested against the back wagon wheel. "Then slice them for me. We'll fry them up with the lard left once I'm done with this bacon."

The smell of supper made Rebecca's stomach growl. She had been on her feet for so long and was famished after such a long day of walking. Her mother had warned her over and over that the meals would get more scant the farther west they went, that they might need to ration and make do, but at least today they had fresh onions and potatoes to feast on.

"I made a friend at the water," she began as she dug through the box of utensils for a sharp knife to peel with.

"Did you? Well, I hope she's going to be part of our wagon company."

"I think so. It was Margaret Hudson's sister, the youngest one. But, what do you mean? Not everyone here is part of our company?"

"Oh, no. All these people? There are far too many. No, this is just a meeting point for many of the companies heading west. That's another reason we'll be here all day tomorrow too. Not all the folks in Independence were ready this morning. And Captain Sullivan wanted to give them a chance. This campsite is the first one outside of town, and it's where many of us folk get hooked up with a company or another. Over the next day a few more will trickle in, and then we can leave the next morning."

"Captain Sullivan? He's not the one leading the wagon train, is he? At the front?"

"No, that's Mills. Captain Mills and his family will be in the lead, and then since it's such a big company, Captain Sullivan and his family will follow along somewhere in the middle. That way folks in the back don't have to ride up quite so far to reach someone in charge if they need to."

Rebecca carefully washed the potatoes, and pulled one of the crates closer to the fire for a seat. She was silent as she fell into the rhythm of peeling the potatoes. Narrow strips of peel dropped into the bowl she had set at her feet. Once the potato slices for supper were done, her mother would fry up these peels even longer, even crispier, and then set them aside to cool. The Stephens children had grown up snacking on such treats, and Rebecca had always made it a game with herself to see how long of a peel she could manage without it breaking.

Ada kept Rebecca busy until sunset, at which point the whole family had eaten and were sitting around the campfire to take a breath after a long day. As the four sat and talked about their day, who they had met and what they had seen, the spirited sound of a fiddle floated on the air from elsewhere in the camp. Rebecca smiled to herself, thinking about Andrew's promise of a dance under the stars. She had been so busy and so taken with all the new things around her that she hadn't much thought of him all day, but she could never escape it for very long.

Later, when she finally went to bed on the little cot in the wagon, Rebecca fell asleep to thoughts of how Andrew would have enjoyed the walk in the spring air that day, imagining him leading the Tenney family wagon while she walked next to him.

The next morning, Rebecca woke with a jolt. She had been dreaming about Andrew, that they were together, but in the dream she had turned to say something and found him gone. The surprise and trauma of that moment had sent a surge of adrenaline through her, dragging her to consciousness. She remained in her cot, listening to the sounds of the camp on the other side of the canvas and giving her heart a chance to slow down.

She would never get used to this. Every morning, for the rest of her life, Rebecca would have to wake to the reality of her life. Over and over again, reminded that her husband was gone forever.

But she couldn't think about that now. She had to get up. There were chores to do, and if she let the tears that threatened overtake her she would never move.

With a steeling breath, Rebecca sat up, brushed out her hair and got ready for her day as quickly as she could before the grief snuck in again. When she climbed out of the wagon soon afterward, she saw that her family had let her sleep late. Breakfast was already started.

"I need you to help me repack the wagon," Ada said as she handed Rebecca a cup of coffee. "I greatly underestimated how much space would be taken up by all the food we have to carry west. Six months' worth! I don't rightly know what I was thinking, but between all that and the space for us to sleep, it's going to be quite a tight fit for a few months at least."

"I'll eat more of that bacon if it will give you more room," Jasper volunteered through a mouthful of food.

"Oh, I don't doubt it," Ada said. "But if I let you eat bacon now, you'll complain when you don't get any more come July. Off with you, boy. Go see if you can't find out if we'll have a butcher in our wagon company. Maybe we'll get fresh beef somewhere along the trail from one of these other families."

Rebecca watched her brother go off to do who knew what with no responsibilities to hold him back. She sighed and turned to the wagon, where her mother was already halfway inside. Hurrying to finish her coffee, Rebecca lifted her skirt and climbed in after her mother.

"Goodness," she said under her breath, when she saw what they were up against.

In the short minute that Ada had been in the wagon, she had already started pulling down the stacks of supplies that had been crammed in the small space.

As Rebecca had been with her mother when the orders for all this food had been placed, she had some idea of what all was in here. One hundred and fifty pounds of flour per person. Fifty pounds of bacon, forty pounds of sugar, five pounds of rice. All of that just for one person, as well as so much more, and then multiplied by four people. Not to mention the rocking chair, quilts, blacksmithing tools, ammunition and a mountain of other supplies that they had brought from Indiana to help make their eventual home in Oregon.

Rebecca had no idea how all of it had fit within the four small walls of this wagon.

"What if..." Rebecca began uncertainly. There wasn't room for her to step farther into the wagon. With the stacks of crates propped against the curving bows of the cover, Rebecca was afraid it would all tumble over any moment. "I suppose we can't leave things outside while we sleep, can we?"

Her mother laughed, but looked thoughtful. "What if we just make Jasper sleep with all the coats and blankets? Convince him it's a soft mattress?"

"Ew," said Rebecca. "Then when it's hot in July he'll sweat all through the blankets we have to sleep under come the fall. I don't want to have to wash those every day."

"Good point." Her mother grinned at her, but turned a thoughtful eye back to the mess of the wagon. "Maybe we'll have to make your father sleep under the wagon too."

"I heard that," Michael called from outside the wagon. "Might I remind you that I already hurt my back getting here."

Ada winked at her daughter, and Rebecca felt a pang of longing. That should be her and Andrew, with their easy teasing and light-hearted banter. Goodness, how she missed him.

She wasn't sure she would ever stop missing him.

Her mother must have noticed Rebecca's lack of interest after that point, and instead of talking through all the changes she intended to make, just gave her daughter instructions. Rebecca was perfectly capable of carrying what needed to be carried, stacking what need to be stacked. Decisions were beyond her, but she was quite able to move things where she was told to.

Once the wagon had been repacked, it was already late into the afternoon. Rebecca was sweating from spending so many hours in the stale closeness of the wagon. She took off her bonnet and fanned herself with it, as she leaned against the back wagon wheel and watched the campsite all around them.

"Go," her mother said, taking pity on her. "I'll be fine. You need a breath of fresh air. Go find a breeze; don't get in trouble. Just be sure you come back in time for supper."

Her face lit up. "Thank you."

Rebecca smoothed down her hair and repositioned her bonnet before darting off. Where to start? She could perhaps seek out Annie Hudson, or Mrs. Buchanan and the children. Or maybe if she lingered by the stream, she would meet more women who could be friends of hers. Or...

Rebecca stood in the middle of a clearing, about twenty feet in diameter, and slowly spun around, taking in the sights, sounds and smells all around her. She lifted her face to the sky as the light scent of apple and cinnamon carried on the breeze surrounded her. Someone was baking, using their choicest ingredients before even setting off. Someone else was crying; Rebecca heard the sobbing of what sounded like a child denied his favorite toy.

There was always so much to life, so much to soak in. Rebecca almost cried herself when she remembered Andrew's expression, urging her to come on this trek without him. That promise she had made was the reason she was here at all.

And how could she best use this one chance?

As more of the wagons settled into place, more of the campsites were populated, and more of the emigrants made themselves comfortable in their new surroundings. The lively sound of a fiddle cut through the air, weaving through the conversations and laughter of all the men, women and children that had just begun their western journey.

That was how she would spend her night—Rebecca resolved to find the source of the music.

CHAPTER TEN

She couldn't resist any longer; Rebecca had set off on her own through the crowded campsite to find where the fiddle music was coming from.

Music had been a part of her life as long as she could remember. When she had been growing up in Indiana, the church organist had been an older spinster woman, and over time had become one of Rebecca's closest friends. This had been the woman that first introduced Rebecca to the possibility of creating music herself, and the reverence for it still stuck with her.

Her friendship with Miss Hotchkiss had begun when she was just a child, after Rebecca had chased the chickens around the yard until one of them had dropped dead from the exhaustion. Though only seven years old at the time, Rebecca absolutely knew better and her mother would see to it that she never forgot again. As a punishment, Ada had sent the little girl to the older woman's house every afternoon for two weeks to complete whatever chores were needed.

That first afternoon, Rebecca had spent cleaning the windows in the parlor as Miss Hotchkiss had played the piano, practicing several songs she would later play that Sunday. By the second afternoon, Rebecca was asking questions. On the third afternoon, Miss Hotchkiss invited little Rebecca to sit down on the piano bench with her. Miss Hotchkiss mentioned it to her parents and once the two weeks of punishment had ended, Rebecca continued to go to the house, though this time to practice scales. Miss Hotchkiss had died a couple of years earlier, and Rebecca would always how remember the woman's strong hands felt, guiding her across the piano keys.

And now, fifteen years later, she still felt the same pull, the same belonging when she heard music.

Just as before when she had walked to the water, not a soul seemed to notice Rebecca as she strolled between the camps. The sun was just setting and the light of dozens of campfires illuminated the whole camp, casting shadows where Rebecca walked. She couldn't linger long; supper would be soon and as a widow she really shouldn't be seen anywhere near a party. But she couldn't resist the temptation of that music, the first music she had heard in months.

Closer and closer that bright fiddle seemed, drawing her in. She moved around the edges of the campsite, looking for the source.

Finally, Rebecca spotted it.

Just outside the circle of light from the campfire, stood a young man with a shock of jet-black hair, utterly focused on the worn, beat-up fiddle in his hands. He stood alone as he played, with seemingly no thought outside of the boisterous music he was producing.

Rebecca stayed in the shadows and watched.

The young man playing was maybe in his mid-teens, as much as she could tell in this dim light. The longer she watched, the more she realized that he was one of a family of all men, or at least, that's all that were present at this campsite. They all had that same black hair and interacted with the ease that came with knowing another person very well. There did not seem to be any women traveling with them. An older man—the father?—with a long gray beard stood hunched over a big pot that sat on the smoldering coals of a campfire. Two other young men laughed and passed a flask around them while their brother played the fiddle.

"Martin!" called the father. "Put that down and come eat."

Martin shook his head and smiled as he kept playing. Rebecca was sympathetic. After the long day, and the stress of trying to make everything fit in the wagon, this escape was exactly what she needed.

The music was attracting other young folk as well. As more of the emigrants finished their supper or their chores, they made their way to the source of the music just as Rebecca had. She held back, waiting in the flickering shadows as the warmth and comfort of familiar music began to draw a crowd.

First they stayed back in the darkness, waiting, watching. But then Martin seemed to notice he had an audience, and nodded pleasantly to the man closest to him. An unspoken conversation was carried on with just those looks. Friendships were forming all around Rebecca, as this community of emigrants found common ground in the appreciation of Martin's fiddle.

When the first couple began to dance, Rebecca knew she couldn't stay. Her feet itched to join them, but widows couldn't indulge in such frivolity. And even if the social rules weren't clear, without Andrew there she would only end up making herself sad.

Ducking back into the dark, Rebecca retraced her steps, weaving between the other wagons back to her own. Now in the dark and crowded campsite, she understood better why some of the families had painted words or identifying marks on their canvas covers. She got turned around, and wasn't able to find her home again until she heard Jasper's hearty laugh floating over the other sounds of the campsite.

"You're back!" Ada said, when she noticed Rebecca. "Supper's just about ready. Wash your hands."

Rebecca slipped back into her family and their campsite unobtrusively, holding the memory of getting to hear music close to her.

In spite of spending all day repacking the wagon, Ada still had not found the most efficient way to make room for all their supplies as well as the sleeping bodies of three Stephens. When Rebecca went to bed, she had to move a small barrel of nails to the foot of her cot. Her mother must have set it there earlier and forgotten to find a new home for it. Rebecca would just have to make do. There was virtually no room for her to even move, let alone be comfortable. But she was tired enough from her day that it didn't matter.

Rebecca had been in full mourning for Andrew for

now six months. If they had stayed in Indianapolis, she would have been expected to stay out of society completely for at least another six months. She was more grateful than ever that she had the memory of that last dance with Andrew. Paul Murphy would never know what a gift he had given her.

CHAPTER ELEVEN

The following morning, Rebecca was up before the sun. She climbed out of the wagon quietly, unable to sit still any longer. This was it. The first day. The first real westward travel. The Sullivan-Mills wagon train was due to leave camp as soon as everyone in the company was ready. Rebecca was determined that she—nor any of the Stephens—would be a reason travel was delayed.

The quiet of the morning made her thrum with anticipation. So many possibilities. So many adventures ahead of her. She wanted to call out, to laugh, to sing, to spread her happiness to every corner of the campground. How were not every man, woman and child not bouncing with the excitement of leaving for Oregon?

In the cool, predawn twilight, few other individuals were awake. She would wait for her mother to start breakfast, but couldn't bear to just wait around their wagon. Instead, Rebecca wrapped her shawl around her and walked slowly through the camps. The paths between the big Conestogas were narrow, and yet the camp seemed to stretch on forever. All around her was what seemed like an ocean of white-topped wagons, the sound enormous animals lowing. The vivacious fiddle of the night before had been replaced by early morning crickets, punctuated with the crackle of campfire and occasional murmured words.

Every one of these sleeping or stirring emigrants imagined a new life for themselves, two thousand miles away. Some would be breaking off and heading farther south, to Los Angeles or San Francisco. Some might be stopping in Salt Lake, with the Mormons. And some of these strangers that surrounded Rebecca in the morning cool would be her new neighbors, her new friends. The thought excited her.

So many adventures. So many opportunities.

So many new things she wanted to share with her husband.

How Andrew would have loved all of this, she thought. He would have patiently listened to her chattering, her ideas and desires. He would have taken on whatever laundry he could so she could have time to gossip or bake with one of the other young married wives. Her husband would have done everything he could to make this the most memorable and exciting adventure they would ever be on.

But Andrew wasn't there.

Now, at the end of April, six months had passed since her husband's death, ten months since they had married. She realized with a start that he had been gone for more time than he had been hers. She had barely had time to consider herself a married woman before she had to grapple with the fact of her widowhood. Where her despair had felt life-ending in the immediate aftermath, now that pain was just a dull ache. Rebecca had been so sure that she had lost her husband forever, but in truth his memory had accompanied her every day, every step. This adventure she had embarked on was theirs together. The promise she had made ensured that he was with her every step of the way.

It was with this comfort of connection that Rebecca went on into the day.

The sun rose higher in the sky, and as the families around them began to stir, Rebecca's excitement grew. She hurried back to her own camp with the few sticks of firewood she had been able to find. With so many emigrants at this camp, the best pieces had already been picked over, but it was enough to boil water for coffee and fry up some bacon. Under the wagon, Jasper was waking in his bedroll. Rebecca dropped the firewood near him, not bothering to try to stay quiet.

She nudged him gently in the ribs with the toe of her boot. "Make the fire, please," she said, as she climbed back into the wagon.

Her father had already risen from the small cot he shared with his wife, and was shrugging on his coat.

"Good morning." He kissed his daughter on the cheek as he tried to squeeze past her in the narrow space.

She tried to lean over out of the narrow walkway to give him more room to maneuver, but lost her balance. Falling onto her cot, Rebecca laughed at herself, pulled her feet up out of his way and waited for her father to pass. Her mother shot her a warning look.

"No one heard me laugh but you, Ma," Rebecca protested.

"All right, then. I'm sorry, dear, but you know how people talk."

Rebecca nodded and didn't protest.

Together the two women made the family's breakfast, coffee, cleaned the dishes, and got everything packed away as quickly as possible. Michael and Jasper had the oxen hitched up and ready to go, but then they waited. Nothing. Rebecca took another brisk walk around the campsite, just to give her feet something to do. The morning seemed to drag on. As should have been expected, with this many families to organize, so many of them new to living on the road, only a portion of the emigrants were ready to leave when Captain Mills had wanted to. Ada Stephens was in the middle of reorganizing their wagon when her husband called to her to finish up.

The moment had come. The wheels were turning. The wagons were one by one being led to the Oregon Trail, which they would follow for another two thousand miles.

If Rebecca had been a boy, she would have whooped with glee.

Instead, she was a woman—in full mourning, no less —and had to content herself with merely observing quietly. Though her mouth had to stay closed, her heart was wide open, grateful for the opportunity. Surely this good had come out of her suffering the loss of Andrew. She promised herself she wouldn't squander it.

With both her father and Jasper on hand to lead the animals and the wagon they drew, Rebecca was on her own for most of the day. Sure, there was plenty to do when the wagons stopped, but she couldn't very well wash her brother's trousers while the wheels were rolling. Instead, she had hours and hours to herself. Hours to fill, hours in which to entertain herself. All the hours that the wagon company was on the trail, all the miles they traversed, Rebecca got to spend however she wished. Or, rather, however she wished within the expectations placed on a widow. There seemed to be so much to see, so many people to meet, and though they had months in which to do it, she still wanted to run ahead and experience all that this life had brought her as soon as she could.

She couldn't help but grin as she hurried on ahead of her wagon to see what was up ahead.

It wasn't until she noticed the judgment and confusion in the eyes of Mrs. Van Anda, the woman in the wagon ahead of the Stephens, that Rebecca pulled herself up short. She was in mourning. Of course. She kept forgetting. Widows didn't run. The memory of Andrew was so fresh, so tender, that the actual fact of his death seemed unreal at times.

But widows had very specific guidelines around their behavior. Even being on the Oregon Trail at all was an exception most women would not allow themselves.

She would just have to stay out of sight of the other immigrants.

With a small contrite smile to Mrs. Van Anda, Rebecca slowed her steps and walked sedately through the tall grass about forty feet off the side of the trail.

In the time she had to walk that day, Rebecca occupied herself by trying to remember all the details about the other families in the wagon company that they had met so far.

The Van Andas occupied the wagon directly in front of the Stephens family in the caravan and would be their neighbor for the entire stretch of the journey. Mrs. Van Anda was visibly pregnant, Rebecca noticed with a shock. If the baby even waited long enough to be born in Oregon, she would be surprised. A woman like that must be unfathomably brave and strong, willing to go on this journey westward in her condition. She wondered how many other women might also be in the family way.

Following the Stephenses was the Keegan family, with two young children who seemed to be close in age and close friends as well. Kate, nine years old, and Jack, seven, had already spent at least an hour with Rebecca that morning, telling her all about their home in New Jersey and the pet rabbits they had to give away. They were delightful and kind to each other, while still retaining that little bit of mischief that made children so much fun.

Ahead of the Van Andas was the doctor and his wife, though Rebecca had not yet met them. Behind the Keegans was a family with three children and a spinster schoolteacher that would be accompanying them all the way to Oregon.

Each family, each wagon, had a unique story about how they decided to leave everything behind and come west. Maybe if Rebecca was diligent, she could meet all of them before the six months of travel were up.

Because they had gotten such a late start, Captain Mills did not stop the wagon for a midday break. Rebecca's stomach began to growl as the day drew on, but Ada had foreseen such a possibility. The fried potato skins she had made two nights earlier were still delicious and helped stave off hunger until they stopped for the evening.

She had been walking by herself through the grass, watching and daydreaming, when she realized that the wagon caravan had all but stopped. Dismayed, she hurried to her father's side where he was waiting with their team of four oxen.

"What's going on?"

"I don't know any more than you, sunshine," he said. "But I'd wager it's not the first time something fell across the trail and proved an obstacle. Patience is the only way we will get through this journey."

Rebecca hid a smile at her father's attempts to offer a life lesson. Sometimes it seemed like he forgot that she was grown and he had missed whatever chance he had to train her. Patience was all well and good, but she still wanted to know what happened. It took a good twenty minutes or so, but finally the row of wagons moved again. Slowly, carefully, they inched forward. The Stephens wagon was near the rear of the caravan, so it took a bit for them to reach whatever the obstacle was. But even from some ways off it was clear that the line of wagons was being led off the trail, around something, before returning to the original path.

Rebecca kept her eyes on the horizon, taking her time, enjoying the beautiful afternoon in the middle of the prairie and wondering what adventure was waiting just around the corner.

As their wagon drew nearer to it, Rebecca finally

spotted what it was that had delayed the wagon company for so long.

She gasped.

There, splayed across the dirt trail and into the grass on the north side, was the wreck of an overturned wagon.

"Goodness," she murmured, as a jolt of recognition stung her.

But as she looked closer, the more acutely the recognition stabbed her.

It was not just an overturned wagon.

It was a man.

A man. A body. Crushed. A woman's scream. Dark blood pooling.

Rebecca's vision went black. She stumbled. She tried to shut out what she had seen. She let out a deep-throated scream that seemed to tear through her.

Her mother was instantly at her side, holding an arm tightly around her.

"Don't look at it," her mother pleaded. "Please, my darling girl. Close your eyes."

She reached out for her daughter, but Rebecca shrank away. She couldn't stand to be touched. She couldn't handle being reminded that she had a physical presence on this Earth, that could hurt so very much.

A man she recognized as Jeb Buchanan was stuck, with his face in the dirt, torso crushed under the overturned, full, heavy wagon.

Just as she had lost her Andrew, her love, another woman had lost her own husband. A man had been crushed, a soul lost.

Her mother's strength is all that carried Rebecca

past the sight. She seemed to have lost the use of all of her limbs in her terror; her throat felt raw from the crying. Still her mother dragged her away from the accident, as far away as they could get while the caravan continued its slow crawl.

Time seemed to stretch and contort and loop back on itself. Rebecca had no thought to where she was. All she had in her mind was the vision of her husband in the dirt, the life crushed out of him.

He had left her. Left her to do life without him.

Rebecca vaguely noticed that she was inside a wagon now, that someone had laid her down, had pulled a blanket over her and left her alone.

Alone. That's all she ever would be. Alone forever.

Just like Jed Buchanan had left his own wife.

What was the point in going on, Rebecca thought, if there would be violent deaths like this on the very first day they were part of this wagon company.

"I can't. I can't." She said it over and over, though there was no one to hear her but herself and whatever ghost of her husband that still lingered in her heart. Mumbling into her pillow she pleaded with him. "I can't do this, Andrew. How could you leave me and send me to do this on my own? What were you thinking making me promise to go on to Oregon without you?"

She raged at him, though he was no nearer than the moon. She raged at herself, at her family for enabling such a reckless promise.

But then the memory of those days following his death flashed into her mind.

She'd had no other option. She had to go. She had to get away.

If she'd stayed in Indianapolis alone she would have been miserable. If she had somehow altered her parents' plans so they stayed with her, she would have felt guilty.

Once her husband had died, she lost the last option for a happy life.

She had to follow through. There was nothing for her in Indianapolis, that was certain, even if she could manage to get back there on her own. The choice had been made for her long ago, and Rebecca Tenney must continue on to Oregon to fulfill her dead husband's last wish.

There might not be anything for her there either. There was nothing for her anywhere.

She could not stay where she was. She could only move forward, but she would detest every minute of it, every step of the way. If she wasn't going to be lonely and miserable in Indiana, she would only end up being lonely and miserable in the wilderness of the American west.

CHAPTER TWELVE

Rebecca Tenney was barely coherent. She had seen her worst memory realized in front of her. The stress of that trauma had consumed her.

Seeing the life crushed out of the man haunted her. It stuck in her head, every detail. The bright sun beating down; the man's wife squinting against it as she screamed. The blood soaking into the ground. The splintered wood stabbing into him. She couldn't close her eyes without seeing it, but she couldn't stay awake in such pain and memories. The scene was chaos, a blur, and Rebecca couldn't be sure where she was. She felt loving arms around her, guiding her, a soothing voice willing her to sleep, begging her to forget what she had seen.

A man had died, right in front of her eyes, precisely the way she had lost her precious Andrew. Exactly the way she had seen the spark drain out of the love of her life. It was as though she had watched her own life end again and again.

And all Rebecca wanted to do was forget all about it.

She cowered in her wagon, quilt pulled up over her head as she attempted to block out the world.

Even after Jeb Buchanan was killed literally while traveling west on the Oregon Trail, the Sullivan-Mills wagon company still did not stop for the day. Even after Rebecca had been shocked and traumatized, taking to bed for the rest of the afternoon, she couldn't halt their progress. It was their very first day on the trail and there were a certain number of miles the captains wanted to travel.

Several men and women stayed behind to help the new widow as best they could, but everyone else had to keep moving. It was only after pushing farther for several hours—miles and miles past the site of the death —did Captain Mills stop for the night.

Lying in her family's wagon for every one of those miles, Rebecca tried to sleep, tried to think of something else, tried to ignore the thoughts that haunted her. Whatever arrangement had been made for the body, or the family, Rebecca didn't want to know. Whatever steps the new widow was taking in light of her new situation, Rebecca couldn't handle. This was all too much for her, on top of everything else, and she wanted to forget it all.

"Rebecca?" her mother called quietly.

The wagon company must have made camp for the night. Rebecca hadn't felt any movement for at least a couple hours, and had dimly heard the bustling sounds all around her outside. But she had resolutely kept her eyes closed, willing herself to fall asleep, to disappear, to hide from the mountain of debilitating feelings that threatened to consume her. The grief felt as though it was pressing in on her from all directions, before her mother's voice cut through the fog.

"Rebecca?" she heard again, this time closer in a whisper. Her mother was approaching. "Are you sick?"

Rebecca contemplated not answering, pretending to be asleep.

"Sweetheart?"

The worry she heard in her mother's voice was enough to prod Rebecca to open her eyes and roll over on the narrow corn husk mattress.

"I'm not sick. I'm awake."

Her mother had a lantern in one hand. She raised it close to where Rebecca lay and peered into her face, looking for some sign or indication of what her daughter needed.

"Well..." she began uncertainly. "You just say the word if you need something from me. I'll bring you supper as soon as—"

"No," Rebecca mumbled, turning face down again to shut out the world. "No food. No talking even. I can't. I just..." Her voice broke.

There was no response from her mother, but Rebecca could feel the woman watching her.

"I want to go home," she moaned. "I wish I had never come. I want to be back on my farm with Andrew like I was supposed to be."

"I know, dear."

Rebecca felt a hand patting her shoulder, but took no comfort from the touch. There was no reassurance in knowing her mother pitied her. There was no relief to her grief and no end in sight.

"None of this is right," she continued. Rebecca sat

up, her knees knocking against her mother's in the small space. Her heavy braid hung down her back, but the wisps of hair framing her face seemed to be loose and chaotic. "This is not what was supposed to happen. We were supposed to be married and have children and a home and live happily ever after. We'd save our money to visit St. Louis, or maybe go all the way to Philadelphia, and spend the rest of our lives sharing stories of that adventure. Andrew was going to build a treehouse for our children and get us a piano. And now—"

A sob choked her words. Rebecca leaned forward into her hands, her shoulders shaking under the force of her tears. Her dream of traveling back east just for leisure was absurd; she knew that. That didn't make the loss of it any easier. Ever since she had been young, every aspect of her future had been imagined and built around the partnership and love with Andrew that she had longed for.

It was gone. All of that was gone.

"I know it's been hard, my dear," her mother said softly. "Everyone has had—"

"No," Rebecca interrupted harshly. "No, everyone has not anything like what I have gone through."

"Mrs. Buchanan—"

"Mrs. Buchanan has children. They had years and years together. She has had what I never will."

"Now, no one can say—"

"Stop," she all but yelled. Even just having to answer to someone else was more than Rebecca could bear right now. Forcing herself to be polite to anyone, let alone her mother who deserved nothing less, was enough to make her lose her wits. "I can't. Please. Just, leave me alone.

Seeing that man die today was enough to... I need to be left alone. I want to go home. I want this all to end. I want to just forget the last six months of my life and go back."

"I'm so sorry."

"I want to go back," Rebecca cried, almost to herself, as she turned her back to her mother, to the rest of the wagon, to the camp outside. She would turn her back on the whole world, if she could, living only in her memories and forgetting her real life. "I want to go home."

Her mother departed without another word, while Rebecca tried to fall asleep, return to her dreams, to the Andrew that existed only in her mind now.

Rebecca made herself scarce the next morning until after the wagon company had pulled out of camp. She was not about to be guilted into attending some stranger's funeral, or made to feel as though she should be supportive to the widow. She simply could not take on another thing. Rebecca was grieving herself, and she was happy to lean on that fact as a reason to keep to herself.

Her mother must have sensed that she could not be goaded or coaxed into doing anything, and left her alone. She tried to shut out the sounds of Jasper asking after her, of the laughter and chatter of emigrants who came near their wagon. After breakfast, Ada would bring a small serving of biscuit and bacon, wrapped in a towel to stay warm and set at the foot of Rebecca's bed. It was more than enough to last her all day. In her grief she had completely lost her appetite.

Rebecca could only stand riding in the hot, dark wagon for two days before she felt too sick to continue.

The jostling and bumps of the rugged trail made Rebecca nauseated from the motion. But during those two days, she had the quiet and solitude to question everything she had assumed about this journey west.

When Andrew had first introduced the idea of emigrating to Oregon, he had painted it as a grand adventure they could share. The new people and new experiences had so called to her. She had imagined relaxing evenings under the stars, or busy social suppers with several families gathered. She had simply assumed that their journey would be full of new friendships and chances.

The reality was far different. And Rebecca could not reconcile the two.

The morning of the third day after she had witnessed such a horrific sight, Rebecca woke up and decided she couldn't keep doing what she was doing. As much as she wanted to block out the whole world, the crowded and uneven ride inside the wagon was more uncomfortable than she could bear. Taking to bed would have been far easier in Indiana, as in fact it was in the weeks following Andrew's death. Taking to bed after such a shock was simply not an option on the Oregon Trail.

Honoring the promise she had made to Andrew had cornered her in this life where she would be surrounded by death—death and monotony. There was no escaping it.

But there would always be plenty of work, and other people, she could distract herself with. Maybe if she could just forget about her loss, she could make it through the day.

That third day was also when the wagon company crossed into Indian territory.

"Well, of course," Rebecca muttered to herself. "Why don't we just head into ever more dangerous waters. What harm could there be in piling on even more stress?" Her interest in seeing an Indian for herself had disappeared with her enthusiasm for the journey.

But the captains were prepared. They called one member from each family to a meeting to lay out all the security restrictions and safety measures the company would be taking in order to guard best against attack. Each night when they made camp, the men would pull the wagons into a tight circle, so tight they could chain the wheels together. The interior of the circle would be the stockade, where they could corral all the livestock to keep them safe. On top of all of that, every night would have men on guard duty, keeping watch in all directions, until dawn.

"There'll be no getting through all that," Michael said when he reported about the meeting to his family. "We'll all be safe and sound until we hit the ocean."

Ada leaned over to Rebecca and in a carrying whisper said, "Well, at least on the nights your father has to be on guard we'll have a little more space in the wagon."

Rebecca knew her mother was making a joke; she must be afraid for her husband's life just as much as any other woman in the company. But she didn't have any of the energy or stamina she needed to comfort her mother. It was all Rebecca Tenney could do to keep herself standing on her own two feet.

CHAPTER THIRTEEN

Another week went by before Rebecca had realized it. Day after day of the wagons rolling ever westward with little to mark the time. Awake at dawn. Mornings were coffee and bacon; evenings were beans and biscuits. Every day with little deviation. Unchanging and uninteresting and unhelpful.

Michael and Jasper had their guard duty, while Ada and Rebecca had their chores. Nothing changed and nothing surprised her and nothing distracted Rebecca from her grieving to the point that she felt utterly consumed. So focused had she been on the Buchanans' accident and her own loss, that she hadn't the energy to worry about anything else. Each day was exhausting and monotonous. Other than small mishaps, like a horse throwing a shoe, each day proceeded more or less like all the others.

And every day it took all of her willpower to make herself get out of bed and face her pain again.

There wasn't much more she could take of this. How

could she possibly make it two thousand miles with such sorrow in every step? Rebecca even considered trying to talk her parents into turning around. They weren't too far from Indiana, she thought. It wasn't yet too late to change their minds. It would be difficult and it would be expensive, but it wasn't impossible. And then she wouldn't have to deal with this day after day being reminded of her husband's tragic death.

But then she heard her mother's insistence that she keep her promise to Andrew. That was the one thing she had anchoring her to this life—the impulsive promise she had made to a dying man.

Rebecca had no choice but to keep going. She had nothing. No options.

Of all the limitations of her sex, not having the independence she craved was the worst. Each day when she had finally forced herself out of bed, the constant bombardment of expectations and work did its part in helping her forget about her pain and grief, but it wasn't enough. If there was ever a quiet moment, the memories would come rushing back and she would find herself paused in her scrubbing, with a dishrag in hand and tears pouring down her cheeks.

Rebecca needed more to fill her time, to hold her attention so she could keep herself from being dragged down into her pit of grief. The only way to get through the day would be to fill those quiet moments with something else. There was plenty of work, plenty of other people. All Rebecca needed to do was find the distraction and fix on it. She didn't have children of her own to care for, and her mother thrived on running their household without aid. She didn't have the freedom that

Jasper had, and she couldn't very well go too far away from the wagon caravan anyway.

Rebecca was stuck, and she was suffering because of it.

But she was determined to find a solution.

There were nearly fifty families in the wagon train, many of them large, with half a dozen children running about. And yet with all of those people, there didn't seem to be anyone who could truly understand what Rebecca was going through, and what she was running from. None of the young women her own age were widowed, and the married ones were all consumed with the responsibilities of their families. She supposed Annie Hudson, whose fiancé had died, might offer a semblance of sympathy, but then, Rebecca realized, having to relive that pain in building a friendship with her defeated her entire goal of distracting herself.

No, Rebecca would need to find something else to engage her mind, something far from her own troubles and doubts.

There must be someone or something who could keep her mind occupied. Rebecca was willing to try anything.

One morning after breakfast, after the wagon company had begun its slow push west, Rebecca found herself with energy to burn and mind that needed to be diverted. Jasper had disappeared somewhere; her parents walked together with the team of oxen. No one needed Rebecca; nothing needed her attention.

She would have to seek it out.

All around her the lush fields of wildflowers beckoned. Bright yellows and oranges everywhere let her imagine that the prairie itself was on fire. It was beautiful, and it was at least a place to start. With a silent plea for deliverance, she strode out into the tall grass, several yards parallel to the trail, by herself. Checking each step for a snake, or the entrance to a prairie dog burrow, Rebecca watched the dirt under her feet and walked west.

The dirt under her feet, just like the blood-soaked dirt under Andrew's crushed body.

As if from nowhere, the dark images flashed in her mind. The crushed torso. The earth being steeped in black-red blood.

Her body reacted involuntarily, with a wave of heat through her whole system.

She paused in her steps, overcome with the terror that the single thought had flooded her with.

She was going to be sick. She leaned over, trying to catch her breath as her heart pounded.

That same fear, that same panic wove through her. The picture of Andrew's death, of Jeb Buchanan's death, blended together in her mind.

Rebecca tried to shake it off, bouncing up and down on her toes while she forced a shimmy down through her body. That was in the past. All she was doing was walking, and far away from wagons at that. She pushed the thought from her and tried to focus on something else.

She looked around desperately for anything to focus her attention on instead.

Anything.

A song popped into her mind from she knew not where. A sweet, lilting song that she had learned as a child. Rebecca could still remember all the words, so she hummed it quietly to herself, holding on tightly to the lyrics in her mind as she started walking again.

Anything to distract her from the memories of her own loss.

It seemed to work, as long as she didn't think too closely about it. Humming that melody to herself, Rebecca continued west, walking through grass and wildflowers parallel to the wagon caravan. As she walked faster, passing the Van Anda family in the wagon ahead of her own, passing the older couple ahead of that, and farther, Rebecca examined each family eagerly. Surely one of these women could be a close friend of hers. Someone who could fill the hole that had been left when Andrew died, and who could now help distract her from these all-consuming thoughts that intruded uninvited.

Though she recognized many of these men, women and children by sight, Rebecca had not yet formally met many of them. She didn't know their stories, or why they were traveling west. She couldn't be completely sure which children belonged to which parents, or how much of a handful they all were.

With all this potential ahead of her, for the first time since she had seen Jeb Buchanan die, Rebecca felt a twinge of hope. Maybe she could make it all the way to Oregon without completely collapsing.

The oxen pulling their heavy loads couldn't travel as fast as one woman with no encumbrances, and so in seemingly no time at all Rebecca neared the front of the wagon train. She had lost count of how many families she had passed. Captain Mills was leading the caravan, and there was only a handful of wagons between her and the very front.

Suddenly, Rebecca spotted a disconcertingly familiar face. Stopping altogether, she didn't know what to do or how to respond. There, just forty feet from her, was the newly widowed Mrs. Buchanan. The woman had just climbed out of the back of her wagon while it rolled slowly forward, and called some command that Rebecca didn't hear to the child running out into the plains.

Her wagon wheel had been fixed, but Rebecca fancied she could still see where it had cracked and bent and crushed the woman's husband underneath.

Again that hot flash of panic washed through Rebecca, and she was vaguely aware that she had stopped walking. Her heartbeat raced. Her palms sweat.

She needed to get out of there.

Rebecca turned on her heel, so quickly that she could not look where she was going and nearly lost her balance.

"Oh! Careful, there," a cheerful male voice said.

Rebecca felt a strong hand grip her upper arm and hold her steady while she got her feet under her again.

"It's such a bother to watch where you step when the grass is this high," an unfamiliar female voice added.

Rebecca tried to calm her heartbeat and looked up to see who had helped her.

CHAPTER FOURTEEN

Rebecca had just accidentally run into a complete stranger. A young couple, both shorter than Rebecca and both a little plump, grinned at her expectantly. The man let go of her arm as soon as he noticed that she had regained her balance, and the woman stood ready to help as well.

"I'm so sorry. Excuse me," Rebecca said. "I should have been watching where I was going."

"No, don't worry, we just wanted to make sure you were all right," the woman said. "Out here all by yourself as you were. You didn't see a snake or something to spook you, did you?"

"No, no. Nothing like that. I just— I suddenly thought it would be better if I went back to my own wagon. Were you out here to talk to me?"

"Well, not at first," the other woman said with a grin. "We like to take walks, too, in the few moments we get some peace."

"Angus Waters," the young man said with a roguish

grin and a thumb pointing at his chest. "There's almost a dozen of us Waterses, so it's strange this is the first time we're meeting."

The young woman slapped his shoulder playfully. "There is not, Angus." Turning to Rebecca, she added, "I'm Sadie Jones. No, sorry, Sadie Waters. I'm sorry, we haven't been married long. And don't listen to him. There are only ten of us Waters."

"Ten is almost a dozen," Angus interjected.

"Rebecca Tenney," she said looking from one to the other curiously.

"Oh, you must be the widow," Angus said seriously.

Rebecca frowned, looked down at her somber black gown, and then back up at Angus to see that he wore a teasing, gentle smile. She relaxed.

"How did you guess?"

Angus laughed. "I've got to be getting back," he told his wife, before kissing her on the cheek. "Be good. Be safe. I'll see you for supper."

"Where were you headed?" Sadie asked as he walked back toward the wagon train. "Can I walk with you? Angus will be busy the rest of the day, I suppose, so I need something to fill my day."

"You were just out walking? That's what I'm doing. I thought I'd... I don't know. Take a look around. See what there was to see. I suppose I had in my head that I would make a friend, but I keep forgetting what I can and cannot do as a widow."

Sadie grimaced sympathetically. "That must be very hard. But you found us, at least."

"It's truly a fortunate coincidence that you also had nowhere else to be."

Sadie nodded. "Angus has four brothers, so it's only his turn to drive a team every few days and we get to spend the rest of the time together. I feel a bit spoiled, truth be told, having so much time together to do what we wish. So many of the other women are just bogged down by chores morning noon and night."

Rebecca felt a stab of jealousy thinking of so much time this woman got with her husband, before quickly brushing it aside. It wasn't Sadie's fault that Andrew had died and sent her on this trail without him. This could be the very solution Rebecca had been looking for.

"Why don't I walk you back to your wagon?" Sadie continued, as she linked her arm through Rebecca's. "We'll walk slow and trade secrets."

Rebecca laughed before remembering that she was expected to be sober and melancholy, but Sadie didn't seem to bat an eye at the incongruity. Rebecca relaxed.

"I'm not sure I have any secrets."

"Other people's secrets then," Sadie said with a laugh of her own. "Angus and me have been trying to meet as many of the families in this wagon company as we can. Everyone's got such interesting stories, coming west for so many different reasons. One couple is here all the way from Ireland, if you can believe it."

"Goodness, really? I'm afraid I have been keeping to myself. I've not talked to hardly anyone, and I don't really know where to start. But I want to change that. If I can."

Sadie nodded. "It must be hard. Being a widow. People probably don't want to impose."

They walked slow steps through the tall grass, far

enough from the wagon train to avoid the clouds of dust that got kicked up by the teams.

"That's exactly it. I'd be grateful for any time you can spare me, Mrs. Waters. Truly."

"Well, call me Sadie to start with, seeing as we're bound to end up there like as not."

"Sadie. And what secrets do *you* know?" Rebecca asked, falling easily into the intimate exchange.

"Nothing scandalous as yet, but with months ahead of us there is bound to be something fun."

Rebecca laughed.

"Lots of these folks, though, are doing as much as they can just to survive. Not many have the luxury of a social hour in the middle of the morning like you and I do. I'd say a bit more than half of these folks have little ones with them. The McKinnons there," she pointed as they passed, "have five or six. Families like that and my in-laws make up for the wagons with just a couple people. Like them. The Harpers." She pointed again. "Brother and sister, from what I hear, and as snobby as the Queen of England. Angus's sister saw her by the river the other day and claims Miss Harper was wearing a silk dress, if you can believe it."

"Silk? In this heat?"

"I know! You'd hope she rethinks that before we get to Oregon." She pointed again as they strolled. "The Sullivan family in the two wagons just behind the Harpers, that's our other captain. William Sullivan and his own wife and five kids. And then after that, I've met... let's see. The Irvings, the Emersons, the Carters, the Coles—"

"Coles, yes. My brother made friends with them.

They have a daughter, right? Maybe a bit younger than us?"

Sadie nodded. "Two daughters."

"And then that's us," Rebecca said, stopping in the grass parallel to her own family's wagon. "Only ten or twelve families from the end of the caravan, including the Hudson ladies, who I know a little. There's so many names to learn. I can't believe how many you've met already."

"You'll learn them. I'll help."

This sounded like precisely what Rebecca had been looking for—something to fill her time other than simply missing Andrew.

"I would love that. Sincerely, please," Rebecca said. "I need something to fill my time, and my hope is with all these people—all these families—someone might need something."

"Stick with me, then, Mrs. Tenney. We'll find the very thing."

Rebecca hesitated before blurting out what she was thinking. "Could we find something now?"

Sadie laughed and looked confused. "Now?"

"It's still so early in the day, and I have nothing else to do until we make camp, and I just find that if I'm left on my own..."

She trailed off, unsure of how precisely to describe the combination of fear and heartbreak that she was trying to avoid.

"What I'm saying is if you have nothing else to do right now, I'm free as a bird," she concluded lightly.

Sadie stood back a step, looking at Rebecca thoughtfully, and then finally nodded as though deciding something.

"I have just the thing."

Ten minutes later, the two women had crossed to the other side of the trail where Margaret Hudson was herding their small collection of goats that the family had brought all the way from Virginia. The older woman seemed thrilled to have the company, while Rebecca and Sadie had their fill of conversation in turn.

"So many of these folks can only think of survival," Margaret said, shaking her head sympathetically. "It would be lovely if you could do something to lighten their load."

As the afternoon finally drew to a close, Sadie and Rebecca said their good-byes, each returning to their own wagon. For Rebecca, at least, the day had been precisely what she had hoped and—even more so—what she had needed. She didn't fool herself that she had helped Margaret watch over the goats at all, but at least she now had a model for how she could spend her next free day.

Rebecca had almost reached her own wagon again. She stood for a moment, watching the crowd pass her by, thinking about all the opportunities these dozens of families represented. Well, she supposed that settled it. Being alone with her thoughts was too much for her to handle, no matter how happy she felt or how easy of a day it was. The only thing that seemed to help Rebecca pull free of her grief was other people.

Thankfully, she had nearly six more months with all of these other people.

And thanks to Sadie, she now knew a lot more names and stories of those around her. It was a place to start.

The company was making camp for the night. As Rebecca watched, the train slowly pulled off of the trail into a defensive circle. It took a moment for Rebecca to orient herself in the circle of wagons, but she soon spotted the Stephenses.

Michael had unhitched the team and was getting their water, while Jasper was chaining the front wheels of the wagon to the Van Andas'.

"Where've you been, sis?" Jasper asked when she approached. "We thought maybe you had run off with an Indian chief or something. You're not trying to get left behind are you?"

She responded by sticking out her tongue at him.

"What are you eating?"

Jasper chewed quickly and swallowed. "Nothing."

Rebecca just stared at him.

"Dried cherries."

Rebecca perked up at that. "Really? Where did you get them? Can I try one?"

Jasper grinned, straightened up, and handed her a couple. When she put them in her mouth the combination of sweetness and tartness startled her. Her eyes widened and she grinned at her brother.

"Where did you get them?" she asked again. "I could eat all you have."

He shrugged, popped another one in his mouth and turned away.

"Jasper Stephens, you are insufferable."

He just waved his hand at her as he walked away.

She just shook her head at him. If only she was a boy

and could go about the campsite charming his way into someone else's store of treats. Or, if only she wasn't a widow and could more easily play a hostess or socialize.

If she was wishing for things, though ... If only she didn't have the harsh memories of watching her husband die to haunt her with every step.

She couldn't go back to Indiana and she couldn't have her life back, but maybe this filling her life with other people could rescue her from her grief. Rebecca vowed to dive headfirst into making friends with her neighbors.

CHAPTER FIFTEEN

Though the upsetting thoughts continued, the farther west they traveled the more Rebecca found to distract her. Sadie inviting her to walk with her and herd goats with Margaret Hudson had set her on the path, and now Rebecca saw opportunity everywhere she looked. Though there was always an awkward several minutes while the other person considered her widowhood and held her at arm's length, most of the emigrants in the wagon company were warm and friendly.

She sought out Margaret Hudson and spent another day helping her with her family's goats. She talked to Mrs. Mills about quilting, and to Mrs. Keegan about teaching the children. She kept up with her family's laundry while still finding time to roam far and wide to find enough fuel for their fire. She even talked her brother into showing her how to manage the team of enormous oxen. Heaven help them if Rebecca ever had to do that unsupervised, but doing so with Jasper helped take up a few hours of her afternoon. If she could fill her days with enough, maybe she could get all the way to Oregon without ever having to remember the pain that she had left behind. It was a tricky balance, with all the expectations that had been heaped on her in her widowhood, but Rebecca was finding ways around that.

But every new thing she took on was one more brick in the wall between Rebecca's day and the looming memories that threatened to overwhelm her.

One morning, a couple weeks into the journey, her mother gave Rebecca the job of frying up breakfast.

"This is the last of the potatoes so make them count. Once these are gone, we'll have to settle for johnnycakes and biscuits like everyone else," Ada said, dejectedly.

"Why didn't we bring more than this?" she asked as she began peeling the final two potatoes.

"Too heavy. Not enough meals to be made from the required weight. Which is a shame, since your brother loves these so. But I suppose it will be nice to have this last treat on our big day crossing the Kansas River. It'll be a long, hard day, so eat up."

"How are we getting across the river?"

Her mother pointed. "You can almost see it from this vantage. There's a ferry and men will push a wide wooden platform across."

Rebecca's face lit up. "That sounds exciting." She peered in the direction her mother pointed and told herself she'd go look closer as soon as she could.

"Let's hope not," Ada said with a wry smile. "Let's pray that it is just as uneventful and simple as it can be. We just want to get to the other side with no complications."

The Stephens family was near the end of the wagon

train, and so had to wait for dozens of other families to cross ahead of them. It took the bulk of the day, and Rebecca could not find enough things to fill her time. Unfortunately, her new friend Sadie had crossed the river earlier in the day, so Rebecca was more or less on her own.

As they were waiting their turn for the platform, she realized that it had been several days since she had thought about that awful sight of Jeb Buchanan crushed under the wheel of the wagon, or of her own Andrew in the same plight. Perhaps it was the time that had passed or perhaps it was merely the distraction of her new friends and neighbors that had driven that memory from her mind.

Either way, Rebecca was happy to keep herself busy doing any amount of work if it meant she was spared the debilitating memories.

Finally, the line of wagons had two by two crossed over the Kansas River and the Stephens family reached the shore. It was their turn to cross. This late in the afternoon, it was clear that the men were tired of the constant traversing, but they remained focused and determined in their work.

Two wagons could fit on the ferry at a time, and the Keegan wagon was anchored on the platform just next to theirs; Mrs. Keegan and their two small children stood near the rail with Rebecca and her mother while the men managed the rest. Thankfully there was plenty of help. Daniel Mills and Junior Sullivan were on hand, as well as at least half a dozen other volunteers. Rebecca felt herself consumed with the fast-paced, violent struggle, as the ferrymen worked to get all of the wagons over the river safely.

Soon everything was in place—the wagons balanced, with small wooden wedges behind two of the wheels to keep them in place. The animals, two teams of oxen as well as the Keegans' cow, were being soothed as best they could. The families held on tight, as the ferrymen gently pushed off from the shore, into the current of the Kansas River.

Rebecca let out a little gasp of excitement. Her mother looked at her in alarm.

"Take this seriously," she hissed.

"I am," Rebecca whispered back. But there was far too much going on for her to simply focus on holding on. Her gaze darted from the man closest to her, pushing the platform along with a pole, to her brother whispering to their lead oxen, to Patrick Keegan gripping the reins of his animals, to the ferrymen on the other side of the platform. Everything had to move in concert, as balanced as possible, slowly if necessary, to guarantee that every man, woman, child, animal and wagon aboard reached the other side safely.

It was a slower traverse than Rebecca had expected, but that gave her plenty of time to watch and take it all in.

Next to her, little Kate Keegan was gripping Rebecca's hand tightly, but kept her eyes screwed shut.

"Don't you want to open your eyes? See what's happening?"

Kate shook her head. "No. If I can't see it nothing bad will happen."

Rebecca chuckled and squeezed the little girl's hand.

She'd had her own superstitions when she was Kate's age.

When the platform crossed the stronger current in the middle of the Kansas River, the westward momentum stalled out briefly.

"What's wrong?" Rebecca asked, trying to quell her panic.

One of the men propelling them across got his pole stuck in the mud.

"Hold tight, miss," one of the men called to her, before yelling instructions at his counterpart on the other side of the platform.

Rebecca couldn't be sure, but she thought she heard a curse being muttered by one of the men, as he pulled at his long pole. Too much was happening at once for her to keep track of where the problem was, what she should be doing.

She held tight to Kate's hand.

Slowly, she felt the boards underneath her feet shift, slightly, as the broad current continued to push the ferry platform downstream and against the effort of the pilots.

Next to Rebecca, her mother drew a sharp intake of breath.

The platform continued to tip, slowly, gently, almost imperceptibly were it not for the growing panic of the men around them.

"What's happening?" Jack Keegan whined.

His mother leaned down to whisper reassurances, but Rebecca had her own questions.

The platform should not be tipping. Not with these huge wagons liable to roll with the slightest jostle.

With wide eyes, Rebecca saw the balance of the platform shift. Time seemed to slow, as the worst thing that she could have imagined began.

As she watched the wagon roll forward, toward where her brother Jasper stood with the animals. He was cornered, blocked in to the rail by the animals, while the heavy vehicle moved incrementally toward him.

Rebecca's heart leapt to her chest. The uncontrollable weight and movement of these vehicles had already claimed one life on the trail. Would life be so cruel as to claim another?

She wanted to scream. She wanted to look away. She couldn't bear to go through such a sight again. Rebecca didn't know what to do. So great was her fear of seeing Jasper crushed under the wheels, or against the side, or even being so crushed herself, that any other option or safety seemed to fly from her mind. She couldn't help. She couldn't do anything. She couldn't even watch. So, she did the only thing she could think of to do—she thrust Kate Keegan behind her, protecting her tiny body against the chance of danger.

"Ow! Mrs. Tenney!"

"I'm sorry," she said frantically. "I'm sorry. Don't look, Kate."

With the little girl behind her, Rebecca curled in on herself, arms up around her head and shoulders hunched over. She shut her eyes to the sight. The idea of watching her brother killed in very same way she had seen both her husband and Jed Buchanan was more than she could bear.

All sounds around her blended together and Rebecca added to the cacophony with her own sobs.

Though it felt like an eternity, only seconds later, the terrifying mess of noise began to sort itself out into individual speakers.

Rebecca listened for a moment and opened her eyes again.

The platform had steadied and they were now almost to the other shore. Ada and Jasper each had a hand on an ox, while Rebecca's father helped Mr. Keegan soothe his own team. Though Rebecca's heart still pounded, she took a few deep breaths, wiped the tears from her face and stood up straight again.

She had gotten better at shaking off the fears, of forcibly pushing these thoughts from her mind, and she needed that skill now more than ever.

"See?" she said, turning to Kate still behind her and injecting her tone with false bravado. "We did it. Everything is fine. We're safe. We're safe."

Repeating the statement helped Rebecca feel as though it were true. In a few short minutes the platform had reached the other side of the river and everyone was safe. Still holding Kate's hand, they stepped off the platform onto solid ground.

It wasn't until she was safely on the shore, far away from the heavy wagon, that Rebecca was finally able to catch her breath. Over the past several days, she had made such progress that she could have almost forgotten how awful the memories were. She had done so well with pushing those memories out of her mind, that now when she had to deal with them it seemed utterly debilitating.

"I have to go," Rebecca told Kate, shaking. "I need to check on..."

She walked away without hearing whatever the child said to her in response. Her family could handle their wagon, and no one would miss her. Rebecca left the circle of wagons that had crossed and found a spot in the shade of the nearby trees, as she valiantly pushed away another wave of panic.

The scene played over and over in her mind. Sitting with her back against the tree, Rebecca noticed that she tasted blood. Surprised, she looked down and realized she had bit her fingernails down to the quick.

The wagon had rolled, but everyone was fine. No one was hurt. No bodies crushed under the weight. Over the previous several weeks, she had learned what she needed to do to keep such thoughts from her mind, so she stood, dusted herself off, and strode toward the campsite, looking for something to do.

By the end of the night, however, there had been another death.

CHAPTER SIXTEEN

Death had again found the Sullivan-Mills wagon company. After all the time Rebecca had spent convincing herself that people were safe, that there was no reason for her to panic, that if she just kept moving west, kept focused on deepening her friendships, everything would be fine, she had been wrong. She had spent so much effort making herself forget the dangers of the past that she had forgotten the dangers of the present. It seemed like she would never be free of the constant pain that reminded her of her own loss.

The Oregon Trail was a wild, uncertain, dangerous place. No one was safe. Not one of the emigrants was exempt. Anyone could be plunged into the same swamp of grief that Rebecca herself had been navigating since the previous fall.

Rebecca didn't know the McKinnon family, but the connection of losing yet another member of this wagon company made her feel closer to them than anything else would. The youngest son, little Alexander McKinnon, had wandered off by himself and accidentally drowned in the shallows of the Kansas River while the rest of his family was elsewhere. Rebecca had heard the agonized wail of the little boy's mother when she had discovered the body. She had had to cover her ears against such pain. It reminded her forcefully of her own keening, her own loss.

The following morning under the trees just outside the perimeter of the company's camp, a small funeral service was held. Most of the company's families were in attendance, though Rebecca herself could not manage the fortitude required to make an appearance. The disappointed scolding she received did nothing to help her mood. It was clear that Rebecca's refusal to attend had disappointed her mother, who set quite a store on the expectations and opinions of their neighbors. Nevertheless, Rebecca had some strong opinions of her own. She was sympathetic, but she absolutely could not handle another funeral at that moment.

Instead, while the pastor prayed over the little McKinnon boy, Rebecca spent her morning scrubbing the breakfast dishes. When she was working, and finding solutions, she could forget her pain. She couldn't do that forever, but she could do it long enough to avoid a child's funeral.

The Sullivan-Mills wagon company left that campsite by the Kansas River immediately following the funeral, but they could not leave the grief behind. In the days that followed, a general pall hung over the wagon company. Rebecca could feel it with every conversation she had. A man like Jeb Buchanan dying in an unfortunate accident was one thing, but the loss of a child so soon after seemed to be more than the emigrants could weather at that moment.

To Rebecca, it seemed like she alone was determined to cheer up; she alone was determined to forget the sorrow. Her attempts to draw out Annie Hudson or Sadie Waters were gently rebuffed. No one had time to entertain Rebecca, as they were all needed to help carry the workload for their families. She soon found herself utterly desperate for company, for distraction. It seemed to get worse with every day.

She could wear herself out hauling water and doing laundry, or helping repack the food supplies, but the moment she stopped, memories of Andrew flooded her mind and dragged her down again.

By the time the wagons had made camp that evening after leaving the Kansas, Rebecca had run through her mental list of available social contacts. Even when chopping onions or gathering water for her mother, her mind wandered and she couldn't help but think about death, inevitable, chasing after the wagon company across the plains.

These dark thoughts were incessant, creeping and insistent.

Rebecca looked one way, and then the other, all around the circle of wagons. It felt as though there was darkness creeping in the periphery of her sight, darkness that had nothing to do with the sun setting.

She needed something. Anything. A person to have a conversation with. An adventure to keep her mind busy.

In her desperation, Rebecca spotted young Kate Keegan near her family's wagon. Though the company of a nine-year-old would be nowhere near as satisfying as someone her own age, the child still needed supervision and stimulation. That's what Rebecca told herself, at least. Maybe taking Kate off of her mother's hands would be a gift. Mrs. Keegan could spend her time resting or getting an extra chore done instead of worrying over her child.

Yes, that's exactly what Rebecca would offer her. Without further consideration, she strode to the next wagon, clearing her throat to announce her approach. Mrs. Keegan was pulling things out of her wagon but halted when interrupted.

"Oh, Mrs. Tenney! How is your afternoon? Did your mother want to borrow the balm for her burn again?" She wiped her hands on her apron.

"No, I was just wondering if maybe Kate was busy, if she could use a friend. We could play jacks, or maybe I could help her with her reading? I'd love to take her back to my campsite, if that makes things easier for you."

Mrs. Keegan looked at her oddly, pausing as though she didn't know quite how to answer.

"If she wants," Rebecca added hurriedly, stumbling over her words in her haste to make her case, "we could go for a walk instead. I thought maybe you'd like a break, right? I can take Kate off your hands. Jack too, if that's easier. Give you some time to yourself and I can play with the children."

Mrs. Keegan shook her head gently. "Not right now, Mrs. Tenney. Rebecca. Not just today. Their father and I need the children to stay close to home. It's just too much to... Not today, dear."

"Oh. Yes. Of course. I... I understand. Of course, I'm sorry."

She stepped backward hastily, almost stumbling over her feet. What had she been thinking? She could have guessed that a mother would want to keep her children nearby after someone else had lost a child of the same age. Faintly behind her, Rebecca heard Mrs. Keegan calling after her, but she had already turned and hurried away and was back to her own wagon in minutes.

She felt her face burning under the embarrassment of the rejection. But not only rejection—of the knowledge of her own selfishness. She had only been thinking about herself and what she needed.

But what else could she do? She was desperate.

No one could know that Rebecca Tenney literally had no one who wanted to spend time with her, not even a little girl.

Her shame was soon subsumed under her despair, however, at having nothing to distract her.

Thoughts of blood, of crushed ribs, of dead eyes, floated up into her consciousness.

Rebecca shook her head, as though trying to shake the images out of it. Instead, she focused on simply putting one foot in front of the other. Concentrating on getting herself back to her own camp, Rebecca was able to push out the agonizing thoughts for another few minutes.

Maybe that was what this would take. Maybe getting past the despair she felt was simply a matter of her filling every minute of every day. Maybe she just needed to be constantly vigilant.

Goodness, that sounded exhausting, she thought. Leaning against the back wheel of her wagon to steady herself, Rebecca couldn't understand how to dig herself out of this.

"Where did you go off to?" her mother called. "Supper is almost ready."

"Nowhere." Rebecca massaged her neck and tried to think.

"You were missed at the funeral this morning. That poor family," Ada began. "To lose a child—"

"Did you hear that the pastor is getting ready to host a worship service one of these nights?" Rebecca asked, loudly interrupting to change the subject.

"Rebecca Tenney," her mother scolded.

"What?" She bounced to her feet.

"Have some sympathy. It's bad enough that you don't seem to care about the child's death, but to actually interrupt me and appear so calloused about it. What if someone else heard you?"

"I'm not calloused," she protested. The overwhelm of it all threatened tears. "I just don't want to dwell on it. I've had too much death in my life already. There's nothing we can do. I can't deal with it, Ma. Please."

"Nothing we can do?" Her mother stared at her, shocked. "You don't think that family would feel blessed by the offer of a meal or an extra hand with the animals?"

"I suppose, but—"

"Weren't you grateful for the meals and the assistance when Andrew died?" Ada continued. "The care and attention everyone in the community showed you?"

"Well, yes, but—"

"I just can't believe any child of mine could be so

hard-hearted as to think her own entertainment was more important than the comfort of a grieving family.”

“I’m not hard-hearted, Mother.” Suddenly, Rebecca felt tired, depleted from all her franticness. All of her efforts to protect herself from her overwhelming emotions had run through any extra energy she had at the end of a long day of walking along the Oregon Trail. Trying to explain herself to her mother was more effort than it would be worth. She leaned back against the wagon wheel again, buried her face in her hands and sighed.

Ada peered at Rebecca, watching as her daughter sank back into herself. When Rebecca looked up again, she couldn’t read her mother’s expression.

“What?” Rebecca asked defensively. “Do I have something on my face?”

Her mother made no reaction to the challenge in her words, and seemed to realize that Rebecca’s lashing out wasn’t directed at her.

After a long quiet minute, Rebecca’s mother finally responded.

“I have an idea,” Ada said brightly. “It’s rather a big project and I need your help, please.”

“Yes, of course, Ma.” She was tired, but after her failure to find anyone to distract her just earlier that evening, she was ready to agree to anything.

“It’s been how many days since we left Independence? I’d wager many of these women are just aching for a decent bath, a chance to wash their hair. There’s not going to be much call for such luxury until we get to Oregon, but I heard your father say that in a few days from now we’ll reach a river and the captains will let us rest for a whole day. I mean to make that a day these ladies won't soon forget."

"How do you mean?"

Ada flashed a mischievous grin. "How long has it been since you've had a long, hot bath? And I don't mean those brisk hair washings you manage with a kettle full."

The mention of a hot bath seemed so foreign to her that she was momentarily confused. Rebecca's eyes seemed to lose focus as she dreamily remembered back; certainly it had been before they left Indiana. Even getting clean at all on the trail, while living out of a cramped and dirty wagon was a catch-as-catch-can endeavor. Add in the possibility of the water being hot and she might as well be dreaming.

"I can barely remember," she said.

"Precisely. I imagine most of these ladies feel the same. Sure they'll be heating up a tub for the little ones, but who's doing the same for them? Their husbands?"

Rebecca grinned at the thought.

"It's just a little something you and I can do for them. We'll set up a fire and a big tub at the side of the river, around a bend, or behind some shrubs or something to give the women privacy," she continued. "All it takes is you and me keeping the fire going, and any of the women who want it can take as much as they like. What do you think? Does that sound like something you might like to help me with?"

Rebecca was surprised by her own reaction—working and serving others actually sounded like something she could get excited about doing. It wasn't as though she was typically so selfish, but neither would she ever have thought about offering something like this to the other women. But bringing all those potential connections to her was more than she could have even hoped for. She would get to spend all day with her mind on things other than her past.

"I think that sounds perfect," she said. "What can I do?"

"Why don't you start, tomorrow, with telling your friends? And they can help us tell others. We should have a day soon that we can make this happen, but if you could help to tell people, that would be an even bigger success."

Rebecca nodded, already formulating plans and imagining how she could reach every single one of the families in the caravan. "I'll make sure everyone knows."

Once the idea had been lodged in her brain, Rebecca could not stop thinking about it. Only a few more days to make sure everything was set. It would almost be like a party—or as close to it as they could get out in the wilderness and with her a widow to boot.

CHAPTER SEVENTEEN

A few days later, everything was in motion. The wagon company had finally reached a narrow river and would be taking a full day off from traveling. Women had been informed of Ada's idea. Plans had been made. It was all falling into place and Rebecca eagerly anticipated the day that she could spend surrounded by people.

About mid-morning, Rebecca started the small fire going in a clear patch of dirt near to the banks of the widest part of the river. She first had to pull up some grass and weeds to clear the area; they wouldn't want risk starting a prairie fire just so these ladies could have warm water to wash their hair. Then she spent close to an hour gathering as many sticks and larger branches as she could find to keep the fire going as long as possible. There wasn't much timber around, after it had been picked clean by other emigrants, but she could do her best. Ada had brought over their largest pot and Jasper had helped them set up the tripod of thick sticks to hold the pot of water steady over the flame.

Everything was set, as much as they could do in the wilderness, to give the women of the Sullivan-Mills wagon company a relaxing day.

Standing up straight again, Rebecca pushed her hair off of her face. All her running around, and keeping the fire going had plastered the light wisps of hair to her forehead in a sweaty mess, and the black dress didn't help, of course. But there was shade near where they were set up for the day and if she had a moment she could always soak her feet in the water. She looked around, waiting expectantly for her first guest.

The several days that she had had to live through since her mother originally voiced this plan had been full of everything from joy to frustration. They had traveled west through the excitement of a torrential prairie thunderstorm, but the resulting mud had become a slog. It was only looking forward to the upcoming social event that kept Rebecca moving forward every day.

Where were they? Surely someone would show up soon.

She had always been the kind of person who enjoyed a party, saying hello to as many of her friends as she could squeeze in. The restrictions that had come with being a widow had made Rebecca feel as though a part of herself had been torn away, and the enormous change of leaving Indianapolis had only compounded that. She couldn't dance, she couldn't sing, she really shouldn't attend weddings or other socials. Even with the leniency of being on the trail, Rebecca felt the expectations stifling.

This idea of her mother's had seemed outlandish at first, but the more time that passed the more Rebecca realized she was excited about it. The days had been long and difficult, not to mention monotonous She needed this change. She needed some excitement in her life.

"I wish we could use a bigger pot," Ada said, standing back to look at the set-up. "You're going to have to keep refilling it all day. There probably won't be any time for resting."

"I really don't mind," Rebecca said. "I like to stay busy."

Now, after days of preparation, the Sullivan-Mills wagon company was in place, in a camp where they could rest and recover and allow the last of the coats and canvas to dry after the big prairie thunderstorm. Rebecca and her mother had even found two extra bars of soap tucked away that could be cut down and shared around. This would be an afternoon full of people and conversation and laughter and, hopefully, relaxation. It would be exactly what Rebecca needed after so long of having to make herself small and invisible.

"Look," her mother said, jutting out her chin to point. "There's Mrs. Sullivan going to collect water. Go run and make sure she knows we'll put her right at the front of the line whenever she's ready."

Rebecca nodded. Even though she was sure at least half of the women here were judging her for being so social and gregarious when she was in mourning, she was far past caring. The anticipation of being around so many women practically gave her feet wings as she hurried to Mrs. Sullivan.

While Rebecca was talking to Mrs. Sullivan, Mrs. Hatchley appeared at the edge of the water. Then another woman with two young girls. Then another and another. Soon, the river was full of women and girls, and Rebecca reveled in the pleasure all around her, the almost palpable joy. If there were moments she was left alone to refill the water or tend to the fire, she could feel the dark thoughts encroaching, but as long as she stayed busy and stayed talking she would be fine.

While Ada trimmed down a piece of the soap for old Mrs. Norton, Rebecca spotted Maggie Kirk walking down the narrow trail toward her. This was the perfect chance to push the overwhelming thoughts from her mind. This was one more woman who she could tempt with rest. She had something like four teenage boys to wrangle every day. If anyone needed a break it was this woman.

"Mrs. Kirk, isn't it?" she said as the woman approached. "Your wagon follows the Waters family most days, don't it?"

The woman gave a flattered smile. "Why, yes, goodness. And you must be Mrs. Tenney, I think. The young widow?"

For a brief instant, Rebecca felt a stab of pain that so many of these people knew her intimate story, but she didn't grant herself the luxury of self-pity.

"I am, yes."

And just like that, the same heat flash coursed through her, bringing with it all the feelings of heartbreak at her loss, shame that she hadn't been able to help, embarrassment that she was a grown woman all alone, still agonizing over something that she could do nothing about. Just the merest mention of the fact that

Rebecca had been married was enough to send her thoughts spiraling.

She pulled herself together enough to mumble out the invitation to Mrs. Kirk. In the time they stood talking, Rebecca managed to catch at least a dozen different women as they walked by. Each was entreated to help spread the word of what they could find at the water's edge that day. Each person she spoke to was one more potential conversation in the future, one more possible friendship for her on this seemingly never-ending journey west.

In no time at all, the afternoon was upon them, the river was full, and Rebecca was stationed by the smoldering fire, maintaining the level of water being constantly heated and helping her mother dole out the bowls-full of hot water as best she could.

There was a measure of chaos to the afternoon, with so many women and so little time, but Rebecca thrived on it. Little by little the askance looks diminished. It helped, of course, that her mother was at her side, that this was her idea in the first place. The expectations for a widow's behavior could be overlooked in some circumstances.

Rebecca smiled to herself as she saw the way this gesture had brought so much happiness to the women of the wagon company. Saying yes to Andrew all those many months ago had landed her somewhere she never would have guessed, but now saying yes to her mother's plan had given her a whole day of conversation and pleasure she never would have had otherwise.

A trio of women came down the path toward them, the last one Rebecca knew well.

"Rebecca!" Sadie exclaimed, with eyes wide. "I know you told me that you would be doing this, but I had no idea…" She looked around in wonder, taking in the couple dozen women and girls all at least waist deep in the river, sudsing their hair, or washing one another's backs. Then she turned back to Rebecca with an expression of pity. "Oh, you poor thing. Having to watch the rest of us all enjoy the fruits of your labor while you suffer over a hot fire."

Rebecca had been fanning herself with the hem of her apron. "You know," she said as she pushed a sweaty strand of hair off her face, "I hadn't even noticed the heat until you said something. My mind has been with Kate Keegan, who keeps trying to dunk her friend," she pointed, "or Mrs. Kirk. Keeping busy like this really helps me forget about the fears that would have brought me down a week ago."

"I'm so glad."

"Thank you. I admit it's an effort. Even now I'm afraid that as soon as you leave the doldrums will hit me again." She laughed, making light of her fear before her friend started to worry too much. "But having this, having a reason to introduce myself to Mrs. Kirk, even playing with soap bubbles with Kate makes a world of difference. Let me get you some hot water, and you can see for yourself."

Over the course of the afternoon, more ladies made their way slowly to where Rebecca and her mother had set up. Mrs. Montgomery, Mrs. Van Anda, Mrs. Benedict and others. Some faces surprised her; some women she expected never showed up. But overall the day seemed to be a success. The tiny fear of what Rebecca would have to look forward to when this was all over was pushed out of her mind.

She could worry about that tomorrow.

About halfway through the afternoon, during a tiny lull in the action, a cheerful young woman Rebecca had seen often walked down the path toward them. Nora Cole held a gray folded towel close to her chest, and looked around apprehensively. Though Rebecca had seen the younger woman around quite a bit, they hadn't exchanged many words since they had originally met back in the campsite in Independence. Since then, Nora had always had her sister, or Claire McKinnon, or both, at her side every time Rebecca had seen her. Now, however, she was alone and she seemed lost without her companions.

"You okay, there, honey?" Ada asked, calling out to Nora. "Can we help you?"

"Mrs. Stephens," she said, with a wide smile breaking across her face. "This is just wonderful. I thought maybe — That is, Jasper told me that, um... I thought I would check to see if I could help you, maybe? If you need it? It's just wonderful what you're doing and I..."

She trailed off looking around again.

Rebecca and her mother shared a smile behind the girl's back. Whatever Jasper had been saying to her over the previous weeks had made some kind of impact.

"I think we have everything under control, dear," Ada said. "But it's nice of you to offer."

Nora turned back and stepped up close to the two women.

"I just—" She blushed and stopped herself, shaking her head before taking a deep breath and composing herself. "I've heard a lot about you both, and I wanted to... to help, too, if you need me, and even if not, I didn't want to miss all this. It seems just..." Nora gestured to the women in the river nearby. "It's just wonderful," she repeated.

"Thank you," Ada responded warmly.

"Your sister didn't come?" Rebecca asked.

Nora grimaced. "Amy is... No. I would have had to really work to talk her into it and I thought it better to just come by myself instead. I'm sure she is perfectly happy inspecting the ant colony she found just outside our wagon wheel."

Rebecca and her mother exchanged another look.

"Well, if you really don't have anywhere you need to be, I'm sure we can find some way to put you to work," Ada said. "Why don't you set down your towel and take that bucket to get us more water? We can always have some ready."

"Yes, of course. I would love that. Thank you. Thank you, Mrs. Stephens."

When she started off, Rebecca and her mother exchanged another smile. Maybe this would be an additional source of friendship and conversation for Rebecca in the future. Maybe, just maybe, she'd be getting a sister out of this journey as well.

CHAPTER EIGHTEEN

That afternoon in the river, with the hot water and soap suds, was the last chance any member of the company would have for several days to so indulge in any kind of relaxation. Time was growing short. The more often they stopped to rest, the harder the immigrants had to push on their travel days. The caravan had to get over the Blue Mountains before the snow fell, and each day that moment was closer and closer.

The Sullivan-Mills wagon company planned to leave camp early the following morning, but this time weighed down with as much fresh water as they could carry. After that quiet campsite by the stream, the trail wouldn't pass any other usable water for days. Instead, they would have to carry it all with them, somehow. Every bowl, jug, canteen, barrel, or container of any kind had to be filled with water. More than that, though, it had to be enough water for each human and each animal that were crossing the plains, and those containers had to be carefully stored in the wagons that jostled along the ruts and stones of the trail. It was far from efficient, but there was no other choice. This was what each person had agreed to do when she chose to start life over again in Oregon.

While her mother packed up the wagon and her father hitched up the animals, Rebecca and Jasper gathered as much water as they could for the family. Multiple trips back and forth to the river took up the early morning. Between the two of them they were finished quickly, with every possible container at hand filled to the brim with water. But, as soon as she and Jasper had put away the last full canteen, Rebecca began looking around almost desperately for something else to occupy her.

All of the wagons were still in camp, and all of the immigrants were occupied with the same tasks Rebecca had just completed. Mrs. Van Anda, in the wagon immediately next to the Stephens, was trying too, though she was now well along in her pregnancy. She had passed the point that she would have been in confinement if she were anywhere other than crossing the Great Plains. There was no such luxury on the Oregon Trail, and so she had to work alongside the rest of the immigrants. Rebecca looked up from her own wagon just in time to see her maneuver her swelling stomach around a tub full of water as she staggered back from the river. It was half-resting on her belly as Mrs. Van Anda's arms stretched around the diameter of the tub to hold it in place.

"Let me help with that," Rebecca insisted, hurrying to take the large washtub from Mrs. Van Anda's hands. "Where is your husband? Shouldn't he be doing this?"

With effort she crossed the distance to the Van Andas' wagon and carefully set the tub full of water down.

"Thank you," the other woman said, following closely behind and panting slightly. "I can't tell you how I appreciate that. It's so hard."

"Heavens," Rebecca said with a laugh. "I don't mean to scold you, but how were you going to get this into the wagon on your own?"

"Oh, I wasn't. My job was just to get all the water here, and then Otis and I would lift it into the wagon together."

"All right," Rebecca allowed, "but I still think you shouldn't be carrying such heavy things in your condition." She blushed, suddenly aware she was speaking to this near-stranger on such an intimate topic.

"She's right, May." Mr. Van Anda appeared at his wife's side. "Thank you for helping her," he told Rebecca. "It doesn't matter how many times I tell her to keep off her feet, she always finds something else to do."

"Strange how that happens out here on the prairie," she said teasingly. "It's almost as though there was not a housekeeper to wait on me or a fainting couch for me to lounge on."

"Well, either way," Mr. Van Anda continued, "we can't have you lifting this tub as high as the wagon."

"Can I help?" Rebecca asked.

The man nodded and between the two of them, they managed to haul the large tub up and over the back of the wagon to sit securely inside. It was heavy, but not impossible. Only a small bit spilled over the top onto Rebecca's hands and cuffs.

"I can handle these smaller ones on my own," he

said, indicating the buckets full of water that were lined up next to the wheel. "I'm sure you have plenty of your own water to be collecting."

"I do." Rebecca took a deep breath. "Or, I did. My brother and I ran buckets back and forth from the river since before dawn. As far as I know all our containers are full. I don't know if it's enough water for all four of us plus the animals. My mother has been talking about rationing for two days now, just to get us ready for it."

"It's going to be rough," Mr. Van Anda agreed as he bent to pick up another bucket of water. "No doubt about that."

"Here." Mrs. Van Anda reached into the pocket of her apron and pulled out a small, smooth stone.

"What's this?" Rebecca took the pebble from her and turned it over in her hands, looking for a marking.

"It's to help with the water situation. My grandma taught me all about them when I was growing up in Florida."

"I don't understand."

"When you get so thirsty you don't think you can stand it, just hold this pebble in your mouth and it will help you make spit."

Any embarrassment Rebecca had felt at referring to Mrs. Van Anda's pregnancy was long gone.

"Make spit?" she repeated with a laugh.

The other woman shrugged and chuckled herself. "That's what she always said. I don't know how it works exactly, but we brought a whole bag of these pebbles from the river near home just in case. If nothing else, maybe it will distract you from wanting a drink of water."

"Well, I don't understand it, but I suppose there's no harm in trying." She tucked the small stone into her own apron. "Thank you."

"You're welcome. We're all just looking out for each other."

"Is there anything else I can do to help?" She peered into the wagon. "More buckets that need to be lifted?"

"We're all good here, miss," Mr. Van Anda said. "I'm sure your own family could use another pair of hands."

Rebecca smiled and didn't argue with him. If there was one thing that could be said about her family, it was that each and every one of them were perfectly capable. That was why she was always looking to others for ways to help, ways to keep busy.

But as she made her way back to her own wagon, the caravan started to move. Some families, like the Van Andas, scrambled to finish loading their water, but soon the whole wagon company was headed west again.

The Oregon Trail cut through the wide-open prairies, with virtually nothing but grass in all directions. As the days passed without sources of fresh water, Rebecca had to try harder and harder to find enough to do to occupy her thoughts. Not only were the memories of her husband enough to derail her for hours, but now the constant knowledge that she should not be drinking water haunted her. The heat consumed her thoughts. The pebble Mrs. Van Anda had given her did help some, especially when she could forget it was in her mouth and busy her hands elsewhere, but nothing could replace the relief of cool water.

Under the heat of the summer sun, in her black dress, the deep thirst was constant.

With so little water in this stretch of country, the wagons churned up dust clouds that stayed aloft for miles. Rebecca covered her mouth and nose with a shawl in hopes to filter out some of the dust rather than breathe it in. With every animal hoof and wagon wheel kicking up more and more dirt, there seemed to be no escaping it. Michael Stephens, and some of the other men, drove their wagons out into the tall grass, to travel parallel to the Oregon Trail and attempt to avoid at least some of the ever-present dust cloud.

Between the penetrating sun above and the parched earth below, it seemed the entire environment around her pleaded for water. She knew she needed to ration it —her family's very survival was at stake—but the temptation was overwhelming at times.

A small cup of water to drink in the morning, another sip at mid-day, and a final mouthful each night. It was barely enough to wet her lips. She could feel her mother watching her with every sip she took. Her very eyes felt dry. They even abstained from washing the dishes for the first few days in order to make sure that the water lasted long enough.

One afternoon, she could stand being near the canteens no longer. It was too much in the forefront of her thoughts, and she left her own wagon to seek out the succor of the open prairie away from the temptation. She held her breath as she darted through the clouds of dust, between the wagons, as quickly as she could. Rebecca was a good half a mile away from the caravan before she found the edge of the dust and relief.

That far away from the wagons, Rebecca held Mrs. Van Anda's pebble in her mouth and hummed to herself.

First all the hymns she could remember from growing up in the church, and then when she had nothing else to distract her, she tried to remember the couple bawdy drinking songs she and Jasper had learned once when they were ten and thirteen.

Anything to distract her.

The journey was far more grueling than Rebecca had expected.

The days passed, and the water just held out. Though the family consumed all of it, to the very last drop, the worry of severe dehydration was unrealized. The Sullivan-Mills wagon company had reached their next water source. The trail crested a low hill, and from the top of it, Rebecca saw the wide, shallow Platte River cutting through the green valley. The slow, meandering river ran parallel to the trail for several days' worth of travel, until they came upon the shallowest part where the river forked.

Fording the Platte River was scary, but not nearly as much so as crossing the Kansas had been. Rebecca was grateful she just had to walk across in knee-high water, rather than risk another tilting platform that could plunge their whole team into the depths. Between Michael and Jasper, the Stephens's wagon got to the other side safely, with Rebecca and her mother not far behind.

Once they had reached the other side of the river, they still didn't have a chance to rest. The terrain grew rocky, almost impassable, but they had to keep moving. To Rebecca, every mile of the Oregon Trail was a new challenge and she simply could not see the end of it.

CHAPTER NINETEEN

Though the Sullivan-Mills wagon company spent much of the day fording the Platte River, they could not stop to rest. On the other side of the river were still several more miles to traverse before making camp for the evening. Rebecca was exhausted when their wagon finally pulled into the circle to make camp for the night. But in spite of her tiredness, Rebecca's mind was whirling.

After the shock of Jeb Buchanan's death, and the fear of losing her brother in a similar way, Rebecca had done her best to put those anxieties behind her. Some days it worked—like when she was busy boiling water so the women of the company could wash their hair. But many days were simply too monotonous to distract her.

Being busy wasn't enough.

Though people would laugh if she voiced this thought out loud, Rebecca could not help feeling there was not enough work on the Oregon Trail to keep her from thinking about her grief. At times she felt like her hands were shaking just from the thoughts of all that was out there to take people she loved.

She needed fun. She needed excitement and friends and joy. But as long as she was in mourning there was no way she would get any of those things. The solution eluded her.

One evening, after the wagon company had stopped for the day, Rebecca stood out of the way of her father and the oxen, nervously biting her fingernails. It was a habit she had broken years ago, but had picked it up again somewhere along the Oregon Trail. Whether it was the monotony of the day or the stress of the trail's danger that drove her to it, she didn't know. As soon as she noticed she was doing it, she pulled her hand away from her mouth and made a tight fist, determined to break the habit again.

"Rebecca!"

She turned to see Sadie Waters walking toward her across the wide circle of wagons. The wagon company had strictly maintained their security measures, chaining the hubs together each evening when they made camp and setting guards at strategic posts. With so many wagons in the caravan, however, the circle became huge. This was necessary to corral all the livestock within it, but it did make for long distances between friends.

Rebecca walked toward her when she saw her friend and waved cheerfully. Though she still adhered to the restrictions of being in mourning—Andrew had only been gone about eight months—the informal banter with friends like Sadie let her be more of herself than she could be in other company.

"I just came to check that you all got across the river

okay. I heard that Louisa Hudson fell all the way in." She chuckled. "Luckily nothing more than her pride was hurt, I think."

"Oh, yes, we're all fine here. I'm sure I almost fell in myself a couple times, but no worse for wear. I was thinking about soaking my feet tonight, maybe. Walking after getting my boots wet seems to have started a blister on my heel."

"That sounds like a good idea, but I won't be doing that tonight. Angus and I are going to the dance."

"Oh! Oh. Well... That's nice." Rebecca tried to hide her surprise and hurt, but the sympathetic look on her friend's face told her that she had failed.

"I'm sorry," Sadie said again. "I thought you knew."

"It's all right. It's not your fault my husband died and I can't even speak to someone I don't know, let alone go to a dance," she said bitterly. "Andrew would have had so much fun. He would have insisted we go to every one, no matter what else happened." She sighed. "I'm sorry. I shouldn't lash out at you."

"You miss him. I can't even imagine. If I lost Angus..."

"But you won't," Rebecca said with false cheer. "He'll be by your side every day until Oregon, and then you'll build your home and have a family, and go to as many dances as you want."

She wasn't fooling Sadie, however. Her friend drew Rebecca into a hug.

"I'm sorry," Sadie whispered.

"It's fine." She laughed self-consciously at herself and brushed away the tears that had fallen despite her best efforts. "I don't even know why I'm so upset. It's really fine. I'll probably be able to hear the music from here anyway."

"You don't know why you're upset?" Sadie repeated. "Could it be because you miss your husband? Your dancing partner? Could it maybe be because you've had to give up every fun and diverting and comforting thing in your life and this is just one sacrifice too many? I don't know. I'm just guessing here."

"Sacrifice?" Rebecca laughed through her tears. "I'm not that dramatic am I?"

Sadie turned serious, and linked her arm through her friend's as she moved close. "No, dear, you're not dramatic. But you are hurting and I hope you know it's okay. You're allowed to be upset that you can't attend a dance with the love of your life anymore."

More tears spilled down Rebecca's cheeks.

"I'm sorry," she said, wiping them away. "I don't mean to cry. I'm just tired."

"Of course you are. Who wouldn't be?"

"But you're right. It's just a lot all at once. I'll be fine."

"Come with us," Sadie blurted out.

Rebecca frowned at her in surprise.

"You should. Come with us. A staid married couple like us, we are perfectly capable of chaperoning you. You don't have to dance, but there will be music, and you could even just watch from the side, away from the firelight. Most people won't even notice you're there, so you won't shock anyone's delicate sensibilities."

Rebecca laughed again, and even felt herself cheering up. She wanted to let herself be convinced, but the whole thing would be a risk. "Do you think so?"

"Even if you do, what are they going to do about it? Shun you? Not invite you to afternoon tea?" Sadie smiled sympathetically. "I know I shouldn't try to draw you into such misbehavior, but for goodness sake, Rebecca Tenney. You are a grown woman. You should be allowed to get within twenty feet of music playing without everyone raising a fuss."

Rebecca hesitated only a moment before letting a laugh escape her lips.

"You're right. I'm going. No one can stop me."

CHAPTER TWENTY

After Sadie left, it was time for Rebecca to be helping her mother with supper. As she scooped out a bit of the bacon fat to help grease the pan for baking, she told her mother she would be going with the Waterses that night after eating.

"I don't like the idea of you being away from our camp after dark. It's not safe outside the circle of wagons."

"There's going to be a dance tonight, though," Rebecca explained. "We'll all be together."

"A dance? I don't know why you care," her mother said. "You won't be dancing, and I should think you wouldn't want to be seen there at all. What would Andrew say?"

"If Andrew was here? Why, you know he would be the first one to call for music. I won't dance. I won't even talk to anyone if I can get away with it without being rude. I just... I want to hear the music. Sadie and Angus are going and invited me. They'll look after me."

"How are you going to maintain the propriety of a widow while Sadie and Angus are dancing? You'll just be on your own, waiting to dance, a temptation for every man there."

Rebecca flushed in embarrassed anger, but before she could respond too harshly, her brother interjected.

"I'll take her," Jasper said, from where he sat rubbing oil into the reins to keep them supple.

Both women looked at him.

"You're going to the dance?" Ada asked. "Since when?"

He shrugged. "I hadn't decided. But if Becks wants to go, I'll take her. I'll keep her tied down and busy so no one asks her to dance. I'll make sure no one even looks at her, Ma. Don't worry. It will all be very respectable."

"Yes, yes, very funny." Ada pursed her lips and looked from her son to daughter and back again. "Very well. I know I can't stop you, either of you. Just, please don't do anything that will embarrass the family."

"We would never," Rebecca assured her mother, who snorted in disbelief. "*I* would never," she amended.

"Hey!" Jasper protested.

With her plans in place, Rebecca climbed into the wagon. At the very least, she could comb her hair and smooth out the loose strands. She didn't bother changing her dress, but taking off her apron and washing her face did her a world of good. As soon as she felt more presentable, she sought out her brother. Jasper was picking his teeth with his knife.

"Are you ready to go? Or do you need to conduct more of your meticulous grooming?"

Jasper chuckled. "All right. All right. Keep your hat on. I was planning on being fashionably late, you know."

"Well, then you walk me over there and you can leave again and come back when you're really late."

"I love this plan," her brother countered.

The dance was to be near the Jamesons' wagon, and as far away from families with sleeping children as they could safely be. As Rebecca and Jasper drew closer, they saw what appeared to be a bonfire, with a wide, flat area surrounding it full of couples and groups of young people talking. At a glance, it seemed as though the guests ranged as young as fifteen-year-old Billy Whitson all the way up to Ernie Schmidt, who might be in his early forties.

"Do you want to dance with me?" Jasper asked quietly, as they drew closer. "I won't tell Ma, and most people here probably won't care."

Rebecca almost stopped walking in her surprise. "That's very tempting... Goodness, Jasper, you have no idea how tempting. I can't." She shook her head. "Don't ask me again."

He laughed. "All right. You got it. If you need me, I'm around, but I'll let you roam on your own. Fair?"

"And when I'm ready to go back?"

"Just tell me," he said, seriously for once. "Honest. Whatever you need."

She squeezed his arm and smiled her gratitude, but they were approaching the crowd and Jasper seemed distracted.

"Go on," she said. "Go find your girl. I'll wait over there, by the fire."

He grinned at her and darted off toward a group of young people sharing a flask.

Wistfully, Rebecca watched him go, but being here at all was better than she could have hoped for. Making her way around the edge of the crowd, Rebecca managed to find a spot in a quiet corner, near the fire and music but not too close to where the couples were dancing. It was the perfect place to watch from, without being visible herself.

Without realizing it, Rebecca had started tapping her foot to the lively music. Her eyes drank in every step, every twirl, every smile. All around her couples were pairing off and whirling around the dance floor—or, rather, the dance dirt clearing. A memory of the last dance she had gone to with Andrew popped into her head, contrasting with the rustic scene before her. How Paul Murphy and his string quartet and his spotless marble ballroom would look down at this gathering. And yet, Rebecca could be as perfectly happy dancing here as she had been there.

If only she had her Andrew.

In all her watching, Rebecca noticed that she was not the only one not dancing. Some couples took breaks to rest, or talk, in between songs. Still others seemed in no way inclined to dance at all, but had cozied themselves up together near the fire's warmth. She spotted her brother whirling Hattie Larson around during a waltz, and wondered if Nora Cole had not come.

Though she tried to keep quiet and subdued, out of sight, Rebecca noticed that someone had spotted her.

A giant, mountain of a man crossed around the edge of the crowd to her. He paused about ten feet away, and she noticed him lean down to say something to Angus Waters. Though there was nearly a foot difference in height, Rebecca noticed the family resemblance immediately. They had the same strong jaw and ears that stuck out just a bit, though the nose of the taller man was straighter than Angus's. Even so, it was clear he must be one of the Waters brothers.

She knew that he had seen her, but didn't realize his intention until he was right in front of her.

"Would you like to dance?" he asked, offering his hand.

Rebecca opened her mouth. She wanted to say yes.

"I can't," she said instead.

"Of course you can."

"No." She gestured to her widow's weeds. Even in the darkness away from the fire he should be able to see she wore all black. "No, I can't. I shouldn't. I don't want to. Thank you, but no."

He paused, amused. "Angus said you'd say that. If I promise I won't judge you will you change your mind?"

Rebecca looked past him to the dozen couples light on their feet, spinning to the beat of Martin's fiddle.

"I'm Beau Waters," he said, gently drawing her attention back to himself. "I mean no offense, Mrs. Tenney, but you look like you want nothing more than to dance."

"I do," she whispered, before she knew what she was saying.

"Then come on." He offered his hand again, stepping closer this time.

She looked up into his eager face, and reached her hand to his. But the moment she touched his strong fingers, and they closed around her, she felt how wrong it all was. This wasn't Andrew. This wasn't her husband. She was still in mourning, no matter how much her feet might want to fly.

"I can't," she said again, pulling away. "I can't. I'm sorry."

Rebecca turned away from him, darting in between other guests and taking no notice of the other voices that called after her. She hurried through the darkness, away from the inquiring faces and nosy neighbors. Frustrated at their freedom and angry at herself, Rebecca's face burned in embarrassment.

She never should have gone.

She should have stayed home where she wouldn't be tempted or reminded of her husband. Running through the darkness, she made her way straight home without stopping.

"How was your time?" her mother asked, as Rebecca stalked by.

"Well, I had to turn down a perfectly good offer of a dance with a lovely man, I'll have you know."

Ada made a sympathetic noise while she continued to pack away that evening's dishes.

"Maybe I shouldn't have gone," Rebecca said. "It just hurts so much to have to miss things like that, but then it hurts again when I have to hold myself back if I do go. What am I supposed to do?"

"I don't want to say I told you so—"

"Then don't." Rebecca cut the conversation short as she climbed into the dark wagon. "I'm going to bed."

With barely a thought to what she was doing, Rebecca took down her hair, took off her shoes, and loosened her stays. She wanted to be safe under her quilt and blocking out the world as soon as she could.

Once in her cot, she rolled onto her side, her face deep in the dark recesses against the wall, with the blanket pulled up to her ears. Try as she did to fight off her tears of frustration, she could not keep from thinking about everything she was missing. Jasper was lit up from within at the joy of dancing, and Rebecca wasn't even certain he had known his partner. The lively music and the joyful young folk all gathered together were some of her favorite things, and she had to deny herself that.

What was the point of all of this?

What was she doing? Was this what Andrew truly wanted for her? To always be on the periphery? To have to turn down the smallest indication of fun she had seen in weeks? Could he have known how hard this would all be when he had made her promise to continue on to Oregon without him?

Rebecca knew that wasn't fair. She turned over on her narrow cot in frustration. Andrew hadn't wanted to die and leave her; he had only wanted the best for her even if she had to be on her own. It wasn't his fault that widows were expected to bury their hearts along with their spouses.

It was a long time before Rebecca finally fell asleep.

CHAPTER TWENTY-ONE

The following morning, Rebecca woke to the sound of her mother unpacking the pans she needed. She was almost surprised to see the sunlight; it felt as though she had only barely just closed her eyes. All night she had lain awake thinking about every little thing she had lost when Andrew died—from the option to wearing colors all the way to a partner to nurse her when she was hurt. She lolled in bed, as long as she thought she could get away with. By the time she had climbed out of the wagon the rest of her family was already awake and breakfast was cooked.

"Morning, sunshine," her mother called out upon seeing her.

"What happened to you last night?" Jasper asked, before sipping at his coffee. "You could have at least told me you were coming back."

"I'm sorry; you're right. I should have." Rebecca accepted a mug of coffee from her mother. "I was upset. I wasn't thinking. Did you wait long for me?"

He shook his head. "Sadie saw you leave. Said she called your name and you ignored her."

Rebecca felt her mother's eyes on her but kept her focus on her breakfast. "Yeah, I was, um, tired. Distracted, I guess. I must not have heard her."

"Well, I'm glad she saw you at least, since my attention was elsewhere."

"That's right," Rebecca said, embracing the pivot in the conversation. "I saw you dance with the Larson girl. Did Nora not come last night?"

She noticed her mother's attention perk up at that, and the two women spent the next fifteen minutes questioning Jasper, until it was time for the company to break camp.

Rebecca's lack of sleep the night before proved to be the first in a long list of struggles she would have to suffer through the next day. If she could have slept better, maybe she would have been more patient or more easy-going. Instead, every step of the trail irritated her more than the previous. Her head felt as though it was stuffed with cotton and she couldn't keep herself from yawning.

Within an hour of leaving camp the next morning, the wagon train reached a rocky terrain that proved just as dangerous an obstacle as the wide rivers had in days past. Each person would need to pick their way through the field of stones, while the men had an even more difficult job of somehow navigating their huge wagons around and over the rocks. Walking all the way around a stone the size of a turkey was inconvenient, but it was far easier than trying to move a wagon around the same.

The stretch of ground covered in rocks of all sizes

was wide enough that Rebecca couldn't see where it ended. Far too wide for the trail go around it. Instead, at the front of the caravan, George Mills halted his oxen to carefully, slowly, painstakingly pick his way between the largest boulders and over the smaller of the rocks. His son Daniel tried to follow immediately behind with the Millses' second wagon, and then the Findley wagon came behind that. Each man in the wagon company tried their best to match the same path that the man before him had followed, but the cost of doing so was time.

It took innumerable hours for all the wagons to get across, particularly when several of the wagons broke a wheel on the attempt. Poor Sean Gilroy, the blacksmith, was kept busy all day next to a hot fire trying to repair the wheels quickly. Everyone worked together as best they could, but the stress of the endeavor was taxing. Rebecca stayed out of the way if only to keep from being snapped at by a brother who was working so hard.

Once the wagons had gotten clear of the rock-strewn terrain, there was still a harrowing journey down into a narrow gorge to be made before they could rest for the night. The campsite where they would spend the night was at the bottom, but first each wagon had to make it down a steep, narrow trail that seemed to have been cut directly into the rock itself. Rebecca hung back, out of her father's and brother's way so they could carefully maneuver the wagon to the bottom of the gorge.

With everything the company had been through that day, Rebecca felt both grateful it was over and completely superfluous. So much of the most strenuous work was handled by the men; all Rebecca had to do was keep clear. Though in some ways a blessing, all it meant was she ended up spending most of the day alone with her thoughts. The stress was not enough to distract her from her feelings of loss. Watching her family delicately lead the wagon down the steep path had been scary, reminding Rebecca of how easily something could go wrong, how easily someone could get hurt.

How easily she could lose one more person.

It wasn't until everyone had reached the bottom safely that she felt like she could breathe freely again. It had been a long, tiring day, but now there was the promise of grass for the animals and water for the humans. They would stay here for another full day, letting the men have time to make what repairs they needed.

Which also meant that Rebecca had another full day to find something to occupy herself, lest she go too far down the dark hole of her grief.

Jasper stood a few feet away, near the foot of the trail and eating a cold johnnycake. He stood close, asking questions and paying attention to how Mr. Gilroy was working as he hammered down an iron tire to replace one that had bent earlier that day. As Rebecca watched her brother, she noticed no fewer than half a dozen men come greet him. She saw the way Patrick Keegan's children sought him out. And she already knew that somewhere else in the camp, Nora Cole was thinking about him.

Jasper seemed to be thriving out here in the wilderness. He was loved and popular, while Rebecca seemed to be deteriorating, even to the point of biting down her fingernails until she bled. She didn't know if it was the fact that she was a woman or the fact that she was a widow that could be holding her back from the same kind of peace in the wilderness as her brother, but Rebecca wanted what he had. She was tired of barely hanging on. He seemed so effortlessly content, whereas she was constantly searching for a reprieve from her grief.

Rebecca crossed the grassy clearing to her brother.

"If Pa's okay with it, I might come apprentice for Mr. Gilroy through the rest of the trip. Useful skills to learn, blacksmithing."

"I don't know how you can be so excited about even more work."

"Really?" He looked at her in surprise.

"I'm just so tired. I feel like I can't think about anything else."

"Becks, everyone is tired. It's something we all have to deal with."

"There are people more tired than you are. Mrs. Van Anda, for example."

"All right, that's probably true." He laughed. "It will all be worth it, though. Just a few months left of all this."

The siblings were quiet together for a few moments.

"Do you never miss Indiana?" she asked.

Jasper took another bite of the johnnycake and gazed up at the sky. The sun had just set, and the stars were appearing slowly through the dark. For a moment she wondered if he hadn't heard her and was on the verge of repeating her question when he finally spoke.

"Indiana wasn't the same for you as it was for me," he said. "You had Andrew and a circle of admirers. You were popular."

"Jasper!" she exclaimed, almost at a loss for words. "What on earth are you talking about? You were plenty popular. Remember Laura Dutton? And Elle Chisholm? They spent months following you from school to home, waiting around till you left again to do chores."

He grinned. "Yeah, that was flattering, of course. Bobby Valenti teased me incessantly about it. But that's not what I mean. None of those girls were true friends. I don't know how to explain. I always kind of felt like I was on my way out."

"That's why you kept talking about New York City," she said, suddenly remembering. "Leaving the farm and all of us behind. I always thought you were just being selfish."

"I was. At least a little. But I also didn't want to up and abandon everything. That wouldn't be fair to Pa."

"So, instead you announced it. At least get him used to the idea while you saved money?"

He nodded.

"That makes so much sense now. What would you have done if we hadn't left for Oregon? Go to New York?"

"I'm not sure. Maybe head off on my own somewhere."

"And break Ma's heart in doing so."

"Likely."

They were both quiet a moment, thinking about that alternate future that they might have had. If Andrew hadn't died.

"Do you think you will feel settled in Oregon?" Rebecca finally asked. Though she and her brother had never been particularly close, she certainly didn't want to lose him.

He finally finished eating the johnnycake and turned to give his sister his full attention.

"I do."

She almost wanted to cry in relief.

"I couldn't say for sure why," he continued thoughtfully, "but maybe it's just something about all these people from all over the country coming together. There's something free and exciting about such a collection of neighbors. And if we're all together in Oregon? Well, then..."

Rebecca watched her brother a few moments longer, as he was distracted by seeing what Mr. Gilroy was doing next. She wanted to ask him about Nora Cole, and how she fit into his carefree life. But then she saw his face light up hearing Mr. Gilroy call him over and realized he had other priorities at the moment. Maybe there would be a time in the future to tease her brother about his sweetheart, but now was not that time. The integrity and almost innocence he showed at the thought of all these strangers coming together warmed her heart.

"Well," she said, finally, "I hope when we get to Oregon you find your place that was never there in Indiana."

"I will. You'll see. I know this is all hard for you, but wait till we get there. You'll keep saying how Andrew was right."

She snorted a laugh and leaned into him. With his arm around her, Jasper squeezed her in a sideways hug.

"You'll see," he said again.

CHAPTER TWENTY-TWO

That day of rest the company passed at the bottom of the gorge went by all too quickly. Rebecca noticed more examples of how Jasper was really finding his place among all these recent strangers and took heart that maybe she could find a way to do the same. She had met nearly all the women in the company, after all, and was trying to keep her heart open to new friends.

It was a challenge daily, though. She woke up each morning afraid for the lives of her family, while also trying to ignore her pain at losing her husband. The emotions overwhelmed her day in and day out, and the only reprieve she found was when she could fill absolutely every minute of every day with other people. Distraction and shallow entertainment.

Of course, then she began to get attached to her new friends like Annie and Sadie, and then went through the same fears of losing them as she had lost Andrew.

She could not seem to break free of this cycle of fear

and grief and distraction, and was running herself ragged even trying.

Only moving forward, ever westward, with the promise of an end in sight calmed her at all.

One morning, in a long monotonous stretch of prairie, the wagon company failed to leave camp as early as the captains had so ordered. Rebecca was bouncing up and down on her feet, eager to get moving, eager for something to happen.

"Why aren't we moving?"

Jasper shrugged. "I dunno, but since it seems like nothing's happening, I'll be right back."

"You come right back when you see the wagons moving, mister," their mother called after him. She shook her head in disappointment when she turned back to Rebecca. "I hope that boy is not chasing after the Cole girl, or any other girl for that matter. The last thing we need in this wagon company is a broken heart on top of everything else."

"He wants to get going just as much as the rest of us. He'll be back."

It was no more than five minutes before they spotted the tall, lanky form of Jasper striding back toward him, his expression grim.

Immediately fear seized Rebecca's heart. What had happened? Who else had they lost?

"Did you find out?" Ada said.

"I heard it second hand, from Nora. It's measles."

Rebecca didn't even have the heart to exchange a knowing smile with her mother about Jasper going to see Nora. The news he brought was too dire.

"What? No! Who?"

"Jeremiah Sullivan. Just him, as far as Nora knew. The little girls went with the pastor's wife, and the older ones can stay with other friends, but it's not looking good. She said the doctor looked worried."

Rebecca let out a long slow breath. She didn't have to be told how bad measles in a crowded camp like theirs could be. With the other Sullivan children staying away from Jeremiah, there was a chance—hopefully—that the disease wouldn't spread. But there was absolutely no way to know for sure.

They would simply have to weather this storm, together.

"So, then are we staying here for the day?" Rebecca asked. "That boy shouldn't be moved."

Jasper shook his head. "We can't. There's no extra days to spare. I hear it was Sullivan's idea to keep going, even if it is his son that's sick."

"The alternative would be to leave the Sullivans behind," Michael said quietly. "No one wants that. How soon until we leave, son?"

"Not long. Should be any minute, I think. Such a shame though. That poor boy."

The day passed as any other, though a tension held the wagon company close together. Each person wanted to hurry along as fast as they could, but at the same time hold back for fear of what the evening would bring. Rebecca stuck close to her family's wagon, too distracted by thoughts of measles in the camp to think about other ways to spend her time.

Both Rebecca and Jasper had had measles when they were very young, but she couldn't remember anything about it. Her mother had stories about the two of them sick together, closed up in one bedroom to limit their exposure to anyone else. Another little girl, about Rebecca's age, had died of the disease during the same outbreak. The one strong memory Rebecca had from that time in her life was being disappointed that she had been too sick to attend the funeral.

Now, thankfully, she knew better than to be so heartless.

Though she was likely not at risk of catching it again, she could imagine what fear must be racing through the mothers of the company. Measles was a lot for a person to handle at the best of times. Now, after living out of a wagon for so long and not getting the same fresh milk and eggs he would have gotten before leaving home, Jeremiah's little body might not be strong enough.

The day dragged on, more tense than usual, until they finally pulled into a tight protective circle when they made camp that night. But even before many of the families had had time to collect wood for their campfire, Daniel Mills was spreading the word that the child had died that afternoon.

The Stephenses accepted the news somberly, but Rebecca nearly spun into a panic. One more loss. One more death. How much longer could they go on in such anguish?

Each day on the Oregon Trail was a strange mixture of danger and monotony.

After the disastrous attempt of attending the dance, Rebecca realized that she was far better suited to one-on-one and small group socializing. After the death of yet another member of the wagon company, and the fear of measles, Rebecca had learned that her thirst for excitement could lead to dangerous things.

And so the days wore on and Rebecca began to rethink her desire for something exciting to always be happening. Attending the funeral of a child every few weeks was far more drama than she was looking for.

CHAPTER TWENTY-THREE

The wagon company pushed west. Day after day the flat landscape offered an occasional change. After several days of monotony, a large stone peeked up over the horizon. Finally, something new. The wagon company was entering a stretch of the western landscape that offered something more than simply miles and miles of prairie grass.

As they drew closer, Rebecca was able to make out the enormous square shape, apparently named after the county seat in Missouri, and it wasn't the first. Though they were few and far between, Courthouse Rock was the first of half a dozen such granite monoliths that peppered the skyline and led the company farther west, with even more to come. Rebecca was fascinated. There was something about these structures that felt ancient, that felt bigger and deeper than she could ever hope to be.

How Andrew would have loved this.

She wanted to slow down to experience each one of

the rocks directly. They were few and far between, but they were better than nothing. The wagon company couldn't spare the time to stop and explore, but she was thrilled each night when they camped. One evening, the spire of Chimney Rock loomed over them when they stopped for the night. Another they stopped at Scott's Bluff, but still they kept pushing westward.

Early one afternoon in June, Rebecca was walking alongside the wagon train by herself, focused on keeping her hands balled into fists so she wasn't tempted to bite her nails any further. She was afraid she would not be able to break that habit until they finally arrived in Oregon and the constant loom of danger was past. Her attention was pulled by a disturbance up ahead in the caravan. The wagons slowed, though she couldn't tell why at first. It wasn't until she spotted Daniel Mills, the captain's son, riding down the length of the caravan, that she learned what the hubbub was about.

Though the wagon company was not set to make camp for several hours yet, all plans changed when the promise of a buffalo herd appeared. While his father redirected the wagons, Daniel rode down to the end of the row, calling for the men to grab their guns and be ready to head north in ten minutes. The company hastily pulled the wagon train into a circle for the rest of the day, and nearly all the men headed off to hunt. Rebecca was wondering how she would spend her quiet afternoon in camp, when she realized Jasper was still lolling under their wagon.

"You're not going?" she asked her brother.

He shook his head. "Naw. Pa'll take care of it. I got

my eye on a nap under the wagon, with fewer people around to bother me."

Rebecca pursed her lips, concerned, but it would probably be fine. If her brother wanted to take the one chance he might have to relax on an afternoon, he should do so. Heavens knew she might do the same thing in his shoes. And plenty of men had gone after the buffalo.

As the men all made their way out of the camp, riding with purpose toward the promise of good hunting, the women and children that remained settled in for a quiet afternoon. Maybe half a dozen of the older boys and men stayed behind, and soon each emigrant had found their shade or cozy spot in which to spend the unexpected break.

Rebecca brushed out her hair before braiding it again and pinning it up. Her mother was collecting the family's clothing that needed to be washed and mended, but Rebecca shut her eyes to the expectant look on her mother's face.

"Nope! Not today. That all can wait," she declared.

"Rebecca, you know if we don't take this chance to—"

"Ma, it will still all be there the next time we make camp. Please. We didn't even stop that close to water. The routine of the trail every day is wearing on me. Jasper's taking a nap. The men are off hunting. I want a break too."

Ada sighed. "All right, girl. You go on, then. Just don't complain when you have twice as much to do next time we stop."

Rebecca waved her acquiescence and set off across

the open space in the center of the wagon circle, looking for Sadie. All the Waters men likely went on the hunt, so maybe Sadie was looking for companionship as much as Rebecca was.

All of the company's cattle and other livestock milled around the broad open area; Rebecca walked between the small herds that would be the emigrants' livelihoods once they arrived in Oregon. Nearly all the horses had been ridden off to chase the buffalo, but she spied a few more horses, goats and dairy cows among the dozens of corralled.

When Rebecca got closer to the Waters family's wagons, she spotted Sadie, her sister-in-law Nancy and the youngest Waters, Faith, lounging in the shade of one of their wagons. Mrs. Waters was nowhere in sight.

"Afternoon, ladies," Rebecca called. "Am I interrupting?"

Sadie put a finger to her lips. "Mother Waters just lay down in the wagon to try to sleep. She's got a bad headache."

"Oh, sorry!" Rebecca said softly. "Is she all right?"

Nancy shrugged. "Hard to say. She's been feeling ill more often. Could just be the heat. And the stress."

"Seems like an afternoon like this could do all of us some good," Rebecca agreed. "You should have heard me telling Ma. I don't care if I have twice as much mending to do next time."

Finding a spot in the shade next to Sadie, Rebecca leaned back and closed her eyes. What she wouldn't do for a hammock or a glass of cold lemonade. The four women lay there, almost dozing in the afternoon heat for not more than twenty minutes before Sadie sat bolt upright in surprise.

"Do you hear that?" Sadie asked with a frown.

"No, I..." Rebecca trailed off as the unexpected sound of a dull roar reached her ears. "Oh, yes. What is that?"

At first, Rebecca wondered if it was thunder, but the sky seemed to be utterly devoid of cloud. Then, in the distance, the distinctive pitch of a war whoop sounded, echoed by answering yells and yips.

The women looked at each other for just a moment longer before the realization of what they heard was all over their faces. The camp was under attack. Those were hooves, tearing toward the wagons rapidly. Those were the victorious yells of the native tribe on whose land they were stationed.

That was the sound of an imminent attack.

They hurriedly climbed to their feet. Rebecca felt frozen in fear.

"What do we do?" Rebecca exclaimed, clinging to Sadie's arm. "We'll be safe in camp, won't we? Won't we?"

Sadie shook her head dumbly. "I don't know. I don't know. Oh, *where* is the gun Angus left?"

At the mention of a gun, Rebecca felt a rush of relief remembering that her brother had not gone off with the rest of the men. At least they would have one decent marksman.

"I have to go," she told Sadie, though the other woman was already climbing into her wagon after Nancy and Faith. Rebecca had to get back to her own wagon, and to her brother's protection. She darted off back through the cattle, across the open space within the safe circle of wagons.

Before she got halfway through, however, another sound arrested her. She couldn't place it, a sound like something heavy was being dragged through the dirt.

She stopped, turned toward the noise, and immediately let out a cry of anguish.

When the men had made camp and gone off after the buffalo at least one of them, possibly more, had not taken that final step in securing the wagon circle. Every night when the company made camp, they were expected to chain the hubs of the wagons together, to keep the circle tight and immovable. But now... As Rebecca watched the camp's attackers came into view. Several of the muscular warriors were physically pulling apart two of the wagons on the north side of the circle.

Rebecca turned and kept running to her own wagon. As she got closer, her mother called out to her from behind the closed canvas flaps.

"Rebecca Tenney, you get in here right this instant!"

Ada was halfway leaning out through the gap in the canvas, gesturing wildly to her daughter. Jasper was still under the wagon where Rebecca had left him, but now he was all alert, all readiness, lying on his belly with his rifle propped through the spokes of the wagon wheel.

"Be careful," she said to him, as she climbed in after her mother.

He nodded grimly, and did not take his eyes from where they stared down the barrel.

In just the minute or so that it had taken Rebecca to reach her family's wagon from the Waterses', the whole north side of the circle had been pulled open, and more than a dozen Indian warriors were pouring into the camp.

Though she shook from head to toe, Rebecca allowed herself to be drawn into a hug by her mother.

"It's okay," Ada assured her in a whisper. "It will be okay."

"Will it?" Rebecca mumbled into her mother's shoulder.

From below them, she heard a gunshot. From outside the wagon, she could hear more war whoops and shouting back and forth in a language she could not decipher. Rebecca pulled back from her mother and sat on the edge of her cot, shoulders hunched over, as though she were trying to make herself as small as possible. She leaned over farther, burying her face in her hands as the sounds of the attack continued all around her.

She just wanted to shut it all out, to block the sounds. She would deal with it later, when it was all over, but the intense fear of living through that fraught moment was almost more than her body could handle.

Her mother gently stroked the top of her head, whispering over and over that they would be all right.

Another gunshot from below.

Rebecca scrunched up her face, wishing she could be anywhere but here.

Another gunshot. And a fourth. Whatever else was happening out there, Jasper was doing his best to defend their wagon. How was Sadie holding up? Or Annie? Or any of the other women whose men had left them without any means to defend themselves?

Rebecca let out a strangled sob.

"I need to see," she whispered. "What if they need me?"

"Who?" her mother whispered back, incredulously. "You stay put, Rebecca Tenney. Don't you dare go out there. Keep out of sight. We don't even have a weapon."

All around the wagon the sounds of Indian cries and horse hooves thundered. There was so much commotion, it was nearly impossible for Rebecca to determine where the enemy was, especially without looking. She gripped her mother's hands and closed her eyes tight, just willing it all to be over.

"Gah!" Jasper cried out, over the ruckus.

Rebecca's heart hammered. He was directly beneath them, and they couldn't see a thing outside the wagon.

"Jasper!" she called, though trying to stay quiet.

There was no response.

Their mother gasped and began whimpering. But louder than her whimpering, even, was the painful groan that came from under the wagon.

"I'll go," Rebecca whispered. "Stay here."

"No—"

"I have to see. I have to help. I can't just sit here. The risk is still better than staying in here not knowing."

"Rebecca, what if—"

But Rebecca had already gone, carefully, slowly, using just the tips of her fingers to gently push aside the white canvas that hung down in the back of their wagon. There wasn't much she could see from this vantage—the front seat of the Keegan family's wagon was pulled close to the Stephens. Sounds of fear and attacks were all around her, but none of that action was in her view.

She would have to leave the relative safety of the

wagon. Her brother's painful grunting was getting louder now. He needed her.

Pushing from her mind all thoughts of fear and danger, Rebecca took a deep breath and climbed out of the wagon. She kept herself small, ducking down low so as not to present a large target, and looked between the wheels underneath the wagon.

Her brother lay on his back, but with his head turned far to the side, muffling his moans in the dirt and clutching his left arm where the shaft of an arrow stuck out. The rifle's barrel was still stuck between the spokes of the wheel, but it was now angled to the sky, with the butt of the gun in the dirt where Jasper had dropped it.

Hiking up her heavy skirt and petticoat, Rebecca crawled on her hands and knees to her brother.

"Shh, shh, Jasper," she whispered, trying to be soothing but she wasn't sure he could even hear her. "Be careful. Let's not jostle it. Don't move."

"What are you doing here?" he hissed. "Go back with Ma. I'm fine."

"You're not fine. I had to see what was going on."

She plucked his fingers away from his upper arm where they had been wrapped around his wound. The arrowhead had lodged deep into the muscle, and he had been gripping that part of his arm tightly. The cramped space under the wagon was no place to perform the careful surgery they would need to clean the wound, even if they weren't still under attack. Rebecca turned back toward the wheel and peered out into the middle of the wagon circle.

It was chaos. Dust flew everywhere under the hooves of not only the attackers' horses, but also the cattle they were driving through the break in the wagons. Her attention was pulled in every direction, as mothers called their children's names, as women tried valiantly to defy the warriors ransacking their wagons. A scattering of gunshot was the only real defense the emigrants had been able to put up.

She felt alive, watching it all. Her body thrummed with excitement. Her heart pounded. The fear she had felt when hiding had been banished in the sight of the chance to actually make a difference. The danger was the furthest thing from her mind. She gently nudged her brother over so she could take his place.

"Help me with this," she said, lifting the butt of the rifle out of the dirt.

"When's the last time you shot a gun?" he asked her.

"A long time. But something is better than nothing, isn't it?"

"No, Rebecca. You could hurt someone you don't mean to. You could injure one of the animals. Only a real marksman should try shooting into that mess."

She was about to argue back when her attention was seized by the sound of heavy steps in the wagon above. Rebecca and Jasper looked at each other with astonishment and fear as they realized who must be in their wagon with their mother.

"I told you to go back," he said in a harsh whisper.

CHAPTER TWENTY-FOUR

Widening her eyes in fright, Rebecca whispered to her brother, "Someone's in there! In the wagon. With Ma!"

"I hear it. I can't believe you left her."

"I— But—"

The wagon company had been under attack by an Indian tribe for what felt like forever, though was likely only ten minutes. The havoc they were able to wreak in such a short time was astounding, including an arrow shot landing in Jasper's arm. Attempting to drag himself with one good arm, Jasper wiggled toward the open space out from under the wheels. Rebecca watched him only a moment before she realized he was in no state to even move on his own, let alone hold the rifle or defend their mother.

More heavy footsteps pounded on the boards above her head. One of the warriors had entered the Stephens family's wagon while the siblings were underneath it. Rebecca looked up, vainly hoping for a crack or knot or some way she could see into the interior.

She never should have left her mother's side.

A second and third man followed, leaving their mother cornered in the wagon.

"What do we do now?" she whispered.

But before Jasper could extricate himself from the narrow space under the wagon, before Rebecca could gather the courage to follow him, several heavy bags were tossed out of the back of the wagon, followed by the big, muscular native warriors who were ransacking the Stephens family's supplies. Three men climbed out of the wagon while Rebecca watched, each carting a bag over their shoulder, the last one handing down a crate holding half a dozen smaller bags before him.

Three huge men were stealing as much as they could carry, an enormous amount. Maybe a full third of all of the supplies that the Stephenses had for the next four months.

Rebecca was frozen in panic, watching these men take so much of what they needed to survive the next several months of the journey. That was hundreds of pounds of food, including what appeared to be all their sugar. Dimly, she heard the sobs of her mother still in the wagon, punctuated by her half-hearted protest. Jasper was still on his belly in the dirt, arrow sticking out of his left arm, and struggling to right the rifle. He would never be able to stop the thieves like that.

She would never be able to stop the thieves from where she was either.

Scrambling after her brother, Rebecca dragged herself through the dirt to emerge from under the wagon. Her heavy skirts and tight neckline constrained her, making it difficult for her to move quickly.

Awkwardly, stepping on the hem of her petticoat, Rebecca falteringly rose to her feet. But by the time she had her bearings under her, the Indians had gathered their arms full of food and were already mounting their horses with it.

"Stop!" she screamed, futilely.

They didn't even acknowledge her with a glance. Riding away across the open circle of wagons, the men left Rebecca standing helpless and weak, taking weeks' worth of food and supplies with them.

"Stop," she said again, more to herself than anything. It was too late now. She looked around and realized that nearly all the attackers were gone or leaving. Detritus and discarded broken furniture were strewn all over the dirt all the way to the opposite side of the circle of wagons. She had missed all chance to defend herself and her family. All she could do now was clean up the mess.

Tears stung her eyes, but she refused to let the despair overtake her. There was plenty to do to keep the sorrow at bay.

"Rebecca!"

She looked down to see her brother still struggling to get to his feet.

Here was something she could help with.

Hurrying to his side, Rebecca gently pulled the rifle from his grasp and leaned it against the wagon wheel. Jasper gritted his teeth as she took hold of his uninjured arm and kept him steady while he found his feet.

"Ma!" she called over her shoulder, while still keeping a careful eye on Jasper.

"Go to her," he said, as he leaned carefully against the wagon.

Rebecca nodded briskly and picked up her dusty skirts, clearing the way for her to climb into the wagon. The rear flaps of canvas had been pulled down against the attack, so it took a moment for Rebecca's eyes to adjust to the dark inside.

"Ma?"

From back against the rear wall came the muffled sounds of her mother crying.

"Mother?" she called again more gently. "Are you hurt? What can I do?"

As the inside of the wagon became more clear, Rebecca could not believe what she saw. The carefully stacked crates of clothes and linens looked as though they had been torn to pieces, broken wood and fabric cascading down like a waterfall. A sack of beans was spilled across her cot; an ax handle, with the sharpened head missing, lay on her parents' cot. Looking down, Rebecca realized she was standing in a scattered pile of spilled sugar, her shoes ruining whatever they might have otherwise been able to rescue.

And through it all were her mother's heart-breaking sobs.

"I'm sorry," Rebecca said, desperately.

She tried crawling over the overturned rocking chair that blocked the path through the wagon. Her skirt caught on the corner of a crate, and Rebecca heard the rip as she tried to pull free. It didn't matter. She needed to get to her mother.

"I'm so sorry," she said again. "I should have been here. I could have stopped them."

In her mind, Rebecca pictured herself standing bodily between the attackers and her mother. She imagined herself making a weapon out of whatever had been on hand, of physically forcing the ax out of their hands. But instead, she had gone after the excitement, instead of staying where she was needed.

"I couldn't do anything," Ada said, getting control of her crying. "They were too strong. They were…"

She looked her daughter in the eyes. Rebecca reached her hand across the mess, trying to get to her.

"I wish you had been here. You should have been here." Her voice cracked as she said it.

That moment of vulnerability was enough to make the tears spill down Rebecca's cheeks. Tears of shame. Tears of guilt. Tears of regret, wishing she had been able to deal with the harder thing for once and not run off to the most exciting prospect.

"I'm sorry."

It took the combined efforts of both women at least ten minutes to clear the mess enough to give Ada a path out of the wagon. As they did, they took inventory of the supplies remaining.

"Well," Ada said as she scooped the spilled beans into a different sack, "at least we know we'll be reaching a fort soon. We should be able to purchase more supplies there."

"What is Pa going to say?"

Ada shook her head. "Those poor men, coming back to find the place attacked. I don't envy them. Your pa may never feel comfortable going hunting again."

When they finally climbed back out of the wagon to assess the rest of the damage, Rebecca was surprised to find one of the other members of the wagon company. Nora Cole, hair loose around her shoulders, stood next to Jasper wincing slightly as she tried carefully to pull back the bloodied shirtsleeve where the arrow had wounded him.

"Miss Cole!" Ada exclaimed. "Goodness, child, you don't have to do that. Let me help you."

"Ma," Jasper gasped. "What took you so long? We didn't know how long you'd be in there. This thing smarts like the dickens."

Relief washed over Nora's expression. "Oh, thank you. I didn't want to hurt him, but... Thank you."

Ada immediately climbed back into the wagon to fetch her medical kit, while Rebecca smirked at her brother. She wondered if he'd even noticed that he had referred to 'we,' as though he and Nora Cole were a team somehow. That would be something she would have to ask him about later, once the poor girl would not be embarrassed.

"Nora, why don't you hold his hand?" Rebecca noticed the girl's blush. "So we can keep his arm steady. It's gonna hurt, and I don't want him to flinch. Jasper, you squeeze if you need to, but you hold your arm still."

"What kind of man do you think I am?" Jasper challenged, though without his heart in it.

"A man with an arrowhead deep in your arm. Come on, now. Don't fight me on this."

Mrs. Stephens returned, and between the three women, they managed to extract the arrowhead and clean and bandage up the wound without too much more damage. The yelling, however, they couldn't do anything about. At one point, Rebecca caught her mother's eye and they both started laughing at the fuss Jasper was putting up.

"How about I dig around in your arm with something sharp and see how you like it?" he blustered.

The women only laughed harder. Charming, good-natured Jasper Stephens was more of a pushover than anything. He wasn't fooling anyone.

"All right. Of course," Rebecca said, carefully placing the clean folded fabric against the open wound. "We're done now. Just don't get shot again."

By the time their father and the other men had returned from the buffalo hunt, Rebecca and her mother had managed to remove the arrow from Jasper's left arm, and clean up their wagon as best they could. Nora returned to her own camp—she had left before seeing to her own sister—and Rebecca and Ada were making coffee when the men returned.

"What happened?" Michael asked frantically, when he rode up to his camp. "Are you all right? Are you safe? Jasper, your arm!"

The other three told their story, speaking over each other in their excitement. Ada tried to calm him, while Rebecca tried to impress upon him how dangerous it was. He asked questions and checked three times to make sure Jasper really hadn't been hurt any worse. Any stories about the buffalo hunt he had could wait.

"I just wish I had been here," Michael said as he held his wife close to him. "I should have been here. I could have done something."

Rebecca watched on, feeling some of the same guilt herself. She had been here, and had let herself be distracted. Instead of staying by her mother's side helping protect their food and wagon, she had run off to whatever her brother was doing. And in that she couldn't even shoot or help defend from under the wagon.

It seemed as though she couldn't do anything right.

The night closed with every member of the wagon company hurt, scared or worried. Not a soul slept soundly that night. Rebecca stayed awake, staring at the canopy above, thinking about how different this journey would be if Andrew were there.

CHAPTER TWENTY-FIVE

The next morning, the wagon company left the site of the attack as early as possible. The unexpected boon of the buffalo meat helped alleviate the loss of so many of their other supplies, but the injuries and fear that permeated the company cast a pall over them all. Captains Mills and Sullivan urged their people on, promising the safety of Fort Laramie only a couple days' travel ahead.

Even with his injury, Jasper was still strong enough to help with some of the chores. Nora Cole had visited the Stephenses' camp the evening before, when word had gotten out of Jasper's injury. She came by again first thing in the morning, to see if there was anything she could do to help.

Even in the midst of her own frustrations, Rebecca grinned at the unmistakable attention from the young woman. Apparently Nora's own sister had been injured, and yet it was by Jasper's side that she remained as much as possible.

"Are you still pretending that you barely know her?" Rebecca asked her brother, after Nora had left again. "Several visits in just a few days. Is that a bit of an infatuation I see?"

Jasper grinned in return. "Can you blame her? After my heroics yesterday?"

"Yes, I noticed you just happened to decide to change your bandage while she was here."

"It's gotta be done sometime."

"Uh-huh. And I'm sure it's a lot easier when there's a pretty girl on hand to help."

"I don't know what you're talking about," he responded airily, before turning to inspect his bandage again.

Teasing Jasper about Nora was a welcome distraction after the terror of the Indian attack, and the discouragement of her own helplessness. The atmosphere of the entire wagon train was oppressive, almost sullen, and Rebecca longed to escape it.

They continued traveling as fast as they could manage and, finally, after several days of walking west and looking over their shoulder at every moment, the wagon train reached Fort Laramie. Though it had begun as a trading post, the fort was now owned by the United States Army. Rebecca took in the tall, sturdy walls and breathed a sigh of relief. There was safety here, at least, and the wagon company could regain some feeling of security.

"I think that must be the first set of walls and a roof we've seen since we left Independence," Ada said, as she began to pull things out of the wagon. "It's a shame we have to make camp outside the fort walls, though."

"Soldiers are right there, Ada," her husband said. "We'll be perfectly safe."

As soon as the wagon was in place, Rebecca's father went off to the fort with the little cash they had to spare and a strict admonishment from his wife to purchase whatever he could. They had lost quite a bit of their food to their marauders, but with luck they would be able to supplement what they were missing. Rebecca hauled bucket after bucket of water from the nearby stream for everything her mother had planned that afternoon. The laundry and mending Rebecca had been meant to help with the afternoon the Indians attacked still needed to be done.

When she was bringing the last bucket needed, her father returned much earlier than they had expected. Rebecca's heart dropped when she saw his expression. She sat the bucket by the wash tub and hurried to her father.

"Did you get enough food?" she asked, as she hurried to take the bag of cornmeal from his arms.

He shook his head. "Some. Not nearly what we lost, but once Jasper's arm gets better and we can supplement this with hunting or fishing, maybe. It will be enough."

"It will be enough," his wife repeated, as she took another sack from his arms.

Rebecca followed her to the wagon, carrying the cornmeal.

"I'll take care of this," she said, taking the bag from Rebecca, "while you get laundry started."

Rebecca groaned. "Always laundry."

"This is our last chance of water for a few days," Ada

said. "So I'll need you to help me wash everything we have before we leave in the morning."

Rebecca suppressed a groan. "All right. Let me just take a little break first, though. I've been working since we got here."

As she walked away from her wagon, she heard her mother call after her. "A short break, Rebecca. Be back in ten minutes, no more."

All around her, other members of the wagon company were setting up their own camp, getting ready for an afternoon of chores, or heading off to the fort to replenish their stores. They all seemed so focused on what they were doing or simply dejected, and that wasn't the kind of person Rebecca was looking to spend time with.

She kept walking, without exactly knowing what she was looking for.

Escape. Relief. Entertainment, or... something.

She spotted Annie Hudson.

Rebecca was just passing the Hudsons' camp and saw her, spread out between the wagon and the campfire with a giant tub of water and drying clothes draped across the canopy of one of their wagons. The blond woman was squatting in the dirt next to the tub, scrubbing hard at the hem of what looked to be a pair of trousers. With a tiny pang of guilt at the laundry she had left her mother with, Rebecca approached.

"Got any time to do some of that for me?"

Annie looked up from her laundry tub and smiled in greeting. "Depends. Is your laundry as absolutely dust-choked as ours is? I thought the days that we had to walk through the mud were bad, but the thin layer of fine dust just gets everywhere."

"Oh, don't tell me that. I was supposed to be doing our laundry today, too." She sat in the grass on the other side of the tub from Annie, and pulled her knees up.

"And if you don't do it today…"

"I know. I *know.*" She grinned. "Ma keeps reminding me. I almost want to go to the fort to get what I need to make more frocks rather than wash what we already have."

Annie chuckled before turning somber. "Were you able to get the supplies you needed at the fort? You lost so many supplies."

Rebecca grew serious as well. If it weren't for the buffalo her father had hunted that day that the Indians had attacked, she wasn't sure how they would have gotten through the past week.

She nodded. "Pa bought what he could. I'm not sure he had enough money for everything we lost. I suppose I may just have to do without sugar until we get to Oregon."

Rebecca was trying to make light of it. Going without sugar wasn't life-altering, after all, but it was a disappointment. So much of this journey was about deprivation. Losing one more of the tiny little luxuries she had been afforded just felt like one too many.

"I keep reminding myself it could have been so much worse," Annie said gently.

"I know!" Rebecca leaned forward excitedly. "You must have been so scared. I can't believe what you did." Annie had shot at one of the attackers herself; the story had gone all around the camp.

"I've been thinking about that actually." She paused in her scrubbing. "I can't really believe I did it either. It seems like I must be remembering it wrong or..."

"Or maybe you're stronger than you think," Rebecca finished for her.

"I don't know about that," she protested.

"Or maybe it's just that traveling across the entire continent has made you stronger."

Annie smiled. "Maybe."

"And, of course," Rebecca said, standing again, "traveling across the entire continent means laundry. I had better go start mine before Ma comes looking for me."

The women said their good-byes and Rebecca completed her long circle around the camp of wagons, before finally returning to her own. She had stalled as long as she thought she could get away with.

Once she reached her family's wagon again, her mother scolded her. "I told you ten minutes," she exclaimed. "Where have you been?"

"How long have I been gone?"

"Long enough. Where were you?"

"I needed a break. Some excitement."

"Always with you. Did you find it?"

Rebecca shook her head. "Around here? Where every day all there is to do is walk westward? Did you really think I would?"

"I suppose the *excitement* of being attacked by Indians wasn't enough for you," her mother said.

"That's not what I mean. It's just that... that..." Rebecca faltered.

"Rebecca, I've tried to give you plenty of time to get over the upheaval of your life and the loss of Andrew, but I'm not sure it's working. I really should not have to ask you to do laundry this many times. You have responsibilities to this family and you are simply not upholding them. We didn't include you in our wagon to Oregon just to carry you like dead weight."

"*Your* trip to Oregon? It was my husband's idea!"

"True, but he's not here is he? I am not trying to hurt you, my dear," Ada said quickly while Rebecca sputtered her protest. "I am merely trying to remind you that the life that you dream of simply does not exist. We need you here, with us, in this real world of darning socks and helping the family you still have living."

"It's not my fault the life I had no longer exists. How am I supposed to reconcile that? I just..."

"Darling girl," Ada said gently. "Maybe instead of looking for something outside of home to distract you, you could find solace in the routine? I know the same thing every day is—"

"Routine is the last thing I want. It's not even that every day is the same. It's not. It's somehow worse than that. We wake up and we do chores and go west as far as we can, and now with all the loss of food..." She threw up her hands in frustration. "How are we supposed to do this? How am I supposed to be able to do this?"

"You need to calm down," Ada said. "You're getting out of control. And I am getting frustrated."

"I can't calm down, Mother. Just because I'm a widow—"

"Rebecca Tenney, this has nothing to do with your being a widow. You know as well as I do that most of the people in this wagon company don't give a second thought to the fact that you're grieving. Everyone here has things that are required of them, and everyone here understands that exceptions have to be made. That isn't what I'm talking about."

"Then what?" she challenged. "What is it I'm doing that's so wrong?"

Ada's expression softened at the pain on her daughter's face. "I don't mean to criticize. I'm just worried about you, child. You seem to be spreading yourself so thin. Between Sadie and Annie and all the others, nothing seems to please you. It's as though you keep looking and looking, never satisfied with what you have right in front of you."

"Of course not!" Rebecca threw up her hands in frustration. "How can I be satisfied with any of this when it's not what I had planned? It's not what I was promised."

"I understand, dear. I do, but—"

"But I'm expected to just put all of that aside, I suppose, right? What I want doesn't matter. What I need isn't as important—"

"Isn't as important as your brother's life, *no*, Rebecca, it's not," her mother interrupted coldly. "The other day, when the camp was overrun, Jasper needed you and you weren't there. You weren't paying attention. He could have bled out because of your distraction. He told me all about it. How you got it in your head that you were going to shoot the Indians too instead of helping him like you had claimed you would. There are things that are bigger than your mere diversion."

Rebecca was stunned into silence.

"You were exactly this way when you were a child," her mother went on. "I thought you would grow out of it, and for a while when Andrew was alive you had. But... then without the anchor of that marriage and that life with him, you seem to be going down a path where I don't know how to help you."

All Rebecca heard was that her mother thought she was acting like a child. Rebecca Tenney, who had been widowed and forced to forget all thoughts of fun at only age twenty-one. Rebecca Tenney who felt like she spent every day doing whatever her mother asked of her, adhering to the rules and expectations of everyone around her, instead of what she wanted.

"I don't need your help," she said, before turning away. She was determined to not let her mother see how much she had hurt her. It was enough that she felt guilty for leaving her without a defense when the camp had been attacked, but to hear her mother say the very things that Rebecca suspected of herself was more than she could handle.

Rebecca stormed off, blocking out whatever her mother was shouting after her. She almost stopped, seeing Jasper approaching camp and feeling the pang of guilt at the truth in her mother's accusation.

But she pushed the image out of her mind.

She was not about to stay to hear what he thought too. She didn't need this. She didn't have to put up with this. Rebecca stomped into the field just outside the circle of wagons and tried to forget all of it.

CHAPTER TWENTY-SIX

Rebecca stormed off into the prairie grass, leaving her laundry and responsibilities behind. She knew she was running away, but she also wanted nothing more than to turn around and make her mother take back every cruel thing she had said. How dare she assume she knew what Rebecca was going through? How could she even hint that Rebecca wasn't doing her part?

She set off across the plains with her mind a maelstrom of defensiveness and indignation. Her breath heaved and she seemed blind to everything around her. Her mother didn't know what she was talking about; she had never lost a spouse. She had never had her life turned upside down. She didn't know a sliver of the grief that Rebecca was going through.

She got far off into the grass before she was able to focus on anything around her. In the fading light, Rebecca noticed the silhouette of a large man standing all by himself some forty yards or so away from all other people and all other structures. She pulled herself up short, and let out a startled gasp; she hadn't realized anyone else was nearby. But he didn't seem to hear her. For just a moment, she let herself watch. She didn't want to have to return to camp, to her mother, or to any of the others who might be judging her behavior.

The man was tall, broad-shouldered and hatless. His arms hung down straight at his side, but even from this distance she could see that he spun something small, a twig maybe, between the fingers of his right hand.

She took a couple steps closer, curious about who this was that had chosen to come out away from everyone else by himself with seemingly nothing to do. He was just standing there.

He seemed so content. So at peace. So untroubled by the same thoughts and fears that haunted Rebecca.

The stranger shifted his weight, as he looked up at the sky where the first stars were beginning to appear. In doing so, Rebecca recognized his profile as that of one of the Waters brothers. It was Beau, the second oldest and the tallest of the brothers. The man who had tried to tempt her to dance a few weeks earlier.

As she watched, he closed his eyes, took a deep breath and smiled to himself.

She didn't want to disturb him. Backing up a couple steps, Rebecca resolved to let this man have his moment of quiet solitude without having her intrude in her temper. But she must not have been as quiet as she had hoped. Before she could turn to go, he opened his eyes and looked straight at her.

"Hello." A kind smile spread across his face. "Mrs. Tenney, are you all right? Are you lost?"

"No, I—" She frowned in confusion, then saw his

smile grow. "Oh, you're teasing me. I'm sorry, I just... I didn't want to bother you. I'll go. I'm sorry, I didn't mean to... interrupt? I don't even know if that's what I've done." She took a few steps away before turning back, unable to ignore her curiosity. "What are you doing? It looks like... Well, it looks like nothing, if I'm honest."

He grinned and shrugged. "It is nothing. Just thinking. It's hard to get a quiet moment with my family, you know. Seems I have to find spots farther and farther away to be able to hear myself think."

"I'm sure," she murmured. Rebecca looked over her shoulder, back to the campsite. "Well, again, I'm so sorry to interrupt you. I'll leave you be. I should be getting back."

He nodded. "I'll walk with you."

"You're not worried about what people will say?"

"Because you're a widow? Or because I'm a handsome devil?"

She laughed, in spite of her worry, in spite of her shock at his language. "*You* know. I haven't even been a widow for a year."

"Why, Mrs. Tenney, what are you implying?" he teased.

"All right, fine, you're right. Better to be seen walking with you than—"

"Than get lost in the middle of the continent as nightfall is coming on," he finished for her. "What are you doing out here anyway?" he asked as they slowly walked through the grass.

"Running away, I suppose."

He laughed. Though ten minutes ago she might have

been offended at such mockery, something about his ease helped her see the humor in the situation.

"You didn't get very far."

"No, I guess not."

They walked in silence another few steps before he prodded her again, his deep, warm voice seeming to welcome confidences.

"I had an argument with my mother. Or, rather, she raised some concerns she had about my behavior—as I suppose is her right as my mother—and I didn't take it well."

"Do you want to tell me about it?"

"No. Well, yes, I do." She laughed lightly in embarrassment. "Very selfishly, I would like to think that you'll take my side and help me feel better. But also, I don't really want to think about it anymore. Too much of this journey has forced me to face things that petrify me and if I have even the chance to push something to the side I will take it."

He nodded. "I've noticed that there's a lot about this journey that folks didn't expect. You've heard talk of some of the families turning back?"

"Yes! I admit I've thought about it. But, has anyone actually gone?"

"Not in this company. Not that I've heard. But, Mrs. Tenney, maybe it could be a comfort to you to know that you are not alone in your frustrations."

She took a long, slow breath and thought about that. She kept forgetting that she wasn't even the only new widow in the wagon company. Mrs. Buchanan had children to raise on top of everything else.

"But what are you doing out here?" she asked.

"Really. You can't really mean to just look for a quiet moment. Why, don't you get bored?"

He laughed at that, and Rebecca blushed.

"What?"

"I don't know if I have ever been bored in my life," he said. "What with all my brothers the house was always plenty lively, and even when I'm by myself... I don't know how to describe it. I find myself plenty of company."

"How is that possible?"

He laughed again.

"I'm sorry," she stammered. "I don't mean to offend, but—"

"When was the last time you took some time to be alone with your thoughts?"

"I... I can't remember. I don't want my thoughts. I don't like them. Not since..." Then she frowned, as the memory came flooding back to her. "Even when I was so upset after Mr. Buchanan died, I couldn't handle being alone too long. Before that would have been just after my husband died," she said, trying and failing to keep her voice from cracking. "I don't remember much about that time. I took to bed, and... it's all a blur, to be honest."

"I'm sorry, Mrs. Tenney. That must have been so hard."

"It's fine." She cleared her throat and looked down at her feet, careful about where she stepped. "It's in the past. I got through it. But you can see why I wouldn't want to go through the same thing again."

"Of course."

They had reached the circle of wagons that had been

stationed just outside the walls of the fort. Rebecca noted that both had been walking more and more slowly, as though to stretch out the time they had together. But now they were within just a few strides of the Stephens wagon, and there was no use pretending otherwise.

"This is where I will leave you," Beau said. They had stopped walking altogether and he looked down at her. "Please understand, I greatly respect the hardships you have been through, but if I might offer one piece of advice from a friend—from a friend's brother at least?"

It was on the tip of her tongue to refuse. This man didn't know her at all; who was he to try to tell her what she should do? But Rebecca caught a glimpse of her mother hunched over the laundry tub and thought about her words, her accusations and criticism. Rebecca bit back the retort. It was clear Beau Waters meant well. Sadie had been a good friend to her, and Rebecca didn't want to be known as the woman who refused kindness. What harm could there be in at least listening to whatever Beau's advice would be? She looked up at him, and though the fading light cast a shadow across his face, the earnestness in his expression could not be missed.

"What is it?"

"All the time you're spending keeping yourself busy and distracted does nothing but put off what is inescapable."

"But, what's wrong with that?" She was too stunned to object.

"Well, maybe nothing," he allowed. "Or maybe you're just putting off the inevitable. Maybe it's like any other wound—ignoring it only makes it fester."

Rebecca frowned. To hear this man talking about her

grieving her husband in the same way he might talk about the hole in Jasper's arm was unsettling.

"I'm not sure I know what you mean."

"I just mean that we're all hurting. Everyone here." He gestured with an arm wide to the entire camp of wagons and the fort beyond it. "Some more than others. And some are able to deal with that hurt better than others."

Rebecca opened her mouth to respond, but found she didn't know quite where to start. She had never heard another person—let alone a big man like Beau Waters—speak about pain and feelings like this. She felt almost dizzy at that incongruity between what she had expected and what she now had on her hands.

"I'm sorry." She shook her head in confusion. "What are you trying to say? I know I came flying out here in a temper, but I have to admit that now I'm just confused."

"This is going to sound..." He paused, tilted his head and squinted at her.

"What?"

He grinned. "I'm just preparing myself for your inevitable laughing at me."

She chuckled; she couldn't help it. "All right."

"This is going to sound probably a bit... foolish. Ridiculous, even. But it's what works for me. With our house as full as it has been my whole life, I've had to come up with various tactics to deal with those feelings of helplessness, or franticness or anger. Anything that makes me feel out of control. All the things that could distort my thinking or keep me from what I need to be focused on."

"I deal with those feelings by... well, by finding something else fun to fill my mind with."

"I gathered. But I'm not sure it's working for you. What you might try instead is a little trick I figured out."

"What is it?"

He took a deep breath and squared his shoulders. "I stand up straight, feel my legs down to my feet connecting me to the earth and I anchor myself. I look to the horizon—to the west, in this case, since that's where we've been traveling—and I just... see it."

"What on earth do you mean by that? You see it?"

"Just that. I notice every little detail that I can between me and the end of the earth. It helps me put my own stress in perspective and the feelings kind of just... course through me. Like a river passing. Then they're gone, and I'm calm. That's what I was doing when you found me. When I'm feeling angry, frustrated, or even very sad, like I'm sure you have felt since the loss of your husband, I stand and look and let myself feel that."

Rebecca waited for the rest of it. When the pause had gone on so long it seemed clear Beau wasn't going to say anything further, she prodded him. "Feel what?"

"That's all. I just let the feelings take me. They never last long, if I recognize them. And then they're done. Or at least lessened."

Torn between laughing and anger, Rebecca spurted out a useless, "What?"

"That's all," he said again.

"Well, I can tell you that won't work for me."

"Why not?"

"Why not?" She cast about her for something, anything, to latch onto to save her from this bizarre conversation. "I can't be wallowing. I can't waste time feeling the way I did after Andrew died. I don't have any of that kind of luxury now, out here, in the wilderness where every day we could be attacked, or could get deathly ill or could get gravely injured. I already did that once out here on the trail."

She faltered, remembering the sight that had sent her to the jostling bed inside the wagon for days. Remembering the haze of pain that overtook her.

Her mother's words came to mind—*There are things that are bigger than your mere diversion.*

"Maybe with all your brothers, your sisters-in-law, your days off from driving the wagons, you can find the time to indulge in such luxury," Rebecca said. "I'm just trying to get through every day."

"Of course you are. We all are." He gestured to the dozens of wagons spread out in the twilight. "Mrs. McKinnon and Mrs. Van Anda and Mrs. Davis with her wagon full of uncontrollably wild boys. Everyone in this caravan has their own unique struggles to be dealing with."

Rebecca felt a wave of shame, but it did not make her any more disposed to be understanding. "Why is everyone attacking me today?"

"I'm sorry you think I'm attacking, Mrs. Tenney. I am merely trying to help. I would imagine that your late husband—"

"You don't know what you're talking about," she answered abruptly. "You don't know my husband, and you don't know me. Thank you for walking me back. Good day."

Rebecca strode off the final steps to her family's wagon without looking back at Beau. Whether she had offended him or not, she didn't care a whit at that moment. Such nonsense as that she had never heard, and the gall of that man to presume to understand what she was feeling, how she was grieving, was unheard of.

Both of her parents tried to get her attention when she returned to camp, but she just shook her head at them and climbed into the wagon.

This was the second time now this man had unnerved her. What was he doing that no one else did?

Rebecca was irritated the rest of the night. First her mother, and then her friend's brother who really didn't know her at all, had the impudence to criticize her behavior. She was not out of control. She was not flighty and irresponsible.

She was just trying to get through every day without the man who had promised to take care of her the rest of her life. And each of those days was full of the toil and hardship that he had made her promise to endure.

CHAPTER TWENTY-SEVEN

After she returned from her strange conversation with Beau, Rebecca made herself get to work. She ensured that all the family's clothes were washed, even to working long after dark so her mother could not accuse her of shirking responsibilities. If it wasn't done now, it wouldn't get done for nearly another week. Fort Laramie was yet another final source of fresh water before the emigrants had to do without for several days. Before they left, the Sullivan-Mills wagon company filled every available container with water from the nearby river. Rebecca drank as much as she could while they were still in camp, not looking forward to the days of thirst ahead of her.

There was much to do before they continued west. In addition to the laundry, Rebecca also helped her mother make two extra batches of biscuits so they had less call for water over the following days. Those biscuits, however, had to last one extra day than they otherwise would have. Since the Stephens family had had so much food stolen by their native attackers, and since Michael could not be certain that more food would be available to purchase at the forts farther along the trail, they had to be extra careful now.

Rebecca was grateful to have the distraction. She could spend her days wandering far from the wagon, looking for edibles and other bits of food to help supplement their supplies. Though she wasn't successful, the busyness was helpful, both for keeping her mind on something other than her grief and for showing her mother she wasn't completely useless.

As the long, hot days passed, Beau's words came back to her at intervals, but Rebecca was too occupied to spend much time thinking about them. He'd had seemed contented and serene, but in Rebecca's mind no amount of calm was worth seeing the expression on her mother's face at her daughter's unreliability.

The caravan had to cover at least fifteen miles of the Oregon Trail every day in order to reach the next potable source of water before everyone had run out of their stash. But other than the pressing thirst, the days that followed were unremarkable.

Ada Stephens seemed to revel in what Rebecca considered monotony. The same thing day after day. No wonder she had tried to encourage her daughter to routine. She rose before dawn, brushed and braided her hair, ate a simple breakfast with just one cup of coffee, before she had to walk west all day until they made camp and did it all over again. She seemed to thrive on routine, while Rebecca, on the other hand, was doing everything she could to not crawl out of her skin at the thought of eating half a biscuit for yet another meal.

Day after day they pushed on, and Rebecca tried to, at the very least, not let her mother down.

One afternoon, when Rebecca was walking with her father next to the oxen, she noticed that the wagon train seemed to be slowing. With so many families and wagons in the caravan, much of what happened near the front was completely unknown to Rebecca until the effects trickled back to where they were in line.

"Are we supposed to be stopping here?" she asked her father.

"Not here, no. We still have quite a few miles to go before we make camp."

"What do you think happened?" She couldn't quite keep the excitement out of her voice.

Her father looked at her strangely before responding. "It could be anything, really. Busted wheel, sick animal, discarded furniture left across the trail. It's nothing good, most likely."

"Or it could be another buffalo herd or antelope or something else we could hunt," Rebecca suggested.

"Maybe. But I doubt it. Jasper ran ahead to see what's what. If we're going to be stuck here for a bit I want to give the animals a bit of water. The sun is brutal."

Ahead of them, Mrs. Van Anda had gone ahead to the Martells' wagon. A couple other emigrants had gathered there, more were passing the Stephens family and even farther ahead up the caravan Rebecca could see more pairs and groups of people stopping to talk to each other. It was tempting to run up to the front herself to see what had happened, and maybe talk to some folks, but she stayed put by her father's side. And waited. Though it seemed to take forever.

Innumerable ideas ran through Rebecca's mind, each more ridiculous and unlikely than the last. Finally, when she had gotten as far as imagining the Indian tribe waylaying the wagon train to return all the food they had stolen, she spotted her brother running back to his family to report what he had found.

"One of the wagons lost an ox," he said breathlessly. "I didn't catch the name. There were too many people crowding around for me to see much, but it sounds like it just collapsed."

"Oh no!" Ada said. She clasped a hand to her mouth in shock. "Oh, that poor family."

"What will they do?" Rebecca asked. She wished that she had gone to see what had happened instead of letting Jasper. True, many of the families she passed would have looked at her askance, in her widow's weeds as it were, but it might have been worth just to see all the excitement.

Jasper shook his head. "I don't know. I suppose if the Mills or one of the other families can spare a cow they might try to use that, but..."

"A cow can't carry the load that an ox can," his father said. They'll likely have to leave some of their belongings. Lighten the load so the remaining team can manage."

"Maybe they lost so much food to the Indians that it won't be a factor?" Ada suggested.

"The weight must be a problem, or the animal wouldn't have dropped in the harness," Jasper said.

"Going without water might have done him in, too,"

Michael said. He rubbed his chin, thoughtfully. "We should be careful about our own oxen. No one can afford to lose an animal out here."

"Rebecca, are you listening?" her mother asked.

"Yes, of course. It's all so interesting. What if they need to get rid of something? What do you think it will be?"

"Rebecca Tenney," Ada said. "I never would have thought to hear you say something so cruel in my entire life. We should be concerned for our neighbors, and be thinking about how to avoid such a calamity ourselves, not speculating over the specifics of their tragedy. Have you no shame?"

Rebecca blinked at her mother, trying to understand what she was so upset about. "What did I say?"

She caught her father and brother exchanging a glance before her mother dragged her bodily away to stand in the shade of the wagon.

"Have you forgotten how much we all gave up when we left Indianapolis? The furniture we left behind was just the start of it. Imagine if you had to give up the cot you sleep on, or if your father had to give up his box of tools. I thought I had gotten through to you—you've been so helpful since we left the fort, but I can see now that you're just as thoughtless as ever. What would Andrew think if he could hear you?"

Rebecca's blood boiled, but at the same time the truth of her mother's words was plain. Looking down, ashamed, Rebecca took a deep breath.

"I'm sorry," she mumbled. "I'm trying. I just.. It's hard."

She kept her eyes on her feet.

"Of course it's hard," Ada said, a little more kindly. "That's what makes it worth it."

She left then, to help her husband with the animals and left Rebecca in the shade of the wagon. Looking up, she caught Jasper's eye. He made a silly face, trying to cheer her up, but all Rebecca could think about was all the ways she needed to stop seeking out the silly and find the same calm equanimity Beau Waters had.

As the days passed, more and more wagons were at risk of the same thing that had befallen the Gladwells.

As Rebecca was not needed to drive the wagon, she spent most of her days walking along the trail with a friend. Sometimes Annie Hudson, or Sadie Waters. Other times she would take the Keegan children with her, to give their parents a break. Occasionally, she would go off on her own. These were always the times that her mother would worry most, afraid that Rebecca would get lost while her mind was wandering or forget to come back in time to help her get the necessary work done.

Rebecca chafed at having to stick close to the wagon, but she knew it was the best thing for everyone. For now, at least.

CHAPTER TWENTY-EIGHT

After the Gladwell ox dropped in its harness, the pressure to get to Oregon mounted. Each member of the wagon company seemed even more anxious about getting westward as quickly as they could, while still making sure the animals had everything they needed. It was a delicate balance, one which Rebecca was glad she was not in charge of maintaining. After leaving the fort, they still had several days of travel to go before they reached another water source; the grass was getting more sparse with every mile.

Walking along the trail with the wagons, there was no shade for Rebecca to rest under, no way for her to keep cool. She tried fanning herself with the hem of her apron, but it made hardly any difference. It was truly a marvel how she could be making so much sweat, when she had barely drunk any water the last few days. Between the sun beating down and the heavy black mourning dress, Rebecca felt like she was practically being baked alive.

They had been walking westward for several days since leaving Fort Laramie. The sky stretched empty blue in all directions; the tall grass of the Great Plains surrounded the emigrants. Big though the wagon company was, on days like this Rebecca felt small and insignificant against the wide expanse of the wilderness. How did the first man even think to cross this land, just to see what was on the other side? Such a sense of possibility and adventure was anchored deep within her, but even Rebecca would balk at such a decision. There had been deaths, and loss and injuries and broken hearts. And yet, when it was all over, each and every one of these men and women she traveled with believed that what they found in Oregon would be worth all of that.

What kind of person would choose to come west, she wondered. The look in Andrew's eyes when he had first broached the idea of them making the journey floated in her mind. He had been so sure that this new adventure would be what she needed. What would he think of how she was handling it now? Thinking of Andrew inevitably led to thoughts of the hole he had left in her life when he died.

And thinking of that hole in her life inevitably led Rebecca to thoughts about how to fill it. No one could take her husband's place, of course, but there were plenty of other things and other people she could spend her time on now.

Rebecca jumped at the first idea that came to mind.

She had been walking alongside the trail, near to where her family's wagon was. The first thing she did was catch up to the wagon and climb inside while it rolled westward. The interior of the wagon was dim, but the early afternoon light was plenty for her to find one of the still-full canteens hanging by a hook near the entrance. They were to be rationing water, but, Rebecca reflected, rationing didn't mean none. She would need some kind of sustenance to get through the day, to get through what she had in mind.

Her family would never know.

Slinging the canteen over her shoulder, Rebecca climbed back down to the dirt and hurried out of the way of Patrick Keegan's team of oxen that were quickly making their way westward.

She waved to Mr. Keegan.

"What a surprise, Mrs. Tenney. Did you need something?"

"I was going to see if I could take the children off your hands for a few hours," she said. "Are they in the wagon?"

"Oh, no. We can't get those two to sit still for love or money. Harriet is keeping an eye on them, more or less, but my guess is they're out chasing prairie dogs or some such."

"What a wonderful idea! I'll go find them. Will you tell your wife? Thanks, Mr. Keegan."

He waved her off as she strode into the tall grass along the edge of the trail. Mrs. Keegan was close to the wagons, but her attention seemed split and she only glanced at Rebecca walking out toward where the children were.

It was getting later into spring and the height of the growing season out on the prairies. In some places the pasture grew as high as her waist. Though they hadn't seen many animals on their journey thus far, Rebecca could imagine herds of deer or bison just past the horizon. Under her feet would be the snakes, bugs and rodents that the bigger animals fed on. All around her was an expansive ecosystem, and with as fast as they were trying to travel through the country, she barely got to see the surface.

She spotted Kate and Jack long before she reached them, the distance in this flat environment disguised by the unending landscape. Jack seemed to be spinning in circles, maybe just for the joy of making himself dizzy. Kate appeared to be looking for something on the ground, walking slowly and peering at each step.

"Can I join you?" Rebecca called when she had gotten close enough for them to hear her. "What are you all doing?"

Kate looked up first.

"Mrs. Tenney! We're looking for prairie dogs. Well. I am." She looked pointedly at her brother.

"I am too!" Jack insisted.

"Do you want to help?" Kate continued.

"What if we played a game instead?"

"What kind of game?" Jack asked.

"Tag!" Kate shouted. "Let's play tag. You're it, Mrs. Tenney."

Both the children shrieked with laughter and ran away. Rebecca thought it spoke well to her reputation for fun that they didn't even wait to see if she would agree—the children just assumed that she would be excited to chase them.

"Here I come!" she called, catching up her skirts before darting off through the grass after them.

As she ran, Rebecca wanted to laugh out loud. It had

been so long since she had given herself such freedom. At least since before she was married. Certainly before her mother began harping on her about her responsibilities. She and Jasper used to play tag all the time when they were growing up; it was one of the benefits of having a sibling close to her own age. Not unlike Jack and Kate, in fact.

Rebecca looked on ahead to where the children were. Kate was running backwards, with a wide grin on her face, watching to see how close her pursuer was. Jack had run back toward the wagon train; Rebecca hoped that he knew enough to stay out of the path of the wagons.

Rebecca ran after Kate, watching with pleasure how happy the little girl seemed to be. Her feet seemed to have wings; even the weight of all her petticoats and dress couldn't keep her from running through the prairie with the children. It was just like when she had been little, playing with Jasper, and she had felt as though she could run straight up into the sky.

But the Great Plains were not the flat, unencumbered surface of her childhood yard.

She had only been running after Kate for five minutes, but as soon as she put her right foot down she knew something was wrong. There was nothing she could do; she had been going too fast to stop herself. The dirt under her heel collapsed. She lost her balance. Her right foot sunk into the hole and as her body continued forward, her leg was twisted in an unnatural angle.

She cried out. "Ah! No!"

At the sound, both children stopped their own running to turn back to her.

"Mrs. Tenney!" Jack cried. "What happened?"

By now, Rebecca was sitting on the ground, grass up all around her, and her right foot wedged in a small hole in the dirt. She felt a lump under her bottom, and pulled out a rock big enough to be felt through her layers of skirt and petticoat.

The children reached her and stood staring and worried, looking down at where she sat in the dirt.

"I fell." She sighed. "I guess that's the end of our game for the day, children. I think I hurt my ankle."

"Oh no!" Jack's eyes were as wide as saucers.

"Help me up, please," Rebecca said.

The two children could do little more than provide her an anchor and balance as she pulled herself to her feet, but it was enough. She had been right in her suspicions—her right ankle had been turned and seemed to be swelling up.

"I suppose it could be worse," she said, testing out putting weight on it. "I think I'll have to ride in the wagon the rest of the day at least. Goodness, how frustrating. I'm more mad at myself than anything."

"Don't be mad at yourself," Kate said. "It was an accident. You weren't mad at your brother when he got shot by an arrow, were you?"

To herself, Rebecca admitted that she was, but out loud to the nine-year-old, she said only, "When did you get so wise, Miss Kate?"

The little girl squirmed under the praise.

"Mama!" Jack shouted, as he ran on ahead of them. "Mrs. Tenney got hurt!"

Mrs. Keegan was at her side in moments, putting an arm around Rebecca's waist and helping her to her own wagon. In spite of her protests, Rebecca had to admit it was rather nice to be taken care of, even only a little. Her ankle wasn't too badly hurt, and she likely would be able to walk just fine by the next day.

"The children will remember this," Mrs. Keegan said before she left Rebecca alone. "Next time they play tag, I bet Kate will be warning her brother about looking where he steps."

Rebecca laughed. "I'm thrilled I can be the model for such a life lesson."

CHAPTER TWENTY-NINE

The rest of the afternoon, Rebecca stayed in the hot, sticky interior of the wagon. With as much food as had been stolen, it wasn't quite so crowded as it had been weeks earlier. At least she didn't have to worry about a stack of crates falling on her. But the jostling and bumping of the wagon wheels going over every stone and rut made her miserable. It was all she could do to hang on to the cot with her foot elevated and not get knocked off.

When they finally stopped to make camp for the night, Rebecca hobbled out of the wagon, grateful for some fresh air.

"Well, I hope you learned your lesson," her mother said, eyeing her daughter's stiffness.

"What lesson is that?" She limped across the dirt to an overturned bucket and sat down gratefully.

Ada smirked.

"That you're not ten years old anymore," Jasper interjected.

Rebecca couldn't help but laugh. "Come on. I'm not *that* old. Not too old to run."

"You may not be too old to run," Ada said, as she brought over a small bowl of water and a rag so Rebecca could wash her face. "You seem to be too distracted and flighty to run, though. Why didn't you pay attention to where you were going?"

"Because I was chasing the children. It was a game, Ma. It could have happened to anyone."

"Really? Anyone?" She took the bowl and rag back, then glanced at Jasper as though to bring him into her side of the argument.

"Nope. Don't look at me." He raised his hands in surrender. "I would have done the same thing if I wasn't driving the wagon. Don't pull me into this."

"But you were driving the wagon," Ada said. She turned back to her daughter and considered her, arms crossed over her chest. "That is my point. Jasper is doing the responsible task. Other women are taking care of children or animals. Even Miss Hudson is driving a wagon and Miss Atkins is teaching the children. And you, Rebecca Tenney, staid widow of not even a year, are playing. Playing so recklessly that you injured yourself."

"Ma, I'll be fine. Tomorrow morning—"

"You don't know that. And even if that is true, it could have been worse. Rebecca..." She shook her head. "It could have been so much worse. You could have been bit by a snake, or broken your leg. You could have had a major injury, and what if we were part of a wagon company that didn't have a doctor. What if Dr. Martell was busy, or sick himself?"

"Ma—"

"Now, honey," she said, crossing again to be close to her daughter, lowering her voice and speaking gently. "I don't want to take anything from you. Your love of life is one of the best things about you. But, darling, ever since Andrew died you have been taking it to such extremes. It's as if you think if you can find entertainment wild enough, you can counter your grief. That's not a thing that can be neutralized, dear. You have to deal with it eventually."

Ada shook her head again in disbelief, but Rebecca felt the sting of truth in her words. That had been nearly precisely what she had been doing. She had been looking for anything to keep her from thinking about how much she missed her husband, even to seeking out the company of children when there was nothing else.

Her mother turned her back on Rebecca. Though she never said a word about having to prepare dinner without her daughter's help, Rebecca felt the bitterness in every bite she took. Her recklessness had made more work for everyone.

Thankfully, Rebecca's ankle was just fine the next morning. It was a little stiff, possibly a result of her being off of it for hours the previous day, but she had no problem walking next to the caravan of wagons as the rest of the immigrants did.

Thinking of that pain now, though, led Rebecca's thoughts to what Beau Waters had said that night by the fort. At the time she had been so insulted that a veritable stranger had had the gall to talk to her about her pain, to make suggestions for how she should be grieving. But as the days since that altercation had passed, Rebecca had reconsidered. She had been avoiding him, but maybe she was wrong. Maybe it hadn't been all nonsense.

It wasn't until she'd injured herself trying to entertain Kate and Jack Keegan that Rebecca finally admitted to herself that maybe what Beau had advised could help her. It was so similar to what her mother was saying. They couldn't both be wrong, could they? She had tried everything else, it seemed like, and seemed to be just spinning her wheels. She was putting herself, and her family by extension, at risk by constantly looking elsewhere to fill her needs.

Her mother was right. Rebecca was a grown woman—a married woman—and she needed to be able to take care of herself without resorting to actions that would get her injured.

There was no time like the present, she supposed. The wagon caravan kept moving, but Rebecca stopped right where she was in the grass. She closed her eyes and took a deep breath.

All around her she heard the sounds of the wagons continuing on, the dogs barking at the livestock they were herding, the light caress of the breeze on the grass. She could smell the buffalo chips, the summer wildflowers, and a hint of some distant campfire.

She opened her eyes and looked toward the west and tried to focus. She was supposed to... what had Beau said? Feel the ground underneath her? Look at what was between her and the horizon?

Grass. Wagons.

She felt silly.

This wasn't working.

This wasn't dealing with any of her pain.

Instead of feeling a peace, Rebecca only felt anxious. There was so much going on around her, so much to see and do and be aware of, and standing still with her eyes closed meant she was missing all of it.

She waited, wondering when the feeling of peace would find her. Even just thinking about waiting for it made her heart start to beat faster until she gave up. It was too hard. Whatever trick Beau Waters had to calm himself was not something she could do.

She looked up and realized that only maybe a minute had passed since she had stopped walking. Her parents were only barely ahead of her on the trail, and she was about even with the Keegans' wagon. She had hardly missed anything and whatever peace Beau had promised eluded her.

Maybe she should try again.

But not now. Now she needed... something.

Rebecca took a deep breath and reminded herself that this was what she had wanted, and what Andrew had wanted for her. This whole journey and experience. Though she may not understand the same motivations that spurred on Captain Mills or the Hudson women to travel all the way west, for example, she did understand her husband. He had seen in her that pioneer spirit that was needed for such a journey. He had understood that the simple routine of staying in Indiana would never make her truly happy.

For the second day in a row, Rebecca had made a promise to herself to seek out the quiet, unassuming moments that Beau Waters had spoken of.

But even as she was having this thought, something more interesting found her. The wagon company slowed down again. When she noticed that the wagon train was slowing, she eagerly looked ahead, walking faster to see if she could meet whatever the obstacle was, to see how she could help, or even just to have some other tiny mystery to occupy her mind.

A cloud of dust was being kicked up, just off the trail, and in the midst of it was what looked to Rebecca to be a wagon going the wrong way, heading east. She ran to where her family were all together, walking next to their own wagon and oxen heading west.

"What is this?" she asked.

"Turnarounds," her mother said quietly.

The wagon had almost drawn level with the Stephens family, and were close enough that Rebecca could see the driver and his companion. It was an older couple, just about the same age as Ada and Michael, with no children that Rebecca noticed. The woman, sitting up on the wagon seat next to her husband, looked so tired and worn down, Rebecca wondered when the last time she had slept was.

"I can't believe they're going back east. After coming all this way," Ada said.

"Why do you think they set off for Oregon in the first place?" Rebecca whispered.

Jasper shrugged. "Don't know. But they won't be making that mistake again. What a mess."

He walked off to see to the animals.

"Do you still want to go back?" Ada asked quietly, when they were alone again.

Rebecca thought for a moment before responding. "I don't think so. Maybe if I could magically go back in time, but to turnaround now and do all of this trip again with nothing to show for it except the same farmland of Indiana... No, that's not what I want."

"I'm glad." Her mother patted her arm kindly. "I know I can be hard on you, but I'm very glad you're on this journey with us."

Rebecca looked after the turnarounds, as the cloud of dust rose up around them.

That could be her. But it wasn't until this moment, when she saw her potential future, that Rebecca could admit to herself that was not what she wanted at all.

She didn't want to be going back to Indiana. She didn't want to return to the quiet life that she had left behind. Maybe things would have been different if Andrew was still alive; certainly she would feel more comfortable and at home in such a case. But he wasn't.

She was on her own. She had only the adventures ahead of her.

CHAPTER THIRTY

The dust the turnarounds had kicked up settled. After Rebecca had watched the older couple head back east to the home they had left behind, she walked off into the grass and tried again to follow Beau's advice. She had failed before, but maybe this new perspective was what she needed to enjoy the present moment and not look for distraction. Again she walked out into the prairie, and again she closed her eyes to settle in. But, again, after only a couple minutes, she felt anxious, like something was crawling over her skin, like her heartbeat and breathing was speeding up. Her body was like a runaway horse and there seemed to be nothing she could do about it.

Rebecca opened her eyes again and shook out her hands, trying to rid herself of the strange tense feeling. Why wasn't this working? She hadn't even gotten as far as focusing on the horizon. She grew so frustrated she was tempted to go find the man to demand he explain himself better. How could she be so bad at something that looked so easy?

She made her way back closer to her family and her wagon, turning over the problem in her mind. Her ankle had healed, but that didn't mean she had forgotten what a mess she had made.

She could do better. She would do better. Just as she had told her mother, it wasn't as though she wanted to turn around and go back to Indiana. She would find a way to make this journey work. She would keep her promise to her husband, and thrive in Oregon.

She just wasn't quite sure how yet.

The unchanging landscape day after day did nothing to improve her mood. If she was meant to be content, to learn to stop looking for the next exciting thing, how could she be expected to do that during a stretch of weeks that seemed to never end. The only change was the rising and setting of the sun, but everything in between was the same, day after day.

The rationed water was running low. The company was tired but determined.

None of the stones were as exciting as when they finally spotted Independence Rock, though.

At the end of another long day of grasslands, wide open blue sky and peering at what might be a granite monolith in the distance, Jasper nudged Rebecca. He indicated farther west with the jut of his chin.

"Do you see it?"

Rebecca was holding a bucket half full of water for their lead ox to drink his fill. She turned partway and squinted into the horizon toward where her brother had indicated. The sun was just setting, so anything

Jasper was pointing out was washed out by the brightness.

"What am I looking for?"

Jasper closed one eye, looked into the sun and pointed. "It's another one of those giant stones. Independence Rock. We're heading straight toward it. Should get there in a couple days."

"Shouldn't we be there already? Today is Independence day, I think."

Jasper frowned. "Yeah. Probably. But it's only a couple days off. We can make up the miles, I bet."

"Hopefully. If nothing else happens. We can't afford many more delays. Especially with as low as our food supply is."

The wagon company covered the final miles to Independence Rock as fast as they could. The captains set a punishing pace, leaving camp as early as possible and stopping again late in the day. At least once, they didn't even make camp until after sunset, and supper that evening was cold, leftover biscuits. Ada didn't want to try to find the dishes and utensils she needed in the dark.

They pushed westward, with the giant rock on the horizon, drawing them ever closer.

With one foot in front of the other, Rebecca walked parallel to the Oregon Trail, making the same slow progress as all the other emigrants in her company. All around her, slowly, the landscape was changing. The flat land continued, peppered here and there with large rock formations and low hills. The sight of the change raised Rebecca's spirits, giving her something new to look forward to, even as far away as it was. At least something around her was changing—or promised to—despite the seeming sameness.

A couple days later, the wagon company finally reached the foot of the enormous granite monument in the early afternoon. Captain Mills led the caravan to a relatively flat circle of land at the bottom of the rock and they quickly made camp. Rebecca couldn't believe they really had time to linger here the whole afternoon, but complaining wouldn't do anything. The excitement of having not only hours leisure ahead of her, but also the wonder of the new location helped her forget her worry.

As she helped her mother unpack the pans she needed for supper, Rebecca kept getting distracted by looking around the campsite, at the shade and trees, and especially up at Independence Rock. Folks streamed away from their wagons, all eager to see it up close and leave whatever chores they had for later. The enormous stone seemed to loom over her, hovering at her shoulder, in her periphery no matter which direction she looked.

Rebecca looked up and up, noticing the silhouettes scampering around the top of the rock.

"Can I believe what I am seeing? Did folks really climb up there?"

"Goodness," her mother said, with a shiver when she followed her daughter's gaze. "I can't imagine having little ones running all over the place getting into that kind of trouble. I'm glad you two are older and wiser than that now."

Rebecca and her brother shared a grin.

"You wanna get into some trouble?"

"How's your arm?"

"Oh." He frowned and rotated his arm at the shoulder, wincing at the pain. "Yeah, okay, probably not a good idea. Happy, Ma? I'll spend my afternoon with my feet safely on the ground."

"Oh, you." She laughed indulgently as her tall son kissed her cheek.

"If we will be in camp the rest of the day, I'm going to find Sadie. I'll be back for supper."

She kissed her mother's other cheek, before scurrying off.

CHAPTER THIRTY-ONE

In camp at the foot of Independence Rock, Rebecca had much of the afternoon free and clear ahead of her. There was a bit of a spring in her step; the promise of the new landscape and the chance of being with friends lifted her spirits.

As Rebecca walked to where the two Waters wagons had set up camp, she was passed by several dozen other people walking the opposite direction. It seemed as though a good third of the members of the wagon company were heading off to Independence Rock as soon as they could. With a grin, Rebecca turned to watch them, even walking backward a few steps to keep the rock in her sights. Pairs and small groups approached the foot of the stone, some walking around the perimeter, but no small number seemed to be attempting to climb the rock face itself.

With a sigh, Rebecca turned back to find Sadie. There were allowances made for a widow on the Oregon Trail, but that did not extend to her being able to climb up the rock. She would have to find some other way to fill her afternoon.

When she reached her friend's campsite, the first thing she saw was a couple of the Waters boys— Rebecca kept mixing up Colin and Davis—wrestling far too close to the campfire. They teased each other, shoving each other toward the flames as only young men who believe themselves immortal could do. She paused, watching them, waiting for one of them to notice her.

As she had that thought, one of the men bodily lifted his brother up on his shoulder, wrapping his arms around the other's upper legs and knocking them both over, until they were sprawling in the dirt at Rebecca's feet, looking up at her in blinking wonder.

"Hello, boys. Is Sadie around?" Rebecca said with a smirk.

The shorter of the two laughed and pulled himself to his feet, dusting his trousers off frantically.

"Mrs. Tenney." He offered his brother a hand and pulled him up too. "I think she and Angus are collecting water. Should be back any minute."

"Thank you."

The two men made their embarrassed excuses, catching up their hats from where they had been discarded in the dirt. They moved out of her line of sight as quickly as they could and left Rebecca alone to wait.

As large as the Waters family was, she didn't antici-pate having to wait long. Faith, the youngest at fourteen, waved hello before she darted off to a group of friends waiting nearby. Shortly after that, another of the Waters brothers approached Rebecca from behind the second wagon.

Beau Waters stopped short in surprise when he saw her, before a broad smile broke across his face. "You're looking for Sadie?"

She nodded. The sight of him had sent her into a confused fluster. Rebecca had spent the last week or more thinking about this man and the strange advice he had offered her. And now with him standing in front of her, she almost couldn't differentiate between the reality and the man she had imagined.

"All right, then," he said, nodding back. "It's nice to see you again, Mrs. Tenney."

Beau tipped his hat to her, and made to leave. There was a peaceful air about him, as though everything was as it should be. She couldn't understand how he could always be so content, and couldn't stop herself from speaking out.

"I wanted to thank you," she blurted out, before he had walked too far. "For our talk the other night. For your advice." She blushed, and was annoyed with herself for it. "I'm just not... I can't do it."

Beau frowned. "What do you mean?"

He had taken off his hat completely, holding it loosely in front of him and giving her his full attention.

"I don't know how to do it. I close my eyes and I try to just... I don't know. Hear what's around me? But I can't do it. After only a few seconds I start to feel antsy. Restless. Like I'm missing out on something and I can't stand it. And then when I try looking to the horizon, like you suggested...? I just feel silly. I don't think this is for me."

He chuckled, but somehow she sensed he was not laughing at her.

"It probably sounds ridiculous, I know," she concluded. "Maybe I'm just not meant to sit still. Like a child."

"I assure you, it is not only children who have a hard time sitting still. You did see my brothers wrestling when you walked up didn't you? They are grown men and never stop. It's all right if it's not for you. Maybe I was wrong."

"No, but..." She squared her shoulders and looked him full in the face. "I want this. I do. I can't keep just looking for the next big, exciting thing. I don't know if Sadie told you, but ... I did something dumb a few days ago. I'm so embarrassed."

She ducked her head; she couldn't look at him while she said it but somehow Beau Waters made her feel safe enough to admit her flaws.

"There's no reason to be embarrassed." His deep voice felt soothing, almost in the way she hoped his advice to her would. "Sadie told me you hurt your ankle. It's better now?"

"Yes, it is. Did she happen to tell you how I hurt it?"

She looked back up at him; he looked as though he were trying to hide a smile.

"Uh..."

Rebecca laughed. "It's all right. I did say it was embarrassing. I was so eager to find something exciting to fill my afternoon that I didn't think it all the way through. It is just so how I live the rest of my life too, I guess. Moving forward as fast as I can without a second thought. I don't know how to do otherwise."

"You can learn, if you really want to," he said gently. "Just keep practicing. It's like a muscle that you need to learn how to use. It's not something you can force, but if you keep looking I guarantee you'll find it."

"Find what, though? You told me to just wait and breathe and watch, but I can't do that and I don't know what else I'm supposed to do. What exactly am I looking for?"

"Peace. You'll find peace. Or it will find you, rather. Just stay open to it."

Rebecca frowned at Beau in confusion.

But before she could ask him anything more, she heard her friend call her name. Rebecca turned to see Sadie and Angus approaching from the sparse trees that surrounded the nearby spring.

"Just keep trying. Please," Beau said, before leaving her alone.

CHAPTER THIRTY-TWO

"How shall we spend our afternoon?" Sadie asked. She shaded her eyes as she looked up at the top of Independence Rock.

She and Angus had appeared from the water, interrupting Rebecca's conversation with Beau, only moments after he had offered more inscrutable advice. Though no one had said anything about it, he immediately made excuses and left the other three alone.

"I heard Pastor Montgomery is holding a worship service tonight," Angus said, as he filled a canteen. "We could go to that?"

"You don't want to climb to the top of Independence Rock with your brothers?"

Angus grinned. "I kinda do, yeah."

"Go," his wife said, shooing him away. "If you break your leg I'll be mad, but I don't want you moping around here either."

Rebecca averted her eyes as they kissed good-bye.

"So, then," Sadie said, watching her husband run

toward the gigantic stone that dominated the landscape. "I ask again: how shall we spend our afternoon? What did you and Andrew used to do on free afternoons?"

"Goodness, I'm not sure I remember." A dozen different things flashed into her mind—berry picking and swimming in the pond and star gazing and picnics and so many other sweet intimate moments that she would never get back.

"All right, a more specific question then. This time last year. Independence Day of 1849, how did the Tenneys celebrate?"

Rebecca untied her bonnet as she thought. She closed her eyes and let the warmth of the sun cover her. What had she been doing at this time last year? She and Andrew had been married for only a month or so at that time, and still had all the obligations to both families to account for.

"I think we had just discussed leaving for Oregon, so we knew it would be our last Independence Day in Indiana, though we weren't yet telling people that. The church we grew up in always has a big picnic where everyone brings something. Mrs. Taylor brought her bean salad. Mr. Dixon brought a big piece of ice, and set up a cool wading pool for the children to cool off in." Rebecca smiled at the memory. "Some of us older ones might have also stripped off our shoes and stockings to cool down too."

"That sounds lovely," Sadie said, smiling. "You must miss it. All those people who knew you your whole life."

"I do." Then she paused, thinking. "But I wouldn't want to go back. Andrew made me promise I would go on to Oregon even without him, and at first I didn't want to. After Mr. Buchanan died I couldn't see the point of going on. I was so dejected and a bit angry at Andrew for forcing that promise on me."

She trailed off, looking up again to the top of Independence Rock where at least a dozen people had climbed.

"I had no idea what I was agreeing to," she continued softly. "This has been so much harder than I expected. I made the promise just before Andrew died, and I hadn't any time to even think about it. I just trusted him, trusted that he wouldn't ask something of me I couldn't do."

"Do you regret it?"

Rebecca looked back at Sadie and shook her head. "I did. More than once. And even now I don't know if I believe that this choice was the best thing for me. But I have resolved to make the best of it."

"That's really brave," Sadie said softly.

"It's not easy."

"It probably would have been easier with your husband."

"I'm not sure," Rebecca said. "Maybe it would have been just as hard, but I would have focused my ire on him and made our relationship difficult along with everything else. But, it is true that one of the hardest things has been just dealing with my feelings about his death, and about missing him. I can't seem to get away from those memories, and they always make me feel so... helpless. And overwhelmed. It's so much."

The two women sat in silence for a few moments; Rebecca thought about that enormous wave of grief that had sent her to bed in the days following his death. She never would have believed then what she was surviving now.

"Can I ask you something and you won't get mad?"

"Of course." Rebecca frowned and looked at her friend. "What could you even ask that might make me mad?"

Sadie paused, leaned forward and asked earnestly, "What were you and Beau talking about?"

"Beau?" Rebecca racked her brain for what else Sadie had said about her brother-in-law, wondering why on earth it would make her mad.

"It's just that... I see that you two are friends, or becoming friendly at least, and after we just talked about your husband I didn't want you to think..."

"Oh..." Rebecca laughed self-consciously. "It's really not anything. Do you remember I told you about that advice he had given me when we were stopped at Fort Laramie?"

"To just hold still?" Sadie laughed. "I remember."

"Right. Well, I tried it."

Sadie's eyes widened.

"And failed completely," Rebecca finished.

Sadie laughed even louder this time. "I'm sorry," she said, still chuckling. "It's not funny."

"It's a little funny." Rebecca grinned. "What kind of grown adult can't just stand still for a few moments? So, today when I saw him, I told him that. That I had tried and failed."

"What did he say?"

Rebecca summed up what Beau had told her, about it being a muscle, and needing to practice. All through her relaying the advice she watched her friend's face. Sadie seemed thoughtful.

"What is it?" Rebecca asked, when she was done. "You look like there's something I'm not thinking of."

"No, I wouldn't say that. I was just thinking about Beau. Did I ever tell you about when I very first met the family? When Angus and I started courting?"

Rebecca shook her head.

"All right, well." Sadie sat up and clasped her hands in her lap, ready to tell the story. "Angus and I met at the wedding of one of his cousins. The bride was a friend of mine from school, and we both attended with no thought to meeting anyone special. Since it was a cousin, of course, all of the Waters brothers were there, and in fact, Beau was the first of all of them to ask me to dance. He was so polite and considerate, very accommodating and attentive. For a brief moment I was smitten. And then the waltz was over and he said good-bye and I honestly didn't lay eyes on him again that day."

Rebecca laughed. "He's unique, isn't he?"

"Unique is the perfect word for it."

"Then what happened?"

"Well, Angus had seen what his brother had done, and that I was a bit lost on the edge of things and swooped in. Asked me to dance. We spent the rest of the evening together. It wasn't until hours afterward that we realized that neither one of us had seen Beau after that dance."

"Where did he go?"

Sadie shook her head and laughed. "I don't know. No one knows, even now. No one saw him again until the next morning at breakfast, and whenever someone asks him—even to this day years later—he claims he went out to look at the stars. I suppose it's possible that he did, that he just went behind the barn or deep into the rows of corn, but I'm certain that no one saw him leave and no one saw him outside. Who really knows what he does? That man is different, that's certain."

"I have noticed he likes to be alone."

"That's the easiest way to put it, I suppose, but really I think that Beau would be perfectly fine completely alone for days on end, if not longer. Angus and I joke that once we get to Oregon, Beau will build himself a cabin up in the mountains and we'll never see him again. Whatever stillness he thinks you should practice he's been doing for years."

"I couldn't do that," Rebecca said. "All that time with my own thoughts. I would probably go crazy."

"Me too, but it seems to be working for Beau."

"Which is why he thought nothing of just telling me to slow down and be quiet."

Sadie smiled. "He's a strange one, that brother of mine."

"Well, now, that's another benefit of coming west that Andrew must have foreseen. All the interesting and —what did we call him?—*unique* people I've gotten to meet."

Sadie laughed even harder, and leaned back in the grass again. "It has been an experience, hasn't it?"

The two women lapsed into silence, both leaning back in the grass and looking up into the wide-open blue sky. Rebecca turned Beau's words over in her mind. Maybe he was right and all she needed was practice. She supposed it couldn't do any harm.

But not now. Now she needed to take advantage of the rest and people that could fill her afternoon.

"Why don't we go to Pastor Montgomery's service?" Rebecca suggested. "Later. Of course. Right now... Why don't we just lay here for a while longer?"

"We should. Wonderful idea. Let's do nothing for a bit longer and then join the rest of our people. Goodness knows when Angus and the others are coming back, so I'm not about to make supper that goes to waste. If we go to the service they'll understand."

For the first time since she started trying to follow Beau's advice, Rebecca could actually see the value in his words. With the sun warming her, and the scent of fresh grass in the air, she closed her eyes and let herself rest.

CHAPTER THIRTY-THREE

The wagon company didn't linger at Independence Rock beyond that day, as they were already several days behind the schedule.

The peace that Rebecca found that night at Pastor Montgomery's worship service helped carry her through the next several days of aggressive travel. Not only did the gathering surround her with people who she cared about, but it reminded Rebecca that there were forces in control beyond her. Beyond the wagon captains. The service combined with the afternoon with Sadie gave Rebecca what felt like a fresh start, even months into their journey. Maybe the rest of the trip from here would be easier for her.

Captains Mills and Sullivan wanted to get the caravan to Pacific Springs as soon as they could, and pushed the wagons more than a dozen miles each day. Jasper's arm was now almost completely healed after they had been attacked by the Indians. Between him and their father, the Stephens wagon was well cared for.

They kept a sharp eye on the animals, who were just as hungry as their humans. Ada always had plenty of tasks to assign to Rebecca, but by this point in the journey everything ran smoothly.

Attempting to travel so far in so few days was a struggle, but surprisingly Rebecca found herself enjoying the routine of it. She had expected to be bored and frustrated, as she had been throughout the journey until now. It seemed completely out of her character for her to be actually thriving with the same activities, the same food and expectations day after day, but she had found a kind of comforting rhythm in it. Maybe this was the practice Beau had encouraged.

Pacific Springs was the last chance for abundant grass and water they would have for a while, and the company stopped in that camp for a half day of rest. As always, there was plenty of laundry to catch up on; Rebecca stayed near the family's wagon to help her mother with the other cleaning and chores that came up.

Well before sunset that afternoon, Rebecca realized she was clutching her elbows, arms crossed in front of her trying to warm herself. Though it was still only July, sometime in the last week the weather had started to shift. Her hands were freezing, and as soon as the sun went down it would get even colder.

She started to climb into the wagon, looking for what would keep her warm.

"Do you know where the winter clothes were packed?" she called over her shoulder.

"Should be a trunk near the back of the wagon, last I saw," Ada said. "When you find it, maybe bring the whole trunk out. We can repack the wagon so the quilts and things are more accessible."

"It's only going to get colder from here on," Rebecca's father added. "We're getting into higher elevation, and fall weather comes early in some of these parts."

"Does that mean we're almost to Oregon?" She turned in excitement, leaning out from between the break in the canvas wagon top.

"Halfway."

"No. What? Really?" Rebecca blurted out involuntarily. "Only halfway?"

Michael nodded. "Thousand miles left, more or less."

Rebecca caught her mother's expression, and almost asked her what was wrong, but thought better of it. Whatever stress or hardships that they would have to suffer over the next thousand miles, there was little she could do about it now. Instead, she needed to do her part to take the burdens of worry off her parents.

"It's too bad that it's getting to be too cold to fully submerge in the spring. It could be fun to do the whole bath day again like we did before," Rebecca joked.

Ada chuckled. "I can't imagine Mrs. Norton being willing to drop her three layers of petticoats if you're cold enough to need a shawl."

Even without such an event, Rebecca enjoyed the little time they had to rest before the wagon company had to keep moving, ever westward.

———

After leaving Pacific Springs, the Sullivan-Mills wagon company suffered a long, strenuous stretch of the

Oregon Trail. They pressed on, even as families ran out of basic staples, and as children struggled to sleep in the chill. As the trail climbed higher, Rebecca grew colder and hungrier. Her mother was valiantly trying to make their food stretch as long as possible, but with as many miles as they were walking every day, it felt as though no amount of food would be enough.

One evening, after a long day of misery and strife, Mrs. Fields brought word to the Stephenses that there was sickness in the camp again. Mountain Fever was a risk as the trail climbed higher in elevation, and at least a dozen of the emigrants suffered under fever, weakness, exhaustion and a loss of appetite. There was no way to guess if someone would fall ill with it, but the captains had decided the company would travel as quickly as they could to reach a lower elevation with grass and fresh water.

Thus they pushed, mile after mile for days, as one after another people fell ill. Taking to bed, finding a neighbor to lead their wagon. Nursing and cooking and animals and every little bit of survival had to be stretched over fewer and fewer emigrants. This continued, until one morning the caravan did not hit the trail just after dawn as they usually did. The break from the expected routine was worrisome, but there wasn't anything Rebecca could do about it. She was exhausted and could think of nothing byt how tired she was. She would have slept later if she had known they would not be leaving on time.

Since the wagons had not yet pulled out of camp, Rebecca thought she might have time to go see if Sadie had heard any recent gossip. Margaret Hudson had mentioned the day or two earlier that Mrs. Mills had asked Annie to lead a quilting circle. Though Rebecca herself had never been much of a quilter, she realized many of the other women in the company might be. There was no word on whether or not Annie had said yes, or when they would move forward with the plans, but Rebecca reveled in talking over all the details with her friend all the same. It was a good distraction from her weariness.

In fact, maybe she would stop at the Hudson camp later to ask Annie about it herself.

As she passed by wagon after wagon, on her way to her friend Rebecca noticed that many of the other families seemed ready to go. There was still no indication why they hadn't left yet.

She had almost gotten as far as the Sullivan wagon, right in the middle of the caravan, when Rebecca heard her name, looked around, and realized Mrs. Martell was calling to her.

"Mrs. Tenney, could I ask a favor of you?"

"Um. Yes, of course. Is everything all right?"

She drew closer to the wagons. Mrs. Martell, the doctor's wife, seemed harried and distracted. The expression on her face worried Rebecca. Something had happened that needed urgent attention.

"No, my dear. I'm afraid things are not all right, and I need help. You see..." Mrs. Martell took a deep breath to steel herself. "William Sullivan is dead."

Rebecca gasped. "Oh no. What?"

"I'm afraid so. It's terrible. It was the Mountain Fever. There was no slowing it." She shook her head.

"We have to get out of the mountains before even more fall ill."

"Oh, my goodness. That would be terrible; we can't lose anyone else."

"It would. I need to get back to Mrs. Sullivan now, and to help the doctor, but news of this sort needs to be communicated as quickly as possible."

"Of course," Rebecca said, though her mind was whirling through what it meant that one of the captains of the wagon company had died. How would they go on? Who would fill that man's shoes, both for the company as a whole and even in his family? Goodness, those poor Sullivans. And after losing Jeremiah so recently too.

"Mrs. Tenney?"

Rebecca pulled her attention back to the doctor's wife. "Yes, I'm sorry. That's just... How can I help?"

"Could you go to each of the family's and make sure they know? Maybe ask someone else to help you too. I believe the pastor will be holding the funeral later this morning. I'm so sorry to ask this of you, but I think your generally upbeat demeanor will help folks deal with the tragedy."

Rebecca blinked in surprise. She'd had no idea she had that reputation. "Oh, well, yes. Of course. Yes. Thank you. I'm sorry. I'm—" Her voice cracked, and she cleared her throat. "Please tell Mrs. Sullivan and the rest of the family how sorry I am."

Mrs. Martell patted her arm in a distracted manner before hurrying away without a word. Rebecca was left alone, and charged with one of the most important tasks she had been given since embarking on this journey.

Rebecca used a quiet moment to still her panic.

How could she get out of this?

Telling the men and women of the wagon company the tragic news went far beyond the normal stresses of survival that each day on the Oregon Trail brought. She was about to rip the safety out from under some of these emigrants. Families that had put all their faith in the wagon company captains getting them to Oregon safely were now about to find out that half of that support was now gone.

And yet, in spite of this challenge, Rebecca felt strangely serene about it. Once she stopped to actually think about what she was about to do, Rebecca realized that she didn't want to get out of it; she didn't want to foist the responsibility on anyone else. Mrs. Martell was right, in that her buoyant personality might serve as a salve for the news she was about to share. Perhaps the months of her own mourning had helped prepare her to lead others through a similar process.

She took a deep breath, closed her eyes and counted to ten. She knew she could do this.

The Sullivan wagon was in the middle of the caravan, and Rebecca decided to start with the family behind them—the Emersons.

The Emerson family—man and wife, and three children, including a niece—were from the same town as the Sullivans in Ohio. They had come west at the same time as the Sullivans; they had been neighbors and the children had been classmates. All of these details Rebecca remembered in a wave, and suddenly wished anyone else could have been available. This family would have known William Sullivan well, and now she was expected to deliver to them the worst news possible.

Mr. Emerson was helping the littlest girl out of the wagon when Rebecca approached, while Mrs. Emerson was trying to comb down the hair of the other two children.

Rebecca didn't quite know how to begin, or even how to gently draw their attention to her. This news was so different from every other reason she might have sought out some of the other emigrants in the past.

"Hello? Hi. I'm so sorry to bother you," she began.

"Oh, hello, Mrs. Tenney." Mrs. Emerson bent down to whisper instructions to the little boy before straightening to greet Rebecca. "Is there something I can help you with?"

"I... I'm so sorry to have to bring you this news."

Rebecca's voice broke. She had thought she would be able to handle the emotion. She barely knew the Sullivans after all; she should be able to kindly impart the news without too much trouble. But maybe breaking the news of a beloved man and husband dying was too close to her own husband dying. Maybe the memory and grief of her own loss was still apt to crop up when she least expected it.

"What is it, dear?" Mrs. Emerson looked concerned, and her husband was soon at her side. "Do you need help?"

Rebecca shook her head. "No. I'm sorry. It's not me. I... It's Mr. Sullivan. The captain. William Sullivan. He died in the night."

"Goodness," Mr. Emerson murmured under his breath.

"How?" Mrs. Emerson asked.

"Mountain Fever, the doctor's wife told me."

"Goodness," Mr. Emerson said again. "I hope the other folks with it pull through."

"I do too," Rebecca said. "I'm so sorry. I know you were probably close. Is there anything... ?"

"No, thank you." Mrs. Emerson looked distracted. "We'll have to tell the children."

"I'll let you get to that." Rebecca backed up a few steps. "I should get on to the next family."

But they didn't hear her. They had already turned inward, toward their family, and their own concerns. Rebecca had a feeling she would find herself on the outside looking in more than once this morning.

The next wagon would be the Owens family. Rebecca took a deep breath, feeling the ground under her feet and noticing the faint sound of firewood popping, before heading off to deliver her news again.

CHAPTER THIRTY-FOUR

Though the task of spreading the news of William Sullivan's death had fallen on Rebecca's shoulders, she felt proud and grateful to be able to serve the wagon company in this way. It was far from a task that she would choose for herself—far too somber and too close to her own grief—but as she was required to do it, she determined to do it well. There were tears, and worry, but in the end, she completed her task later that morning.

They wasted no time in burying the man. Proper funeral rites and extended grief were a luxury on the Oregon Trail, and they had many miles still ahead of them. Rebecca stood with her neighbors to honor one of their captains, her heart breaking for the widow and her children.

Not long after Mr. Sullivan's funeral, the other captain, George Mills called a meeting of all the men in the company to discuss the next steps. They had to keep moving and decisions must be made. Both Michael and

Jasper attended, and returned to camp to let the women know that they would be following the trail around by Fort Bridger, rather than take the cut-off across the high desert.

It was a risky choice, given that several members of the wagon company were still sick, and how many of the families were running low on food. This was the longer route by a whole week, but the hope was that the gains in letting the animals have plenty to eat would make up for the time it would add to the journey. This branch of the trail would take them to Fort Bridger, stationed at the fork of three different creeks. The route would allow them enough grass and water for the animals, and the hope was that the fort itself would have supplies that the families could buy.

Rebecca could see the strain in her mother's face, though she never said a thing about it. She had already noticed how paltry the family's meals were growing. The little bit of food they still had was barely enough to keep the family going for more than a couple weeks, let alone the month or more they still had ahead of them.

In truth, Rebecca only had a vague idea of how much longer the journey to Oregon would be. They had passed the halfway mark; at least there was that. But how much longer could they go on under this much hardship?

But she trusted the men's decision. She trusted her mother could work miracles with the food they still had. It was far easier for her to continue her habit of distracting herself with something more interesting than to worry about the state of their wagon and supplies. She didn't want to think about it. Someone else would worry about it.

Partway through the journey to Fort Bridger, however, tragedy again struck the wagon company. William Sullivan had not been the only person to succumb to Mountain Fever. As the wagon company continued westward several other members came down with fevers, aches and a more acute exhaustion than they had felt thus far.

Caroline Harper had to drive her own wagon while her brother was laid up. Alma Valentine, Josie Hudson and several others lost full days to fever and delirium. Rebecca felt helpless in the face of so much sickness, but her father assured her that the best thing they could do was keep pushing west. It was the altitude that brought the sickness, so they needed to keep pushing toward Fort Bridger.

But not all of the emigrants recovered.

Just before they reached Fort Bridger, young Ralph Davis brought the news that Louisa Hudson had passed.

Rebecca gasped when she heard. She felt helpless and heart-broken for her friend. How much more of these losses could the company take?

The funeral for Louisa Hudson was sparsely attended, compared to that of William Sullivan. Louisa was not particularly popular, though that was likely owing to how hard she worked to take care of her family and how seldom she had the energy for any socializing.

Rebecca made sure to be there, regardless of anything else.

She found a spot in the crowd, standing just behind the row of family and directly behind Annie. As the pastor spoke about how much Louisa Hudson had added to their community, Rebecca chided herself for not being a better friend, for not checking in more when she heard Louisa had gotten sick. Annie had been so kind to her since the very beginning of this journey and Rebecca had allowed herself to seize on so many other things, so many other people to entertain her.

She put a hand on Annie's arm, just briefly, just so the other woman knew she was there. That reassurance would have to be enough. That poor family; already without a man to do the more strenuous chores, now they had lost one of their most stalwart members as well.

It was truly heart-breaking that Louisa never got the chance to get to Oregon, given all that she had sacrificed to help her family get there.

Losing so many members of their wagon company in such short succession was more excitement than Rebecca would have ever wished for, and yet somehow she didn't seem to need the distraction. Each day she had been trying Beau's method of looking toward the horizon, of anchoring herself here and now as a way to manage the stressful feelings that cropped up. It wasn't easy, and she didn't feel like she made much progress each day, and yet somehow she managed to get through the funerals without wanting to run, or hide her head in the sand.

Maybe Rebecca was finally finding a way to handle the grief of all her losses.

They only had another day of travel before they reached Fort Bridger, and with it the promise of food and rest. Over the past few days, Rebecca was finding more and more peace in being on her own as she walked with the wagons. Sometimes Kate and Jack walked with her. Sometimes she walked with Jasper. But each day, she kept her eyes on the horizon, focusing on her future and what she had to get through before Oregon.

As she walked over the top of a low hill, she saw the fort waiting for them by the curve of the river. It wasn't very large, though the sturdy walls surrounding it seemed more than enough to hold off any attackers. There was no allowance made for any kind of comfort, but the company would be camping at the water's edge for the rest of the day; they would have a chance to get clean.

The wagon company had not had a break in more than a week, since before William Sullivan's death—and each person was looking forward to the chance. Half a day spent here at the fort could refill much of their stores of supplies as well as energy.

The row of wagons pulled into their secure circle, chained the wheels and unyoked the animals to make space for the rest of the day.

"Anything you can find, Michael," Ada called to her husband. "I mean it. *Anything*, please. I will make anything work. Flour, oats, even some type of rice you have never heard of. It doesn't matter. Whatever food you can buy, please do."

"I hear you," he said. "Give me a minute."

She watched him carefully as he went through all of the steps of getting the animals and the wagon settled for the rest of the day. Though he moved quickly, and had Jasper's help, it didn't seem to be fast enough for Ada.

"Other families will be trying to buy supplies too," she reminded him.

"I know, dear. I'm going now."

Michael had not even left the vicinity of their camp-site before they noticed a wave of emigrants returning from the fort. At their head was Mrs. McKinnon, shaking her head and seemingly talking to herself as she made a beeline for her own camp.

"Oh no," Rebecca said. "What does that mean?"

"I'll go check," Michael said, heading off any assumptions. "We don't know."

"There's nothing there," Samuel Findley called to Michael when he passed the Stephenses' camp. "Cleaned out completely. Not even a bullet to be had. I don't know what we're going to do now."

Rebecca's stomach dropped in fear. No more food to buy and they were reaching the end of their stores. How would they survive to get to Oregon?

CHAPTER THIRTY-FIVE

Upon hearing that Fort Bridger—the destination they had pushed so hard and added a week to their journey to reach—was completely out of food, Rebecca went cold with fear. So many of the wagon company were running low on supplies and so many of them had been counting on the respite they could take here at the fort. Her own family was among those suffering the worst from deprivations and she had no idea what they would do.

Rebecca instinctively glanced at her mother, who had turned pallid. If Ada was worried, then the situation was far more dire than Rebecca had realized. Her heart started pounding, and she couldn't think about anything other than how hungry she was. Before the news, she would have been fine, not thinking about food until her mother called them all for supper. But now knowing how dangerously limited their supplies were, Rebecca felt the urge to eat everything in sight.

Before seeing what her mother would say, before letting any more of their problems enter her mind,

Rebecca walked off briskly to find something, anything, to distract her from thoughts of food, of survival, of what other scarcities she would have to endure. Every day was more of the same, and she wasn't sure she'd ever master Beau's cool detachment.

First she strode toward the Keegans' wagon, but the scent of coffee brewing gave her another sharp pang of hunger. It was more than she could handle. She turned right, then left, finally spinning in a slow circle, trying to figure out where she could go. Rebecca felt unanchored and lost, thinking only of how hungry she was and how hard the days and weeks ahead of her would be.

She stumbled away from the campsite, and from the smell of food. Wandering into the middle of the circle of wagons, Rebecca lost sight of where she was going. Her stomach growled again, and she turned back, maybe to return to her own wagon, maybe to... what? Where could she go? She was in the middle of the continent without a husband, without food, without any idea how to solve even the smallest of her problems.

A simple game of tag with a child couldn't save her now. This entire journey had been a mistake.

Again, she felt that urge to eat everything she could find, just to make sure she got some, to make sure she had enough right now. In some ways, it felt like the same compulsion she had had to dance last summer, the last night of such revelry she had had with her husband.

What was happening to her?

She spun again, looking for something—anything— to hold on to. Something to quell her anxiety. Something to be solid and reassuring.

She turned again to see Beau Waters striding toward her across the open grass.

"Whoa, whoa," he said, as he got close, holding his hands up to forestall her further stumbling. "It's all right, Mrs. Tenney. Whatever is wrong, we'll figure it out. You'll be all right."

"Is it, though? Is it? The fort doesn't have food and some of the families here are running so low on supplies that people are going to die. We're all going to starve. It will be like that group in California two years ago, stuck in the snow and eating their shoes. We're going to be like that. And now, with Mr. Sullivan gone we're at an even bigger risk and I can't believe I ever agreed to come on this trip in the first place."

She only stopped speaking when she had run out of breath; there were far more things Rebecca was concerned about. She was so tired of putting on a cheerful face for everyone. This was the end of her patience.

"I promise you will not have to eat your shoes," Beau said with a smile.

"But—"

"Try looking out to the horizon."

"I don't—"

"Please," he insisted. "Humor me. Just try it."

"I *have* tried it!"

"Again. Please. Just one more time, while I stand here and do it with you. Please."

With hands shaking, Rebecca turned toward the west where he was pointing. The wagons were in a circle all around them, and then past that the short grass and water south of the fort. The sun was still overhead, casting harsh shadows on the ground.

"What do you see?"

He stood close enough to her to help her feel safe, but not so close that anyone watching would think it inappropriate. Beau Waters seemed to always know exactly what to do.

"Feel your feet on the ground," he said gently. "Feel the sun on your shoulders. Look toward the horizon, toward where we are going and what comes next. Tell me what you see."

And so, Rebecca took a deep breath and started talking. The short grass under their feet, already picked clean by previous herds and wagon trains. The low fire of the Emerson family's camp, with Bridget sitting nearby writing in a little notebook. The dirty white expanse of the wagon canopies, stretched under the afternoon sun.

"And beyond that?"

More dirt, short grass in patches. Two different streams forking. She could hear the babbling of them from here, even over the other noises. Past that a stretch of flat land, with a worn trail winding farther away.

"And what is beyond that?"

She shook her head. "I don't know."

"Yes, you do. Not the details, not like you can see closer up, but what is in the distance?"

She looked again. "Mountains. The tallest I've ever seen."

"Mountains," he repeated. "That's where we're headed. Those mountains have been there for centuries, millennia, in fact. Those mountains will be there tomorrow and the next day and the next day, until finally we are over them. Whenever you're worried about uncertainties or scarcity, remember those mountains. Whatever else you're missing, they will always be there."

Rebecca took a deep breath and kept her eyes on the mountains.

Hundreds of emigrants had made it that far on the Oregon Trail; nearly every single one of them had made it over the mountains. Fretting would not put more food in their pots.

She was amazed at how much difference just a little surety could make.

"How do you feel now?"

She tore her eyes from the horizon, looking at him finally. "A little better. I guess. I suppose it is helpful to think about the permanency of those mountains. But... I still don't know how we're going to get out of this, though."

"Well, let's think through this calmly. Now that you have a little more peace. First, you are with your family who love you and will support you, right?"

She nodded. "Yes, but I don't want my father to go hungry just because—"

"But also," he continued, raising a hand to slow her speech, "also you are in a community of other emigrants. Most of the families here know how much food you all lost to the attack. Many of the families find themselves with enough food, some even extra. There is help all around you, if you're willing to ask."

"I just hate to remind anyone that there are even more in need," she said, dejected. "There's already so much suffering going around; I don't want to add to it."

"All right. Well, beyond the community, then, we are traveling through the veritable land of plenty. The men chose this route by the fort specifically because we would be near water and grass. Maybe you could... learn to fish?"

Rebecca's mouth fell open in shock, before she noticed the twinkle in his eye. "Oh, you're teasing me."

"Only a little. I do mean what I say, though. If not here, then in a few days we'll be traveling through the Bear River Valley where the hunting and fishing is supposed to be bountiful. If your brother can get a chance to go out, I'll go with him."

"You don't have to do that."

"I know. But I meant what I said about there being a community around you willing to help. I'm part of that. If I can bag a rabbit or quail, or even a deer, maybe, that could feed your family, the Gladwells, and others who are in similar straits. We'll all pull together."

"You would do that?"

"Of course I would. Not one member of this wagon company deserves to go hungry if there's anything to be done about it."

"Thank you. I'm sorry I worried you." She was humbled and a bit embarrassed by her outburst.

"It's really not something to apologize for. Besides, I don't want you to be eating your shoes."

Rebecca grinned. "Very funny."

"Are you hungry now?"

She wanted to say no. She wanted to save some pride and prove that she was fine on her own. People expected that of widows. But then that same scent of coffee wafted over from a nearby camp and her stomach growled against her will.

"Come on," Beau said, indicating to where his family's wagons were set up. "I'm sure we have something, and you can take it back to your parents."

"I couldn't..."

"Neighbors, Mrs. Tenney. This is what we do."

Feeling both grateful and self-conscious, she followed him to where the Waters family was starting to make supper. This, this friendship and working together and interesting people and adventures she had never had before. *This* was precisely what Andrew had had in mind for her when he had made her promise to continue to Oregon.

CHAPTER THIRTY-SIX

The time the wagon company spent in the Bear Valley did make Rebecca feel better, just as Beau had promised. The Stephenses weren't the only family running dangerously low on supplies, and while the men drove the teams of oxen, the older boys would spend the days off hunting and fishing, supplementing as best they could. There was food all around them, if they could take the time to find it.

Though she wasn't nearly as skilled in it as others, Rebecca contributed by foraging for edible plants. Or, rather, she accompanied Sadie and the youngest Waters, Faith, in their foraging. Her childhood in Indiana had not required any such labor of her, so she was grateful to her friends for helping teach her.

"Is this anything?" she asked, calling after the other two who were already well ahead of her.

"Probably not," Sadie said over her shoulder, but Faith came back to check.

Rebecca held out the small plant she had plucked

from the dirt near the roots of the maple tree they were walking under. "I don't know," she said. "It looks kind of like the top of an onion? But I think you said that there should be a flower? I think?"

She trailed off as Faith approached and looked at what Rebecca clutched in her hand. Then she looked back up at Rebecca's face.

"That's... just grass."

Rebecca looked at the girl. As the youngest of the Waters children she was barely into her teens, but already far more capable and in some ways more grown-up than Rebecca was almost ten years older. Faith went back to studying the handful of greens, and seemed to be avoiding Rebecca's eyes.

"It's okay to laugh," Rebecca told her in a carrying whisper.

"Oh, thank goodness." Faith cracked up and stepped away, no longer pretending to be interested in the grass Rebecca had collected. "Good try, though. But if it was an onion, when you pulled it up by the roots you'd see..."

"An onion?"

"An onion." Faith grinned. "Not roots."

"All right. I think maybe I'll know better for next time."

Their few days in the Bear River Valley was all too short. Rebecca's time with Sadie and Faith taught her a lot of things, and allowed her to bring home a collection of edible plants to supplement the game. She treasured each second they had been there and for the first time since setting foot on the Oregon Trail, did not try to distract herself out of her present moment.

The trail climbed out of the valley on the north side,

and the landscape shifted from the lush, green valley to the stark high desert. Jasper, with the help of Beau and others, had managed to catch enough game that his mother had dried meat to feed them for several days. They had more than enough at the moment to carry them through to the next fort, though Rebecca knew that the chance of Indian attack, or a wagon turning over in the water, or any other manner of losing their stores was still possible.

But she kept looking forward, toward the horizon as Beau had taught her, feeling the safety anchored beneath her and the freedom to trust on what she had. Not only did such reassurance keep Rebecca from being dragged down by feelings of doubt and fear, but when such emotions did find her, she was better able to weather them.

They traveled through the scrub brush and baked earth for two days before reaching Fort Hall. Though situated near the Snake River, the elevation of this part of the country had stunted all the growth and vegetation the emigrants had experienced elsewhere. There was barely any grass for the oxen, and many families had to supplement their feed with oats from the wagons' stores.

The fort itself was two stories tall, built from roughly hewn logs and windowless. It was no more than a box, sitting in the middle of a virtually barren landscape. But for the emigrants who had come so far and needed so much, it was the respite they needed.

The families of the Sullivan-Mills wagon company were not the only emigrants that had camped outside the walls of Fort Hall that day. As the Stephenses made camp with the rest of their company, Rebecca looked around eagerly at the crowds of families who had also stopped for the day. She hadn't seen this many people in one place since at least Independence, before they left in April. The thrum of so many people lifted her spirits just as much as the chance of adding to their supplies.

After the camp was set up, Rebecca helped her mother pull from the wagon all their clothing and bedding to wash, while Michael and Jasper went to the fort with all the cash they could spare.

"I appreciate the help, love," Ada said, as they hauled water from the river back to their campsite. "But I understand if you want to spend the day with your friends. It's really all right."

"Ma, thank you, but I'd rather stick close to home. Today at least."

"Or until you know if you're going to have to eat your shoes."

Rebecca looked at her mother in surprise, before seeing her smirk. "Don't tease me like that!" she said with a laugh.

"I'm sorry. I overheard you and Sadie joking about it the other day. It's not funny, though. Those poor people. I'm just glad to see you more lighthearted. After Andrew died..."

"I know. I was doing everything I could to not have to think about that pain, but it was always still there. I know I got a little... wild, I guess. I'm sorry."

"Even to twisting an ankle to avoid having to think about missing someone." Ada smiled. "You seem to be doing better now though."

"I think I am. Sometimes the hurt still surprises me. When I'm least expecting it, but also when I pull out something that has been packed away since Indiana. The most random things seem to remind me of him."

"It will get easier with time."

"It already has." Rebecca smiled at her mother, but the older woman was distracted by something behind her. When she looked over her shoulder, she saw her father and brother approaching with their arms full of sacks and crates of food.

"Goodness," Ada said. "That's more than I even hoped for. What all did you get?"

She crossed to them and took one of the sacks out of Jasper's arms.

"A side of bacon, ten pounds of sugar, thirty pounds of flour, thirty pounds of cornmeal. A few other things. We'll go back to get the rest." Michael set the crate in the dirt at his feet. "We probably could have picked up another side of bacon, but I know there are a lot of other families in just as dire straits as we are."

Ada paused only briefly before responding. "That's enough. It seems perfect. There's another fort a few weeks ahead, too, isn't there?"

"Fort Boise. Hopefully they'll have some supplies left, though it will likely be quite late in the season by the time we get there."

Rebecca continued to scrub at the pan while her mother organized and packed all the food they had acquired. She looked around at the collection of people who had stopped here for the night. On its surface, the landscape and the structure were stark and bare. But Rebecca was able to see past that; for that she was grateful.

The crowd of so many people reminded Rebecca of

the new life that was waiting for them once they got to Oregon. This could be their new community, this collection of neighbors. This constant drudge and struggle was only for a small period of time compared to the time they would be in the paradise of the Oregon Territory. With its rivers full of fish and fertile farmland and whole towns full of new friends and neighbors, Oregon would be even better than their life in Indiana had been.

The only thing missing would be Andrew, but she would always have the memory of their few months together, and the heart of the promise she had made to him to continue her life in this new environment.

After leaving Fort Hall, the trail turned west, to the Snake River, where it followed along the top of a canyon for several days' worth of travel. As the river headed west, it had cut through the bottom of the canyon, rapids and shallows far below the trail. Where the wagons had room to travel was narrow, though level, and dozens of feet above the running water. They could hear the river, though not see it for long stretches.

With as narrow as the trail was, Rebecca spent her days close to her family and their wagon. There was no wandering off into the plains or playing games with the children. It was all she could do to stay far enough away from the edge to not worry.

She was walking behind the Stephenses' wagon, humming a hymn to herself when she heard a strange sound from up ahead. It sounded like a low moan, or even the groan of livestock. Rebecca didn't know when she had ever heard something like that.

Then, only a couple minutes later, the wagon drew to a stop. She tried to crane her neck to see past the wagon, see past the family in front of them, but she couldn't understand why they weren't moving.

She hurried up to her brother who was leading the team.

"What's wrong? What was that sound?" Rebecca demanded. "Why are we stopped?"

Jasper looked back at his sister, and grimaced. "Um..."

But Ada seemed sure of what was happening. "Rebecca, go see if Mrs. Van Anda needs help."

"Why me? Now?"

"Yes, hurry. You can go faster than me."

Bewildered, Rebecca darted up to the wagon that had stopped just ahead of them. When she reached the front of it, she noticed that the wagon ahead of them had continued on the trail. The Martells didn't seem to notice that the wagon behind them had stopped.

The second thing Rebecca noticed, though, was even more worrisome. Mr. Van Anda was nowhere to be seen. He had completely abandoned his team. The reins were dragging in the dirt, and the enormous animals seemed to be fretting.

Rebecca went cold with fear. What had happened here?

"Jasper!" she called back to her brother. "Come here, Jasper, I need you."

She took a deep breath and picked up the reins. Trying to soothe the lead ox, Rebecca had trouble keeping her voice from wavering. There was a reason she had never done this herself. Animals of this size—animals that could crush her under their strong hooves—scared her.

"Where did he go?" Jasper asked as he approached.

Rebecca shook her head. "Take these. I'm going to check inside the wagon."

Making her way back to the rear of the Van Andas' wagon, Rebecca heard that same low moan again, this time it was punctuated by a cry of pain. She hadn't even had to climb completely into the wagon before her eyes adjusted to the dimness and she saw what had made that sound.

Mrs. Van Anda, now at the end of her pregnancy, was doubled over in pain even as she sat on the cot pushed against the side of the wagon's interior. Next to her, her husband sat rubbing her back and trying to shush her.

Rebecca gasped and they both looked up at her.

"I'd hoped the babe would wait until we made camp," Mrs. Van Anda said with a wry smile.

"I'll fetch the doctor," Rebecca said breathlessly.

CHAPTER THIRTY-SEVEN

As Mrs. Van Anda went into labor in her halted wagon, Rebecca ran ahead, to where the wagons had continued moving. Though breathless, she was able to catch Dr. Martell and explain to him the situation. The family in front of the Martells was the Gilroys, and ahead of them the Coles, and between all of them they were able to carry the news up to the very front of the wagon caravan. Soon the whole company was stopping their travel for the rest of the day while Mrs. Van Anda had her baby.

Rebecca tried to help, but there wasn't much she could do that wasn't already under control by the doctor and his wife. She kept busy taking messages to the other end of the caravan, or collecting water from some of the other families. Having a baby would be a harrowing experience in any environment; she couldn't imagine how difficult it must be for Mrs. Van Anda here at the side of the trail.

Amidst the excitement of Mrs. Van Anda's baby

being born, Rebecca had missed the other major upheaval that had come to the Sullivan-Mills wagon company. When the caravan had stopped, one of the men—John Harper—had risked climbing down into the canyon for fresh water. Though several other of the young men had done the same over the previous days, terrifying their mothers, John didn't have their same luck. In his attempt to climb back up, he had fallen to the rocky floor below from nearly the top of the cliff, dying instantly.

When Rebecca learned that the poor girl's brother had died, a franticness came over her. It was as though she wasn't able to even grasp the fact of one more death in their wagon company. Especially as it only reminded her about the risk of losing her own brother. She was exhausted from her day running around for the doctor, and yet at the news of John Harper's death, Rebecca felt an urge to run around even more, looking for something fun, seeking out more distraction.

"Jasper!" she called to her brother.

He was at the back of their wagon, reaching inside for something. "What?"

As he turned to face her, she rushed up, stood directly in front of him and stared at him for a long moment.

"What?" he asked again, frowning this time. "Why are you looking at me like that?"

Rebecca threw her arms around his neck, squeezing him tightly. "I'm glad you're here. I'm so grateful we're here together."

He patted her back awkwardly. "All right... any

particular reason why? Is this your way of getting me to do your cleaning chores?"

She pulled back and grinned at him, not even caring that he was making fun of her.

"No. Just... No. Nothing."

How could she explain to him how afraid she was for his life every moment of every day? How could she detail what a difference it has made to her grieving to have his sense of humor to buoy her up? How could she properly convey how much better her life was because she had her brother by her side? His warmth and his sense of humor and his reliability and all of it.

"Nothing," she said again, stepping back. "Just don't climb down into the canyon, please."

He laughed. "Ma would kill me. Don't worry; that's not in my plans."

The next morning, yet another funeral was held, the friends and family of the deceased bleary eyed as they said their good-byes. But there was no lingering for anything. Captain Mills had already promised that they would have to push their teams as hard as they could to make up for fewer miles covered the previous day.

The wagon caravan continued down the trail as it wound along the bank of the river. There were so many miles to cover that day, it was near dark when they finally reached Shoshone Falls and their camp for the night. Rebecca could hear the strong rush of water even in the dark, even as far away as they were camped from the falls themselves.

"I wish I could see the falls now," she said as she finished washing the dishes after supper. "Aren't they supposed to be enormous? Can you even picture it?"

"Biggest falls this side of the Mississippi, at least," her father said. "Hard to believe Lewis and Clark missed it, though, if it's really that big."

"Well, I guess we will have to wait and see tomorrow morning," Ada said. "I will not have you all wandering off in the dark, liable to stumble over the edge before you even realize it."

"Your mother's right. We'll have plenty of time in the morning. I don't think we will be leaving camp until mid-day or so."

And so Rebecca went to sleep that night with visions of rushing water and magnificent views. Though the falls were named after the local Indian tribe, that made the site even more interesting to her. Imagine growing up your whole life near a wonder like that.

She resolved to explore on her own the next morning. For the last ten months, ever since her husband had died, Rebecca had looked to other people to keep her busy, to entertain her, to distract her from her thoughts. After coming so far on this harrowing journey, being through so much and making it out the other side, she finally felt ready to be alone. It may have taken almost thirteen hundred miles to get here, but she had done it.

And so, after breakfast, she sought out the trail that would take her to the top of the falls. It was narrow, barely enough for her, but she wasn't cutting her own trail. Previous wagon companies had come this way; she would not be the first emigrant to want to look out over the powerful natural wonder.

She found her way and began the short trek toward the sound. The falls roared, muting the sounds of everything else. Rebecca joyfully looked at the nature all around her and walked toward the sound. There was a narrow trail from the emigrants' campsite, through the trees to the top of the falls. There was a second trail from the campsite to the pool below the falls, where most of the women were headed that morning to collect water, so Rebecca had the other almost to herself.

The trail covered a slight incline, with grass and low bushes on either side. The few trees were far between, the elevation in this part of the world not allowing for the same enormous foliage that they had seen closer to Missouri.

The roar of thousands—millions—of gallons of water pouring over the falls grew louder, so loud that Rebecca did not hear her own footsteps.

As the trail reached the top of the ridge and leveled out, Rebecca finally saw what had been drawing her since the evening before. Cautiously, slowly, she approached the edge of the water, keeping her eyes on the gorgeous view the whole time. She could smell the fresh river water in the air, where it sprayed up against the rocks at the bottom of the pool.

It was unlike anything she had ever seen or would likely see again, and she drank up the sight. There she sat and watched and thought, peacefully alone for the first time in a long time. Her thoughts were calm; her faith in her future was stable. The uncertainty of this life would never go away, but Rebecca knew now, after so many months of widowhood and travel, that she could handle whatever came her way.

She didn't know how much time had passed, but by the time she felt ready to return the sun was passed the top of the sky. Though she could easily sit here and be entertained for hours, it was time to head back.

With a deep sigh of contentment, Rebecca stood, brushed the dirt off of her skirt, and headed back down the trail to the campsite. The chance to see this natural wonder was once-in-a-lifetime, and she was thinking about it all through her stroll back.

The trail curved away from the water, to the mostly flat section of land where the wagons and their livestock could stay overnight. But when Rebecca got to the flatter part there was nothing to be seen. No white-topped wagons. No oxen pawing at the dirt. No children squealing in delight.

Nothing. No one.

Where had they gone?

CHAPTER THIRTY-EIGHT

Where had everyone gone?

As she stood under the afternoon sun looking around, Rebecca felt panic well up in her.

She had spent her morning sitting by the Shoshone Falls and for once enjoying her quiet and solitude. Those hours alone had been exactly what she needed. She had felt refreshed and more herself than at any time since before her husband died. But somehow when she returned to camp, the camp was no longer there.

She kept staring at the empty space in front of her, in disbelief.

Maybe she had come up the trail the wrong way. It was so narrow, and the foliage so sparse, that maybe she had mistaken a bare strip of earth for the actual trail.

She stopped, forced herself to take a breath and look around more carefully.

And the first thing she laid eyes on was the remnant of a campfire, still faintly smoldering. Similar remains not covered over by dirt were peppered around the wide-open space.

So then, she had not come up the trail the wrong way. She was, in fact, right where she was supposed to be, but the wagon company had left. Somehow, in the few hours she had been away, the entire fifty wagons had packed up and disappeared and no one had thought about her.

She was too late. She had been left behind.

Rebecca Tenney had been left in the middle of the wilderness without friend or support or supplies.

She had been abandoned.

Everyone had forgotten her and she was on her own.

No matter how many different ways she considered her situation, it seemed utterly unbelievable.

How could this have happened? Was she really so forgettable? Was she really absent often enough that her parents didn't think to look for her?

Her heart pounded. She felt as though she could not get her breath. Rebecca pulled at the high neck of her dress, certain it was choking her, that her very gown was closing in on her. Her fingers trembled. She felt as though she was going to be sick.

"Hello?" she yelled, as loudly as she could. "Anyone?"

It seemed to come out in a whisper. Her voice cracked. All strength had drained from her.

There was no one.

She had been so reckless, so unthinking.

Her love, her husband. She had let him down. Andrew had made Rebecca promise to make the journey to Oregon without him. She had meant that promise; she had so wanted to do this for him. Maybe she hadn't thought it all the way through at the time, but nevertheless keeping that promise to him was the most important thing she had in her life.

And now, she had thrown away all her progress by looking for a fun diversion.

Rebecca collapsed in the dirt, her legs all but giving out on her.

What had she done?

She fell forward, leaning her face in her arms and curling into a ball of despair on the ground. Tears fell into the dirt as she sobbed out her hurt and disappointment.

She was all alone.

How could she stand it?

What could she do?

And yet, somehow, being completely alone in the world was something that Beau Waters voluntarily sought out.

At the thought of Beau, Rebecca sat up again, her one chance at salvation, at calm and preparedness, hitting her like a bolt of lightning. She knew what she needed to do.

Though her hands were still shaking, and she felt like she could throw up from the fear, she forced herself to stand. Though goodness knew it might not do anything but waste time, there was one thing that Rebecca could try to at least help her get a hold of herself. The help and support that Beau had given her since they first spoke outside of Fort Laramie all those weeks ago was far more useful than she had initially realized. It couldn't hurt, and it might actually help.

That advice to truly be present in the world, and to

anchor herself had been the foundation of how she had spent her days since that very first conversation. Even when she failed at it, the benefit of taking the time to calm herself had stuck with her.

She didn't know how, exactly, but Rebecca knew that if she could just calm her heart, if she could just stop shaking, she could do something. She would be able to see the next step she needed to do, and then the next and the next. Rebecca Tenney was the only person who could help her, and she needed to find her again.

Her breathing slowed as she grew to accept the situation.

The first thing she needed to do was stand on her own two feet, and feel the solid ground beneath her, holding her up. Trusting her legs would stay beneath her, Rebecca stood up as straight and as tall as she could. Never had she felt less confident, or less like standing, even, but she had to do this. This first step. Forcing herself to do this was the only way she was going to get through to anything better on the other side.

Wiping the tears from her cheek, Rebecca opened her eyes, and spun in a slow circle. This broad expanse where the wagons had been felt even more empty than it really was, because she had the memory of nearly fifty families with all their animals filling the space. She swallowed hard.

But she couldn't let herself think of that. She had to figure out which direction was west and look toward the horizon.

Shielding her eyes against the sun, Rebecca looked up and for the first time was grateful it was so late. The sun had passed the halfway mark in the sky and was beginning its descent. The sun would set in the west. She had a place to start.

Turning to face fully in the direction of Oregon, Rebecca took another steeling breath and slowed down to examine each and every thing she saw.

The mostly flat expanse of dirt and trampled dirt where the livestock grazed during the night. Charcoal, ashes, charred stones where the campfires were.

The trail down to the pool of water where the falls emptied, with the footsteps of travelers light in the dust. A damp, almost muddy patch under a bush where someone must have spilled water.

The scrub and bushes. The few pine trees, with starlings flying out at intervals. And then beyond that...

The mountains.

The same impossibly high mountains that had been drawing her for weeks. The same mountains that had steeled her before when she couldn't see past her own panic. The same mountains in the west, the same mountains where she should be heading along with everyone else in her wagon company.

That was where she should be headed.

That was where she would find her family again.

She sighed in relief. Everything would be fine.

Beau Waters had been right all along. All she had ever needed was an anchor, a solid foundation under her feet that she could trust, even when the worst happened, even when her fears ran away with her.

The mountains in the west would guide her way. Once she knew where to look, finding the trail to follow the wagons was easy.

CHAPTER THIRTY-NINE

Rebecca picked up her skirts and ran west, down the trail, toward her new life in Oregon.

The wagon company couldn't move any faster than the slowest, weakest ox, and as long as she did not lose her way she should be able to catch up with them in no time. It was only mid-afternoon. They couldn't have been gone too long.

As she headed west, toward the mountains, toward where the wagon company had likely gone, the trail wound away from the water. She hesitated only briefly before trusting that this was the right way. The dirt here was packed down, from the weight of enormous wagons. The plant life along the edges was stripped bare, eaten by dozens of animals. There were enough clues that a group of vehicles and animals had passed this way that she kept going, running down the trail.

For the first time since she had noticed the company was gone, Rebecca actually felt hope. She had pretended to be confident before, but now that she was actually moving westward she felt that certainty surging through her.

She would not be left behind. She would not be stuck in the past.

Rebecca ran toward her future.

The trail curved again and began to head down into another canyon. Rebecca paused at the top. If she was wrong, if this was not the direction the wagon company had gone, she would need to climb back out of the canyon again or die trying.

She walked a few more feet, down past the next curve of canyon wall.

Under the pounding of her heart she could hear the bustle and voices of a group of emigrants.

She ran again toward the sound, heading down the steep trail that led to the bottom.

As she rounded the slight corner, there they were. All fifty wagons, the dozens of families, the hundreds of heads of livestock. She had done it, had taken care of herself, had conquered her fears and found her family again. Her presentiment had been correct and Rebecca had caught up to the Sullivan-Mills wagon company after being utterly lost. They were congregating slowly at the foot of a trail that climbed up out of the canyon.

She almost cried in relief, but instead she kept running. Past the Goldmans, past the Franklins, the Taylors, the Hudsons, until finally she passed the Keegan family and reached her own family's wagon.

Her mother was walking immediately behind the wagon and reaching in, while it continued forward. She found what she was looking for, and turned just in time to see Rebecca run up.

"Goodness, child, where have you been? I needed you to help choose items that we could give to the Indians for the toll. I just had to guess which of your old dresses you were willing to give up."

"I was…" But Rebecca couldn't continue. She was too out of breath. She moved to the side of the trail, out of the way of the Keegans' team, and bent over to try to catch her breath.

"And why are you breathing like that?"

"I ran." She placed a hand on her bosom, in hopes of calming her heart. "I ran here from the falls."

"Why on earth did you do that?"

Rebecca shook her head. She didn't know where to start, especially with her heart still pounding like this. How to explain to her mother that she had been left behind? That she had panicked so completely? Though things could have gone very wrong, fortunately they did not. Rebecca had mastered herself and returned home.

She was home.

She smiled and threw herself into her mother's arms, forcing a hug onto her.

"Rebecca!" she responded, surprised but returning the hug. "Are you all right, dear? Goodness, be careful. Let's get out of the way."

Ada extricated herself, lest the two women block the path for the wagon behind. There was a story that Rebecca would need to tell eventually—she inwardly cringed at how Jasper would tease her—but none of that needed to be done now.

She was here. She was home. And her family needed her.

Her father appeared around the side of the wagon. "There you are. Just in time to help."

"What?" Rebecca looked from one parent to another.

"I don't know where you got off to, but you're here now. I'd like you to carry this crate of dishes," Ada said.

"What? Why?" She was only just getting her breath back.

She pointed, toward where the wagon was heading. "We need to get the wagon up this steep trail cut into the side of the cliff, and the less weight the animals have to drag up with them the better. It's not much, but maybe it will help."

"We can't afford to lose an animal the way the Gladwells did," Michael added.

"And we certainly don't need to make the same mistake others have made." Ada pointed to the foot of the trail, some thirty feet behind Rebecca.

She turned to see what her mother meant, and saw a chaotic pile of personal belongings, most of which seemed to be well loved. There was a medicine chest, still a third full of supplies, and crate full of well-loved books. A heavy wooden trunk that had been emptied and turned on its side. She even spotted a side of moldy pork that was so rotten even the animals were steering clear of it.

"What is all that? Did a wagon turn over?"

Ada shook her head. "Getting rid of extra weight was the only way some of these wagons were going to make it up out of the gorge. Breaks your heart to look at it, but when you see how boney some of those oxen have gotten, I don't know what other choice they had."

All of these items had not only been brought so far west on the Oregon Trail, but they had been cherished and selected from maybe as far away as Massachusetts or Georgia. Some family had spent the time and energy to bring this collection of books more than two thousand miles, months of travel, wearing down the oxen and taking up space that could have been used for food.

This first edition copy of Washington Irving had been treasured and brought so far, only to be discarded at the side of the trail because the family had to get up out of this gorge and had spent all the energy to do so. And now her own family was facing the same choices.

"I understand," Rebecca said. "Just let me catch my breath."

Within a few minutes, Rebecca had recovered from her wild dash and was ready to climb the trail. She marveled at what she could do, how much she could handle, in the name of survival. But beyond a mild surprise at her own capability, she didn't have time for any other such introspection. There was work to be done.

Rebecca picked up the crate that had sat at her mother's feet. The clinking of the dishes padded by dried straw reminded her to be careful with it. The crate wasn't light, but as long as she focused, Rebecca could make it to the top of the trail with it. She made her way slowly to the foot of the trail, waiting her turn with the other women walking up between the wagons.

"What's that?" Kate Keegan appeared at Rebecca's elbow. "Are you walking up with that?"

"It's my mom's fancy dishes."

"Did you bring that all the way from Indiana?" The little girl's eyes got big.

"Sure did. Let's hope they make it to the top of the trail now, huh?"

Both looked up the steep trail, where animals were struggling under the weight of all they were expected to haul. The stone wall where the trail was carved was all black jagged edges and scraggly weeds.

"Do your parents know where you are?" Rebecca asked, suddenly more aware of such things.

Kate pointed back to where her father was helping Michael chain their wagons together. In order to get everything up out of the canyon, the teams of oxen would be doubled and the wagons paired off.

"Ma wanted me out of the way."

As Rebecca watched, Mrs. Keegan looked up, saw her daughter, smiled and waved her on ahead.

"You want to walk up with me then?"

"Yes, please. Jack is with the Jones family but I didn't want to."

"Well, I appreciate the company," Rebecca assured her.

There seemed to be a lull in the traffic while the men had to hitch their teams. Rebecca picked up the crate of dishes again, heaving it gently and balancing the weight in both arms. This was no light load, but she thought she could make it to the top.

"Let's hurry," she said, leading the way. "I don't want to have to set this down and rest partway through."

"It'd maybe slide all the way back down," Kate added with a giggle.

Rebecca was too busy concentrating on carrying the

crate and not breaking anything to be able to hold up her end of the conversation. Luckily for her, Kate Keegan had plenty of news.

"...And then my brother almost caught a frog himself, but then Bobby Jones splashed him and he accidentally dropped it."

"Well, that doesn't sound very nice," Rebecca said, though her attention was ahead of her, at the top of the gorge, where she could finally put down this crate.

"No, but Jack wasn't mad. He says it just means he has to practice more, so he doesn't drop it next time."

Rebecca smiled down at her. "That's very smart. Practicing something, even if it's hard at first, is the best way to get better at it."

CHAPTER FORTY

Once they reached the top of the gorge, Rebecca and Kate moved aside, off the trail and out of the way of the others coming up behind them.

The animals were heaving breath, barely hanging on from the strenuous work of pulling the wagons up such a steep incline. As each wagon reached the top, it was pulled out of the way as fast as possible. This left room for the wagons still coming to reach the top, but also gave the oxen a small break as they waited for the rest of the caravan. They were given water, oats, and whatever other treats the men could spare. There was still so far to go, and they needed every single one of these animals to make it the whole way.

"Do you want to wait here for your mother?" Rebecca asked, setting the crate of dishes at her feet and shaking out her aching arms.

"Yeah. Jack will probably be with the Jones boys, I think, until we make camp. I don't want her to worry about me too."

"Well," Rebecca began, squatting down in the dirt next to her. "I learned a trick recently that might help you, if you're ever in a spot where you can't find your mother while we're traveling to Oregon."

Kate frowned suspiciously. "What do you mean? Why wouldn't I be able to find her? Where would she go?"

"I'm sure you will always be able to find her. But just in case. It's good to know where we're going. Do you know which way Oregon is?"

Without hesitation, Kate pointed toward the west, toward where the wagons were slowly making their way once the animals had been fed and watered.

"Wow," Rebecca said. "You're very smart. How did you—"

"When we left New Jersey, I asked Father how he knew where to go, and he told me about directions and things. And the sun setting. And I just..." She shrugged. "It's easy."

Rebecca laughed. "You are a lot smarter than I was at your age, Kate. You might actually be smarter than I am now, at some things. I won't tell you how long it took me to actually pay attention to something like that."

Kate's eyes got wide, but Rebecca shook her head.

"Maybe when you're older. It's too embarrassing to tell you now." She winked at the little girl. "Just trust me. You're going to grow up just fine."

Though the ascent out of the canyon was treacherous, the Sullivan-Mills company did not have a chance to rest. There were still two hours of daylight left, and Captain Mills pushed them the whole time. With as many families in the company as were struggling to ration their food, there wasn't the luxury of a break. Even a mile further helped cut down on the amount of food they would still need. They kept pushing westward, desperate to get over the Blue Mountains before snow fell.

They were still crossing Shoshone land. The wagon company had paid a toll for the privilege of crossing unmolested, but the agreement was the emigrants needed to move as quickly as they could out of the territory. Captain Mills set a double guard each night. There was no doubt that members of the tribe would be watching them from hidden places, but the emigrants saw no other glimpse of the Indians.

One evening, as the company made camp, Rebecca went out into the flat stretch of land away from the river to look for fuel for the campfire. This late in the summer, most of the available sticks, twigs and even buffalo chips had been collected by previous wagon companies, but she had to look. Ada, smartly, had kept the emptied-out crates after they had eaten all the food that had been stored there, and Jasper periodically broke down that wood into smaller pieces for burning. But they were nearing the end of the supply.

They had made camp right at dusk, and now there was just enough light for Rebecca to see by. She kept her eyes at the ground and the few feet surrounding, hoping to spot every little bit of fuel that was available. It took at least ten minutes, but she finally had collected enough to fill her apron. Standing straight again, Rebecca took the opportunity to look around her, in the quiet and the dusk. She took a deep breath, looked toward the west and smiled to herself.

Just about everything was in place. Though there would be questions of food and fuel until they reached Oregon, her heart was calm.

A week ago, she would have hated this. She would have hurried back to a crowd and warmth as soon as she could, clutching at the closest person to talk to her. But now she felt a peace, knowing that she had come through such a frightening experience and knew what to do next time. It was practically impossible that she would be left behind by the wagon company again, but if she was she would be all right.

Growing up, with visions of marrying Andrew Tenney always in the forefront of her mind, Rebecca had never truly considered that she needed to worry about anything. He would always take care of it. He would always take care of her. When he died, she had her family and community around her constantly, making sure she had food, and a roof over her head. Keeping up her spirits and giving her the support she needed to get through the hardest part.

And she had done it. It had been difficult, but she had done it. She had made it this far toward the Oregon Territory, and she had done it while finding a way to work through her grief. The rest of the journey would be difficult, but the obstacle of figuring out how to manage her pain was behind her.

She returned to her camp, fuel for the fire in hand, ready to settle into an evening of helping her mother take care of everything.

After getting to the top of the canyon, the Oregon Trail followed the curve of the Snake River. They would be near this source of water, blessedly, for at least three days, heading west. They would need to cross the water again, before heading northwest across the flat open plains toward Fort Boise.

For several days the wagon company traveled as fast as they could; it wasn't very quickly given how hungry and exhausted each person and animal was. Rebecca could not remember ever being so worn out. This journey had already been one of the hardest things she had ever done in her life, but this final stretch, these last few weeks with little food and even less energy was the hardest thus far.

They were reaching the end of August, and from what Rebecca had overheard her father and brother say, were not nearly as far west as they had hoped to be by this time in the summer. Each wagon company that left Independence or St. Joseph, Missouri, in the spring had the goal to be over the mountains and into the Willamette Valley by the first of September. That was mere days away. Now they would be fortunate if they made it to Oregon before October.

The Sullivan-Mills wagon company had been delayed by sickness, death, broken wagons, and so much more. They still had several weeks to go before they could stop. Several weeks in which there was no guarantee they would be able to add to their food stores. Several weeks in which the risk of Indian attack was ever-present. Several weeks for someone to get sick or injured and further delay the journey.

Though Rebecca had gotten far better at being calm with her thoughts when she was alone, that didn't mean she wasn't eager to seek out her friends when she had the chance. In fact, conversation with people she cared about energized her. She could easily forget the blister forming on her heel when she had gossip or stories to chat about.

Though she felt satisfied as much as she could, Rebecca wouldn't truly feel right until she had made it to Oregon, and she had fulfilled the promise she made to Andrew.

CHAPTER FORTY-ONE

After following the curve of the Snake River for several days, the emigrants finally reached the best point to cross so they continue heading west, away from the water. Previous water crossings had been difficult, but the Sullivan-Mills wagon company was already desperate to cover ground as quickly as they could. It would take two days to get everyone across the water, and there could be no shirking.

Throughout much of its length, the Snake River was rapid and deadly. Shoshone Falls was just one of many points along the river that a man had to avoid if he wanted to make it across the water. Early fall was the only time of year the river was shallow enough to be slow and to not overwhelm the wagon wheels. Further, this spot was called Three Islands Crossing for a reason—across the width of the river were three small sand dunes that acted as respites in the middle of the otherwise wide water.

Even with everything lined up and efficient as it

could be, only half of the wagon company could cross in a day. The Stephens family, being in the back half of the caravan, made camp with part of the company for one day while they waited for their turn to cross the next.

The Waters family crossed early, so Rebecca didn't have Sadie's company during the day they were in camp. But as she hummed to herself while walking between the wagons that remained, she realized she was just fine on her own. A few weeks ago, she would have been desperate for someone to talk to, but now it was enough to simply observe as she walked.

"It's getting to be our turn, Rebecca," her mother called to her. "You about ready?"

Rebecca returned to where her brother was soothing the oxen, getting them prepared for the plunge into the river. Her mother had just climbed into the wagon, and was leaning out the back, between the canvas flaps of the cover.

"Do you want to ride the wagon with your mother, or ford across on your own?" her father asked.

"Ugh. Last time I rode in the wagon it made me sick." She looked up ahead and noticed how many of the other women were hiking up their skirts to wade across the shallowest part of the river. "No, I'll go through the water. It'll be fine. Maybe I'll see if Mrs. Van Anda needs help with the baby or something."

"You sure you're all right on your own, Becks?" her brother asked as she made to walk away.

"Do you mean am I afraid you are going to leave me behind again?"

He grinned, which prompted her to shake her head at him.

"Well, seeing as you need to wait your turn to cross with the wagon, I guess I'll get to the other side before you. If you still lose me after that we might have a problem." She grinned back at him, and strode on ahead to see if it was possible to wade across the river with a friend.

Half a dozen families were lining up their teams and wagons to cross, including the Hudsons with their two wagons. Ever since the Hudson family had lost Louisa, the whole company had been surprised by how well they seemed to be progressing, not to mention being grateful that the blow had not been more debilitating. Annie had taken over driving one of the wagons completely, and Margaret and Josie had been able to fill the other gaps left by their sister. In circumstances like this, however, the loss of one of their own was even more evident. There was always something more to do that they just didn't have enough hands for. Rebecca walked toward their wagon to find Margaret and Lawrence discussing how they would get all the animals across the water.

"If we move the chickens' coops to inside the wagon, they'll be fine. It's the goats I'm worried about," Margaret was saying.

"Would they ride inside too?"

"Goodness, can you imagine? We'd have to tie them down at the very least, and then who knows what they might do when irritated."

Rebecca stepped into their circle. "Do you need help?"

When Margaret turned to see Rebecca, her face lit up. "Like you wouldn't believe. Even just another pair of arms to help carry one of the goats over. I don't trust these creatures in a current this strong. They're liable to get distracted halfway across and just float on downstream, never to be seen again."

With that agreement, Rebecca gathered up the smallest of the goats in her arms. It was just as heavy as the crate of dishes had been and much more squirmy.

"Is there a trick to this or...?"

"Here." Margaret bent down and gathered the lower part of Rebecca's skirt. Leaving her petticoat showing, she wrapped the fabric of the dress around the goat in Rebecca's arms. "Is that all right? It will help her feel more safe if she's wrapped up like that, but I know showing your petticoat to all and sundry isn't ideal. You say the word and we'll find some other way."

Rebecca had been taken aback, at first, both by Margaret's forwardness and the situation she had put her in. But upon reflection, Rebecca realized she didn't mind at all. Her legs were well covered, and would be even more so when they got in the water. And, goodness, who really was paying attention to how modestly she was dressed at this moment, anyway.

"Well, you have been a widow longer than I have, so if you don't think it's a problem I won't either."

"Not with these folks."

"Just let's be sure to get across before my mother sees," Rebecca added with a laugh.

Three Islands Crossing was no casual stroll. One of the wagons broke an axle in trying to get across, and another woman had to be rescued after the current had pushed her too far downstream. But to Rebecca, it was the kind of challenge that invigorated her. This seemed like precisely the kind of challenge Andrew had envisioned for her when he made her promise to come to Oregon. Rebecca almost dropped the goat from laughing too much when she imagined the look on his face if he could see her.

After crossing the river, the flat high desert seemed to flatten like a johnnycake. Far in the distance she could still see the mountains and the western territory where they were headed, but between here and there was a long stretch of nothing. No trees, as far as she could see. Only scrub, low bushes, weeds with periodic patches of grass, and flat, flat land. The wagon company passed several days across this bleak landscape, heading north-west toward Fort Boise.

Many of the women, including Ada, had baked as many biscuits, johnnycakes and oat muffins as they could manage in the days the company had traveled next to the river. At least there, the emigrants had had some semblance of fuel for the fire. Here, on the open desert, Rebecca had to give up coffee for a couple days, since they simply did not have enough wood to burn long enough to heat up coffee for everyone in the family.

It was such a small sacrifice—she had gone far longer without coffee—but on top of every other thing she had given up over the previous months, it felt almost personal.

After all the physical obstacles and deprivation they had had to endure on the trail already, this stark stretch of desert felt most like the landscape was trying to destroy them.

As they were higher in elevation, the temperature wasn't too hot, but the sun was unrelenting.

On the prairies, nearer to when they had left Independence, there were some trees. There'd been enough water to grow tall grass.

Here, there was nothing.

And yet, she knew that Indian tribes must be nearby. And they would have to live on something. Her father had told her that there were uncountable animals all around them, that just didn't cross the emigrants' path. In spite of the seeming lack of any sign of life, this great basin was just one more of the myriad of wonders she had seen on this journey.

As their journey wore on and more and more folks seemed subdued under their hunger and exhaustion, Rebecca just kept putting one foot in front of the other. She no longer felt as though distracting herself was the most important thing, if she could keep making progress westward. She still wasn't as enamored with the routine as her mother was, but at least she no longer felt the urge to run away.

After several days of passing through such stark landscape, the small structure of Fort Boise appeared on the horizon, drawing the wagon company with its promise of food.

This fort was a veritable oasis compared to some of the other places they had stopped over the previous months. The caravan arrived at the fort in the early afternoon, and everyone drew a sigh of relief when the captain declared they would camp there for the rest of the day. The fort itself was just a handful of small buildings behind a stockade wall, but they had supplies in stock for the men with money to buy it. Michael Stephens collected as much as he could afford, as much as the fort could spare with all the other families who also needed to add to their food stores or ammunition.

But more than just having the supplies needed, Fort Boise was located on a wide, slow stretch of the Boise River. Though they stayed only half a day, in that time the emigrants finally had as much water as they could collect, and the chance of fresh salmon for those willing to fish.

At least half of the families in the wagon company had someone with a fishing pole and net lounging on the banks of the river that afternoon. It was impossible to say the next time they would have such abundance until they finally reached their destination of the Oregon Territory.

CHAPTER FORTY-TWO

Rebecca knew that Fort Boise might well be the last pleasant day they had until they finally got to Oregon. And even then, they would only have a few weeks to find shelter and supplies before settling in for the winter. Every day for the next several months would be a struggle for survival—she could not fool herself about that. It may not be until the following April when they would have the same slow, plentiful afternoon as they had had at the fort.

But in spite of this stress, Rebecca felt ready for the challenge ahead. There was only a short time, just a few more weeks, before they would be safely in Oregon. She had made it this far, and she could make it the rest. They were so close.

After leaving Fort Boise, the wagon company had to make up so much ground that the captain drove them west for days without stopping for a midday break. The men would have to get what nourishment they could while they walked alongside their teams. They could not afford to let up even for half an hour. Ada had dried some of the salmon when they were stopped at the fort, and baked extra when she could. That meat added to cold biscuits was all that they had to keep them going day after day, mile after mile.

Though Rebecca could not ease the burdens that were on her father or Jasper, she did try to lend a hand not only to her mother but also the other women in the company. She had the energy and time to spare, when many women did not, and the joy of helping others around her gave Rebecca a peace that she had been missing in her franticness earlier on the trail. Sadie had taken on more of her mother-in-law's chores, so Rebecca spent several mornings with that family, helping out as they had all helped her in the past.

Several days past the fort, the wagon company began their gentle climb into the foothills. Though each day seemed exactly the same, Rebecca knew that they must be making progress. It was impossible to see in the hour-by-hour daily increments, but one day she looked up to realize that the land around her was no longer the interminable flatness of the Great Basin. Though they were still somewhat in the distance, low hills cropped up around them. She had her eyes on the western horizon as she walked parallel to the trail.

"Sister," Jasper called. When she closed the distance to him, he said, "Can I ask you something?"

"Well, I'm obviously quite busy right now, Jasper, but if you'll leave your card with the housekeeper—"

"Have you spoken much to the elder Miss Cole?"

"Nora?" Rebecca shoved his shoulder playfully. "Why

ever would you be asking about Nora Cole, dear brother?"

He opened his mouth to answer, but then closed it again and looked ahead.

"What?" she prompted.

"Just deciding how much to tell you."

"What? Really?"

"Why not?"

"It's just... I didn't realize you were serious at all. Ever. About anything."

"Ha ha," he responded dryly. "Never mind. Forget I said anything."

"No, no. Let me think. I admit I noticed her flirting and eager for your attention, but I didn't realize that went the other way as well."

"A gentleman does not divulge details about his lady's attentions."

Jasper had always affected an unconcerned manner, but if there was anyone in the world who could see through that, it was his sister. She watched him for a few moments without saying anything, and the silence seemed to unnerve him.

"What?" he asked, a hint of concern in his voice.

"She seems lovely, Jas," Rebecca said gently. "We haven't spoken much, but she seems kind and earnest. She seems like the kind of woman who would be an excellent support."

"She is, yeah," he agreed.

"And she's almost certainly too good for you," Rebecca continued.

"Hey!"

"So just don't go and do that thing that you've always

done. Remember Laura in Indiana? How she came over every day for a month pretending to want to have tea with me because she was so convinced that you were going to fall in love with her any day?"

"Oh." He winced. "Not my finest hour. Sorry 'bout that."

"Right. So let's not do that again, please. I don't have time for tea every day, for one thing. But then, I'm not sure Nora is the type to moon over you. Maybe when we were leaving Missouri at the very beginning when everything seemed uncertain. That girl seemed more than smitten, showing up as many times as she did when you hurt your arm. But now? I saw her at the river crossing. What did you two talk about?"

He shrugged noncommittally.

"Well, I admit I haven't spoken to her myself, and this is just going off of the little I've seen, but I would say... Jasper, if she is important to you, you should tell her. She seems like she is perfectly fine whether you are in her life or not, so if you want to be you have to make it happen. You can't just wait for her to show up outside the house again like you did with Laura."

Before he could respond, Rebecca felt a drop of water on the back of her hand. When she looked up at the thick layer of gray clouds, she felt another handful of raindrops on her face.

"Looks like it's gonna rain. We should get—"

But before she could finish the thought, the sky had completely opened up, rain pouring down on them in buckets all at once.

"Too late!" Jasper said with a laugh, as they darted to the back of their wagon to take shelter.

Ada appeared from the other side of the wagon just as they got there, and all three climbed in. From trunk near the front of the wagon, Jasper grabbed two oilskin wraps, and headed back out to take one to their father, leaving the two women alone.

Lightning flashed across the desert plain, and Rebecca peeked out through the canvas at the sight. The rain was falling so thickly she could barely make out the Keegans' team behind them. She watched in wonder as all around her the landscape was transformed into something unrecognizable.

"Incredible," she said in a whisper.

"It really is," her mother agreed from next to her.

True the rain would make their travel even harder; the wheels would stick in the mud, and even in later days when it dried, the trail may be all ruts and bumps. It was also true that the animals had already been struggling, and were weak. Someone could get hurt. A wagon could get broken. An ankle could be twisted.

And yet, in spite of all this risk, Rebecca could also see the wonder in it.

Thunder cracked.

The storm wasn't quite on top of them, but it seemed to be getting closer every minute.

As with everything on this wild journey westward, this storm was a mix of both struggle and excitement. Dangerous and extraordinary. Though Rebecca still didn't quite see how Andrew could have thought her capable of all that the trail had asked of her, she knew he would have loved this wonder for her.

And would have equally loved teasing Jasper about a young lady.

Rebecca smiled.

CHAPTER FORTY-THREE

The amazement and wonder at the storm didn't last long. The luxury of sitting and watching the weather did not belong on the Oregon Trail.

In days, the wagon company had climbed even higher into the foothills, and were hit by the cold chill that came with it. Rebecca dug her gloves and heavy coat out of the trunk in the back of the wagon and walked briskly along the trail to keep warm. The cold had seeped into the bones of the rest of the emigrants as well. Where two months ago she would have engaged in a teasing conversation with Kate Keegan, now it was all Rebecca could do to smile and nod when she passed the little girl.

Everyone was simply too hungry, too tired and too cold to do much more than survive to the end of the day. Then, at least, they could get some small amount of rest before they had to get up and do it all again the next day.

The trail climbed higher into the mountains every

day. Rebecca tried to remind herself that they were making progress, that they were near the end of the journey, even if it didn't feel like it. Any day now they would reach the highest point and start back down the western side. Any day they would finally get a glimpse of their future home, the rolling farmland of Oregon.

But the grass for the animals got scarcer, and the cold biting through her coat grew stronger. She found herself wishing for the long afternoons of a few months previously with the warmth of the prairie sun on her cheeks.

One morning, a cold wind had blown through overnight, and the bucket of water Jasper had left out for the oxen froze over. In the morning, he barely had time to break into the ice before the wagons needed to start the climb up the trail again.

"Be careful," Ada said, watching as he hurried to chip away at the layer at the top. "We can't spare a drop."

"No drops here, Ma. I think you mean a chip."

His grin was disarming, and Rebecca noticed her mother soften a tiny bit under his beam.

"He's got it, Ma," Rebecca said.

"I know." She sniffed. "I just worry. We're so close; I would hate for anything to go wrong now."

"We're close," Rebecca agreed. "Nothing will happen. Just a few more days. A few more miles."

"I don't know how we're going to cover those miles. I heard little Joshua Goldman has worn completely through his shoes," Ada said, shaking her head pityingly.

"Oh, that poor child," Rebecca said.

"I don't know how he's going to last those final miles, riding in the wagon. But, he couldn't walk across all the stones and things without shoes." She shook her head again. "I just don't know."

"We'll get through it," Rebecca said. "Somehow. We have to. We have no other choice."

And still the Sullivan-Mills wagon company pushed on. They had lost one of their captains, multiple children and several other members to disease and accidents. They had lost thousands of pounds of food and supplies. They had used up every bit of energy and willpower they had.

But they had also gained a new life—the Van Anda baby—and new love. Two different couples had announced their engagements in the previous weeks. No matter what the Oregon Trail had taken from the emigrants, each person had also gained a strength and hope that they had not expected. And there were still many miles of traveling to go.

One afternoon late into September, the wagon company was plodding up through the mountain pass when they stopped for a midday meal. Most of the families didn't have more than a mouthful to eat, but the captain could not keep them moving for twelve hours each day without rest.

"The rest will do folks good," Ada said, as she sat heavily on the rear lip of the wagon.

"But the longer we rest the closer we get to running out of food before we get there," Rebecca said.

"Without food, we don't have the strength to keep going all day every day."

"There's no simple solution," Michael said, stepping between them to pull something out of the wagon. "Captain Mills is doing his best."

But was his best enough to get all of these families down into Oregon before anything else happened?

The previous night, Rebecca had lay in her cot in the now significantly less crowded wagon, and she could have sworn she heard the crying of a child. Maybe even Jack Keegan; their wagon was close to hers. Between the miles they had to cross every day, the thinner air up here in the mountains, and the minuscule meals, it was a wonder that more emigrants hadn't had complete breakdowns. It was only by constantly looking forward, looking toward the horizon, that Rebecca managed to get through the day without crying herself.

Now, when they had stopped at noon, Rebecca tried not to think of food. There was nothing to be done about it. Ada didn't even take the steps to build a campfire. The little food they had left the family would eat at supper that evening, and searching out the small bit of fuel in the area would simply take more energy than it was worth. Instead, Ada wrapped another scarf around her neck, and they fell into a quiet torpor.

Leaning against the back wagon wheel, Rebecca suddenly remembered that they had run out of the last of their sugar that morning. After her father had acquired more at the fort, they had stretched it to last as long as they could, but now it was gone.

And now it was all she could think about.

She needed something to distract her from her hunger, but just as much she needed to be far away from her mother. Rebecca couldn't much help her stomach rumbling, and she knew if her mother heard it she'd feel terrible, or insist on Rebecca taking a handful of the bit of oats they had left for the animals.

No, it would be better for her to go off on her own, and find something to occupy her. She didn't know how many days of travel they had left, but it couldn't be that many. They must be getting close. By the end of the week, perhaps, they could buy more food at an actual general store, or convince a local farmer to sell them eggs. It might be too much to hope that the first town they came to in Oregon had a restaurant, serving her favorite: mashed potatoes, dripping with butter and gravy, with roasted carrots and a thick slice of pot roast.

Rebecca's stomach rumbled again as she imagined such a meal, sitting down in a warm room and having someone serve her. Goodness, even being off her feet and not having to wash the dishes afterward was a luxury she could barely remember.

She got up and strode toward the rest of the camp.

"Where are you off to?' Ada asked as Rebecca passed her.

"Just to see what I can find. There's probably none of the mushrooms that Sadie taught me about up here, but maybe I could find some acorns or some wild greens that we can boil."

Ada offered a small smile. "Good luck, love. I'm sure if there's anything to find you will find it."

The company was only stopped for an hour, so instead of a secure circle of chained wagons, the vehicles were scattered at intervals all over the mountainside. Rebecca made her way slightly higher up the mountain to where the thicker forest was. So far she hadn't seen any oak trees where she might find acorns, but that didn't mean there weren't any. With her eyes on the ground, Rebecca walked toward the line of trees, hoping that something would catch her eye.

Were pine needles edible? There really wasn't much more around here.

She stopped before walking into the trees, hands on hips, and looked up. She took a deep breath. They certainly smelled nice. But scent wouldn't fill her stomach.

Maybe she had taken too deep of a breath; Rebecca felt a bit unsteady, a bit dizzy. She blinked several times, but her vision was blurring. The wagons around her, the trees, the mountain, it all seemed to be spinning. Her legs couldn't hold her weight; her ankle turned.

And then it all went black.

An unknown length of time later, Rebecca opened her eyes to the feel of a cold soft hand on her cheek and someone leaning over her saying her name.

"Rebecca," the voice said, urgently, pointed, prodding her brain to wake up. "Open your eyes. We've got to get you up. Please open your eyes."

Her head swam, but Rebecca managed to open her eyes and focus on Sadie leaning over her.

"What happened?"

"You fainted." She furrowed her brow. "When was the last time you ate?"

"Last night, I think. Not too long ago."

"Well, clearly it wasn't enough. Come on." She wrapped her hand around Rebecca's arm and hauled her up. "Let's get some food in you."

CHAPTER FORTY-FOUR

Sadie had her arm around Rebecca's waist, all but holding her up after she had fainted.

"Come eat," Sadie said, gently guiding her back to the wagons. "Please. We have enough. It's not a lot, but it is enough."

"I couldn't. There are so many other people—"

"You are the one who just collapsed, Rebecca Tenney. If need be I'm sure Angus's mother will share with others, but right now you're the one I'm worried about."

Rebecca didn't have the energy to argue with her friend. "Thank you," she said weakly. "Maybe just a bite."

But when they approached the Waters family's campfire, and smelled the beans, the rumble of her stomach betrayed her. Much of the rest of the family had already served themselves, all taking small portions to share what little they had with as many people as possible.

"Good thing I found you when I did, right?" Sadie teased gently, as she dished out a few bites onto a tin plate. "Sit. Eat."

The serving was small—barely enough to make a difference—but Rebecca was more grateful than she could find words for.

"Thank you," she said in a small voice as she took the food from her friend. With a shaking hand she lifted a bite to her mouth. It was warm, and exactly as comforting and nourishing as she could hope for. She closed her eyes as she chewed, enjoying the unlooked-for treat. Who would have thought she could get so much pleasure out of a few bites of warm beans?

The rest of the Waters family surrounded her, each focused on their own food or chores. No one seemed to mind Rebecca sitting in their midst, eating their food. From where the oxen had been corralled, Beau approached the family's campfire. He looked at Rebecca, looked at the plate balanced on her knees and nodded in satisfaction.

As he sat to join the conversation, he pulled Angus's attention.

"You haven't seen them, have you, Beau? I was just telling the ladies here that we should be in Oregon any day, so it's too bad we can't go faster."

"Seen who?"

"Daniel Mills and Benjamin Findley," Sadie said. "They left to go scout ahead, and maybe bring back help but no one has heard from them."

"Mills and Findley left almost a week ago, wasn't it?" Angus frowned. "You don't think something happened to them, do you?"

"We should go look for them," Beau said. "If they're in trouble, maybe we can find them before it's too late."

Rebecca looked from one man to the other, eyes wide at the thought of heading off into the wilderness.

"Oh, no," protested Sadie. "We can't leave the camp. What if we get lost? Plus then we'll just have to walk back up the mountain to the wagons. It seems like far more trouble than it's worth."

"I dunno, Sade," her husband said in a low voice. "People here need help. Mrs. Tenney fainted, for goodness sake, and she is one of the strong ones. If Mills and Findley have found anything, it could be worth helping them bring it all back."

"They've been gone a week," Rebecca reminded them. "They could be anywhere."

"But, if we're really as close to the other side as I think we are," Beau said, "maybe we can at least get a glimpse, go on ahead, scout ourselves."

"I don't know... It seems like an awful long shot."

"I think we need to go," Angus said, standing.

Sadie looked at her husband for a moment before slumping in acquiescence. "All right. But I'm going too."

"Me too," added Rebecca.

The men both frowned.

"Well—" Angus began.

"Of course," Beau said. "But you know what this means. Sadie already detailed some of it, but you also need to remember that if we find either of the men, we may need to carry them, or supplies, back with us. It's not going to be easy, which you already know. But beyond that it could be nigh on impossible. Especially as weak as Rebecca— as Mrs. Tenney is."

He looked more serious than Rebecca had ever seen him, so much so that she easily overlooked his familiarity in calling her by her Christian name. The emigrants had been through so much together, there was no question of him being respectful as he carefully outlined all the hardships they were choosing to take on.

"I understand," she said.

"Sadie?" He turned to his sister-in-law.

"I know. You don't think I'm going to let my husband go off alone in such circumstances, are you?"

Angus smiled wryly. "I should have known."

"Well, what are we waiting for?" Rebecca stood; she held a spoonful of the last bit of beans and quickly put it in her mouth.

Beau raised his eyebrows in surprise, but didn't say anything. Instead he turned to the wagon, reached inside and pulled out two canteens that must have been hanging just inside the canvas.

"Do you need to tell your family or anyone else?"

"No," Rebecca said. "They left me behind once already. I'm not sure they've worried about me since."

Sadie laughed. "We won't go far. They might even catch up to us if we don't go very fast."

Rebecca looked at Beau who shrugged. "Ready?"

The four of them left the collection of wagons and easily found the next stretch of trail, taking them farther west through the mountain pass.

Rebecca walked off ahead, quickly, eager to see something—anything—that might show them how close they were to the end of their journey. Where the trail curved around the mountain she slowed, taking tentative steps toward the edge. Tall pine trees from the slope below framed the view, and Rebecca cautiously looked down over the rim.

It was beautiful. Autumn was beginning in the Pacific Northwest, and a riot of color met her eyes. Orange, yellow, red, green, in all shades.

She felt Beau come to stand next to her, neither saying anything for several moments, looking out over the side of the mountain. Of every person in the wagon company, he seemed to be the only one Rebecca felt comfortable being silent with. It was no wonder this man was able to help her calm her heart and sort through her grief.

At the thought of her grief, Rebecca felt a pang of sorrow, that she was now so far from Andrew, from the life they had had together, brief though it was.

"It seems like every day there's something new that I wish Andrew could be here to see," she said finally. "This whole trip was his idea in the first place. He would have loved so much of it. It's been almost a year since he died."

"I'm sorry."

She shook her head, but couldn't answer. Even just saying his name out loud to another person hurt right now.

"I had a sweetheart who died," he said quietly.

"What?" She blinked up at him in surprise.

"We weren't married, not even promised, not yet. But we had been courting for almost a year when she took ill. Galloping consumption, the doctor called it. It seemed one minute she was the bright, constant, love of my life, and before I could turn around again she was gone."

He didn't look at her, seeming to focus on the line of trees just down the mountain in front of them.

"I'm sorry," she whispered.

"So, no, it might not be quite the same thing as you went through when your husband was killed." He looked at her then, with an intensity that made her quake all over. "But believe me when I tell you I know something about grieving."

Rebecca was quiet for a moment before answering. "Thank you for telling me. You always seemed so... So solitary. I never would have guessed."

"I wanted to tell you that day at the fort," Beau said. "I'm one of the only ones who remember her now. Even both her parents have passed."

"I'm so sorry," Rebecca said again, unsure how to comfort this stoic, strong man.

"Thank you. I don't know if she would have wanted to come to Oregon, so I suppose all of this could have gone differently and I never would have seen this view... or met you. Or met any of the other fascinating folks in this company. It'd be a totally different life."

"It is a totally different life," Rebecca agreed. She was a different person than she had been a year ago, when her husband had been alive.

They stood together, looking out over the view, for another quiet moment before being interrupted.

"Do you hear that?" Sadie called.

When Rebecca and Beau turned back toward her, she and Angus were peering down the trail, around the corner toward the sounds.

It was hooves, muted in the dirt, but unmistakable.

"Someone's coming," Rebecca whispered.

They took a few steps forward to meet the new arrival.

CHAPTER FORTY-FIVE

Rebecca didn't realize she was holding her breath at the sound of hooves coming up the trail until the horse and rider came into view. As she stood on the side of the mountain with the Waters family, she thought about how far she had come to get to this moment. Everything was about to change.

"Benjamin Findley," Beau said in a tone of surprise when they saw who it was. He closed the distance between them. "You're back. I wasn't sure we'd find you."

Though his father was not one of the company's captains, the Findleys were very close to the Mills family. He had regularly been paired with Daniel for many of the tasks supporting the wagon company. This wasn't the first time Benjamin had been enlisted in similar scouting all along the trail.

Before Benjamin could respond, however, two more horses with riders came around the bend, followed shortly by another half dozen.

"What is all this?" Rebecca asked in wonder.

"We were just hoping to see you," Angus clarified. "Who are…?"

Rebecca took a few dazed steps toward the group of men and older boys that had suddenly appeared on the mountainside, heading up the trail toward their camp. Each and every one of the eight strangers rode or led a horse that was weighed down with full saddle bags. Most of the men carried more on their own person.

"Relief mission," Benjamin said with a smile. He gestured to the group. "Daniel was supposed to come up ahead to spread the news, but maybe he's already in camp and you missed him. These folks are from down in the valley, from Dempsey, and are here to make sure we all make it down safely."

Sadie laughed a little hysterically, tears of joy welling up at the same time as she threw her arms around her husband. "A relief party," she said, over and over.

Rebecca was too stunned to feel any such emotion. She had been so tired for weeks now, and the sudden appearance of relief was more than she could wrap her mind around.

"This is…" She couldn't even finish the thought.

Beau touched her gently on the shoulder, drawing her attention away from the sacks of flour and beans that were slung over the horses' backs.

"Why don't we walk back up to camp with these men," he said. "I'll make sure you get back to your own wagon all right."

She nodded, still stunned, and allowed herself to be led.

The men followed, with their food and their salvation.

Within an hour, every child who had been crying from hunger that morning was sitting down to a full meal. Every mother who wondered how much longer they could go on like this was giving thanks for the plenty. Every family in the Sullivan-Mills wagon company who needed even a little bit of sustenance now had all they would need to get down the mountain.

Rebecca learned later that for the last several years, all the small towns in the foothills had relief parties waiting to be called for weeks every fall. When Daniel and Benjamin had scouted on ahead, the men of Dempsey, Oregon, had jumped into action. Now they had enough food to make sure that all of the wagon company had the strength and fortitude to make it the final day of travel into the valley. There was every chance that they would not have all made it without this food, without this charity. Without this generosity and thoughtfulness.

The Oregon Territory was a true community of helpers.

The next morning, every member of the Sullivan-Mills wagon company was up early, ready and excited to get moving as soon as they could. The boon of the supplies from the rescue company had put a spring in everyone's step that hadn't been there since Independence. As Rebecca sipped at her coffee, laced with sugar fresh from the relief party, she noticed Kate and Jack chasing each other around their camp, and even her father whistling as he hitched up the team.

When was the last time she had heard him whistle so cheerfully?

Not long after the sun crossed the horizon—higher now, this deep in the mountains—the draft animals started tugging, the wheels started turning, and the wagons made their way to the crest of the hill.

Rebecca walked up ahead. A group of emigrants— the ones who were not responsible for a team of draft animals—had hurried down the trail ahead even of Captain Mills's lead wagon. Rebecca moved to join them, walking fast past the Martells, the Sullivans, the Gilroys and on and on past the long caravan that she had been part of for almost six months now.

Rebecca waved to her friends, but this was one instance when she didn't want the distraction of her mother's meddling or her brothers' teasing.

This was where it all ended.

The journey that her husband had initiated more than a year ago now had brought her all the way west. It had been far harder than she expected, both in terms of the physical toll on her body and in the emotional upheaval she had suffered in her grief. But she had made it, just as Andrew had known she would.

Ahead of her were several members of the Waters family. Their father and Colin must be driving the wagons; she easily spotted Beau's head and shoulders above the rest, along with several other recognizable Waters hats. Behind her somewhere were the Keegans, the Hudsons, and so many of the other families who she had made friends with along the journey.

But, at this moment Rebecca was alone on the trail.

She hung back a bit from the crowd ahead, not

wanting to share this moment of reflection, of missing Andrew, with anyone else. All of the men and women she had traveled west with had their place in her life going forward, but only Andrew Tenney belonged in these last few steps at the end of the journey.

The folks walking at the front of the group sped up a bit, as the trail wound lower on the mountain. It was as though merely having a full meal for the first time in weeks had given them more energy and vim than they had had since Missouri.

When Rebecca got to that same turn in the trail, she stopped in her tracks. This was what they had all been hurrying toward. After two thousand miles, countless injuries, innumerable cups of coffee and a handful of torrential storms, this was it. From this vantage point, Rebecca could see down the mountain into the Oregon countryside she had been dreaming of.

After a presumably wet summer, the farmland was almost an emerald green, in low rolling hills cut through by wide, meandering streams. Stands of thick trees, maple and pine, peppered as far as she could see. Though it was nearly impossible to make out at this distance, there was what looked like a small town, or at least a collection of tiny rooftops and chimneys collected around one of the larger rivers.

And beyond that, she knew, would be the immense deep blue expanse of the Pacific Ocean. She had started in the flat farmland of Indiana, and had made it all the way west to the Willamette Valley, and the luscious, fertile land of the Oregon Territory.

Rebecca Tenney had done it. She had fulfilled the

wild promise she made to her husband. She would spend the rest of her life here in Oregon.

She smiled, and quickened her steps to catch up with her friends down the mountain.

THE END

Download your free book — *HANNAH'S HOPE* — at ATButler.com/Hannah

When Hannah Sullivan's family decides to head west to the Oregon Territory, she's exhilarated. The small town where she grew up was fine when that's all she had to choose from, but as soon as the horizons and opportunities open up, Hannah finds a whole new world, just built for someone as competent, kind and warm as she is.

Sign up for A.T. Butler's mailing list today and receive Hannah's Hope for free! Dive into a story where romance blossoms against all odds, and be the first to hear about new releases, exclusive content, and special offers. Don't miss this chance to fall in love with Hannah and Benjamin's story.

ATButler.com/Hannah

When I was about twelve years old, I noticed a big, fat hardcover book on my parents' shelf. It was one of those fancy Readers Digest editions; they had perhaps a dozen or so different classics all from the same publisher. The book in question I didn't know anything about, but I recognized the title. And because I have always been a big reader, I sat down and got to work on this 1000-page opus.

The book in question? *Gone with the Wind.*

Yes, I read *Gone with the Wind* in middle school. I'm not sure either of my parents have ever read the book, nor knew specifically what was in it. I loved the book. I ended up reading it several more times over the following years. It is because of that experience that I believe that kids should be allowed to read whatever books hold their interest (but that's a conversation for another time).

All that to say that when I knew I wanted to have a widow character as part of my Oregon Trail series, I decided to give her a similar personality to Scarlett O'Hara, young and itching to have fun but restricted by the expectations placed on a widow in 1850. Our poor Rebecca could have had such the life with her beloved husband and didn't even get the chance.

Fortunately, she's always up for another adventure.

If you're interested in Rebecca's continuing story, look for *Frontier Fortune*, book five of my Oregon At Last series that follows this same wagon company as they are settling their new homesteads in the territory.

This was also the book where I was able to start crossing over more characters. Writing similar scenes from Rebecca's point of view, instead of Annie's for example, offers a fun challenge. It felt as though the whole series shifted, up-leveled with this book. I enjoy every new book more than the last.

I hope you do too. Thank you so much for being here with me, reading through my Courage on the Oregon Trail series, following along as these characters learn more about themselves, survive hardships and build their new lives.

We have a bunch more books to go!

— A.T. Butler
March 2025

FREE PRINTABLE OREGON TRAIL MAP

Sign-up to download a FREE custom printable map of the Sullivan-Mills wagon company's journey on the Oregon Trail.

You'll also get news of future releases, updates for promotions and discounts, as well as occasional other exclusive goodies, created just for my subscribers.

https://atbutler.com/ot-free

The next book in COURAGE ON THE OREGON TRAIL series is available now.

Grab FIERCE DREAMS here!
(on Kindle and Kindle Unlimited)

Surely love must be waiting for her in Oregon.
Nora Cole has been in love with Jimmy Rayburn since she could walk, but when he becomes betrothed to her best friend, she has to rethink all the big idyllic plans she had for her future. Luckily, her parents decide to try their fate in the Oregon Territory. Nora and her sister Amy go with 

them, and she easily starts rebuilding her dreams of a life-long love, family and children.

Throwing herself whole-heartedly into the romance of her journey west, Nora soon learns that the reality of survival must take all precedence. Any dreams she had of meeting the love of her life are dashed.

Will Nora regret leaving everything she knew, or will she find bigger dreams in her new life?

All the books in the Courage on the Oregon Trail series take place within the same wagon company's trip west and run concurrently. They can be read in any order.

She thought the hardest part was behind her.

The Oregon Territory, October 1850: After nearly a year of living out of a covered wagon, day after day of grueling work and heart-breaking tragedy, Caroline Harper has finally reached the Oregon Territory where her new life will begin.

She thought she had given all she had to give; she thought she had become the strong woman the frontier requires. But every day brings a new challenge for the settlers.

When unexpected obstacles appear that keep her from getting married, from finally finding her security, Caroline learns that

becoming the woman she needs to be will be far more difficult than she had realized.

Can Caroline find her new path or will this journey be the end of everything she thought she had achieved?

For all the stories of how these brave pioneers got to Oregon, look for the book series Courage on the Oregon Trail by A.T. Butler.

Oregon At Last Series:
Journey's End (Caroline's story)
Christmas in Oregon (Annie's story)
Snowbound Promises (Nora's story)
The Pastor's Baby (Olivia's story)
Frontier Fortune (Rebecca's story)
Reluctant Spring (Sadie's story)
Summer of Promise (Margaret's story)

ALSO BY A.T. BUTLER

Courage On The Oregon Trail Series:

Westward Courage

Faithful Trail

Frontier Sisters

Unyielding Heart

Wild Promise

Fierce Dreams

Seeking Home

Trouble and Grace

Oregon At Last Series:

Journey's End

Christmas in Oregon

Snowbound Promises

The Pastor's Baby

Frontier Fortune

Reluctant Spring

Summer of Promise

Juniper Falls Series:

The Juniper Hotel

Building the Dream

Snowflakes and Sugar Cookies

Marrying a Sweet Sister Series:

The Sweetest Bond

The Sweetest Spark

The Sweetest Shelter

The Sweetest Gamble

Jacob Payne, Bounty Hunter Series:

Trouble By Any Name

Danger in the Canyon

Justice for Jasper

Blood on the Mountain

Outlaw Country

Death By Grit

Desert Rage

Arizona Legend

Fool's Demise

Silent Night

Bountiful Justice Series:

Loyalty's Price

Riding for Justice

Trail of Redemption

Other Western Novels by A.T. Butler:

Hawke's Revenge

Short Stories from Juniper Falls

ABOUT THE AUTHOR

I grew up in the southwest—California Missions, snakes and constant threat of drought weaving the backdrop of my childhood.

But it wasn't until I moved to Texas a few years ago that the magic and mythology of the American West began to seep into my soul.

I'd love to write about western adventures, strong women and noble men for a long time.

If you enjoyed this book, a review on your favorite retailer would be greatly appreciated.

- A